THE CYBORG REDEEMER

By

Willie Fordham

Publisher: Willie Fordham, LLC

Editors: Vaughn Foster, Jr, & Hannah Pallotta

ISBNs:

978-1-7364829-9-5 (Ebook edition)

978-1-7364829-8-8 (Paperback edition)"

To my parents

Prologue

Durin' the era of Nevi'im, technology had advanced beyond measure. From hover cars to intergalactic travel, the new wave of technology was desired by everyone. However, Yah, the creator of the universe, only granted such advancement to one group, Neo-Edens

The greatest of the new wave was the Praise. Configured as a golden band on the right arm, the Praise created a neuro-digital link between both the Neo-Edens and their creator. This allowed a shared cloud of thought wit' knowledge and wisdom downloaded directly from Yah himself wit' simple utterance of the word, Hallelujah . No one quite understood how the Praise, or its two-edged motherboard-fatherboard processor worked, but they saw the results: the Neo-Edens risin' to one of the most advanced societies in the world.

Unfortunately, good moments don't last forever. The Neo-Edens rebelled. They desired to control their technology wit'out Yah, similar to the surroundin' kingdom that chose to operate wit'out connection to the creator. This rebellion led to a deadly virus infectin' the Praise. The virus, coined popularly as Lewdness, obliterated their firewalls, destroyed their two-edged mainframe, and caused fear to closed the mouths of the voice-activated technology. The capital city, Neo-Eden, was left open to enemies and plagues.

Famine, fear, and discord fell on the land as Yah pulled his Word from all but a select few. The technology created by last wave of Praises was still used amongst the Neo-Edens, but only those that stayed obedient and remained connected to Yah received a powerful upgrade: Holy Spirit.

Table of Contents

PART I:
MOABOLIS - THE LIFE AND TIMES OF ELIME EFRATHAT

CHAPTER 1

When Elime was 7

"In the future, Yah will create the Cloud and the Hard Drive. And the Hard Drive will be wit'out form and void; and full storage will be upon the face of the deep. And the Upgrade, will hover over the circuits, decodin' the chaos. Then Yah will say, …" The cyborg teacher, Mrs. Wires, scanned the class, waitin' for a student to answer.

"Let there be Light Code, and there will be Light Code. And Yah will divide the corrupt files from the eternal backups." Elime didn't miss a beat, rewirin' and reprogrammin' his Praise as he spoke. Sparks flew like a short-circuitin' droid, but he didn't mind. He always wore his safety goggles. Safety first, he heard Mrs. Wires' words repeat over and over in his head like the algorithm he had to learn to get here.

"That is correct. Of course Elime got it." She smiled. "Class, it wouldn't hurt for you all to learn the Word of Yah. It isn't just the motherboard and fatherboard. It helps you in the physical realm, but also in the spirit realm, or cyber realm, as it is known." Mrs. Wires glided her way back to her seat. Sneerin' expressions flew at Elime like any other day. This was fourth grade and Elime was promoted early. He'd shown advanced intelligence early on in his life.

When he was 4, he was already programmin' his Praise, gifted to him earlier than most. At 5, he took a vow to listen to Yah no matter what. So it wasn't a shocker when school began, his reputation as a genius of both tech and Yah preceded him, causin' the teachers to place him above his age group. He could've been promoted again, but he wanted to enjoy bein' a child. You'd think bein' a genius made him feel left out, since most didn't like him 'cause he always knew the answers, but no. Another seven-year-old was in his class: his brotha-cousin, Boaz.

Boaz and Elime had been brotha-cousins since birth. They did everything together, includin' inventin'. Boaz was Elime's mirror; whatever one did, the other would do, or try to outdo. It was a healthy competition that kept 'em sharp.

Elime removed his goggles, lookin' around. The sneers were gone; every face was now buried in a screen for Mrs. Wires' latest assignment. Elime and Boaz never had to do theirs; they knocked out the whole year's worth of work in a week. So Mrs. Wires let 'em roam, doin' whatever grew them as inventors and innovators.

"Hello, Mrs. Wires." Boaz strolled in, half-covered in flour.

"Hello, Boaz!" Her slightly robotic voice carried a happy push. "You may go to your seat. Did you enjoy yourself today?" She was so used to seein' Boaz covered in some food substance that she didn't even bat an eyelash.

"You already know!" Boaz strutted to the back where Elime waited. "Hey cuz, how was it?"

"It was awesome, as usual. To Yah be the glory!"

"To Yah be the glory!" Elime grinned. "So, you know what I'm gonna say." He chuckled.

"Elime, we go over this all the time. I like usin' my intellect to cook and feed people. You like usin' yours to invent and spread Yah's Word. That's why you're back here, upgradin' your Praise, while I'm in the cafeteria kitchen makin' meals the whole school actually eats."

"That's true. Ever since you took over, the food's gotten a hundred times better. And I keep reminding myself of what Nana always says: not everyone is raised like you, and not everyone thinks the way you do."

"That's right." Boaz smiled. "Elime, you'll grow up to be the greatest inventor, innovator, and Yah-lover to ever do it. I'll grow up to own the most popular restaurant the multiverse has ever seen."

"The multiverse?" Elime slipped off his gloves, restin' them in his lap. "You really believe everyone will come eat wit' you?" He rubbed his hands to keep the blood flowin'.

"Of course! And wit' you by my side, I can't lose." Boaz extended a fist.

"You already know I got your back!" Elime bumped him. "I'm gonna invent somethin' that gets me a chance to meet royalty. I just don't know what yet."

"Don't sweat it. Yah's already given us what we need." Boaz lifted his wrist, showin' his golden Praise. "Ain't nothin' more powerful than this. It's our greatest weapon and best-kept secret."

They laughed, starin' at their wristbands. It was always a joke hearin' other nations try to replicate the Praise for their gods. It never worked.

"Yes, I'll Praise my way into new recipes and, eventually, my restaurant."

"And I'll use mine to invent somethin' that'll change the world and, maybe, meet royalty."

"I'm sure we'll both fulfill our dreams."

"Hallelujah," Boaz whispered into his Praise.

A screen popped up, slidin' onto the desk as he started scribblin' a recipe. Elime followed, slidin' his gloves back on and tinkerin' wit' his Praise. Before they could dive in, Mrs. Wires' voice filled the room.

"Class! Class!" Her speaker projected her tone. She was never a yeller, not even before the cyber upgrades. "Attention, I have news for you all."

Heads lifted. A cinnamon-skinned girl wit' an afro almost bigger than she was stepped in, smilin'. She stood beside Mrs. Wires, who mirrored her grin.

"Class, this is Naomi. She'll be wit' us for the rest of the year. Say hi."

"Hi, Naomi," the class droned.

"Would you like to say anythin'?" Mrs. Wires asked.

"Umm, hi. My name is Naomi. I love to fast, pray, and give to the poor. I'm seven years old."

The class groaned in unison. Naomi blinked. "Did I say somethin' wrong?"

"No," Mrs. Wires assured her. "It's just… we already got two other seven-year-olds in the back. They tend to answer all the questions and one-up everyone. But don't worry, they'll welcome you wit' open arms, especially the two in the back. That's where you'll sit."

She clapped twice and a desk lowered beside Elime, landin' right in the middle of him and Boaz.

Naomi bounced to the back, slidin' into her seat wit' a calm smile.

"Hi, I'm Naomi. Nice to meet you guys."

Elime looked, silent. He'd never felt this way 'bout another human before. Science and Yah had consumed him, leavin' no room for emotions outside the family. Now his heart raced, his blood pressure ticked higher. He wanted to speak, but the words jammed, caught in the circuits of his own chest.

"Hi, I'm Boaz." He leaned forward, hand out for a fist bump. She met it.

"Nice to meet you, Boaz. So, you two are the other seven-year-olds?"

"Yep, sure are!" Boaz grinned wide.

He plopped a Hallegraphic screen and wrote Elime's name down. Naomi made a face, tryin' to decipher how to pronounce the name.

"Haha, I do that all the time when it comes to his name. People always make that face. It's pronounced 'E-lime'. This is Elime, my brotha-cousin."

"Oh, okay," she chuckled. "Hi Elime." She smiled but, again, silence. Elime just stared.

"Is he okay?" Naomi tilted her head.

"Yeah, he's fine." Boaz covered for him. "He's just shy. Once he warms up, he's the best to talk to."

Naomi shrugged, slidin' a smile back on. "Okay. Since we're the only three seven-year-olds, we should stick together. Be friends. The others don't seem too friendly."

"You're right," Boaz said. "That's why me and him stick close." He stretched his arms around them both. "From this day on, we're not just friends, we're best friends. Deal?"

Naomi hugged them both. "Deal!"

CHAPTER 2

When Elime was 10

Elime sat at the steel table floatin' off the ground, the seat driftin' alongside him. He was pickin' at his lunch when he spotted Boaz and Naomi makin' their way through the hungry crowd of teenagers. They slid into the seats across from him, worry flashin' in their eyes.

"This place is huge!" Boaz spread his arms wide.

"Is the place huge, or are we just small?" Naomi countered, tiltin' her head.

She had a point. They'd been bumped up a few grades 'cause they'd already mastered their old ones, and now, at only ten years old, they were high school freshmen. None of them thought life would look like this so soon.

"You think we can handle this?" Boaz asked. "I mean, socially. We're only ten."

"Yes, we can handle it," Naomi said wit' that radiant smile Elime adored. He talked about her smile to Boaz all the time.

"I agree," Elime added. "If the admin didn't think we could handle it, we wouldn't be here. We've survived two months already, so what's another two?"

"See?" Naomi smiled wider. "Elime believes we can do it, so we can do it."

"Okay, okay," Boaz gave in. "But why do we gotta have different classes? Shouldn't we stick together?"

"Maybe, but bein' separate will help us grow. We can't lean on each other forever. Besides, we still got lunch and a study hall."

They grinned in unison. They couldn't have imagined life like this, but they were open to whatever Yah had in store.

"And don't forget, we still get recess." Boaz smirked. He loved recess. It was where he cooked up most of his wild recipes.

Naomi leaned forward. "So, how does it feel bein' in charge of the menu for the whole district now?"

Boaz sipped his lemonade like a champ. "Feels great, actually. I get to serve delicious, nutritious meals to every school in Neo-Eden. To Yah be the glory!" He bit into a deep-fried mushroom, then waved it off. "But enough 'bout me, how's it feel bein' curator for Home Eco?"

Naomi lit up. "Home Eco is my callin'. I knew I was a wiz kid, but it wasn't until I got placed in Home Eco that I realized how I could use my tech brain to make homemakin' easier." She squealed softly, sippin' her water. "And how's Theology, Elime?"

Elime's whole face brightened like the sunrise. "I always knew Yah and science went hand in hand, but bein' in charge of Theology for the district means I can show people that the two aren't enemies. They're allies."

The three relished their newfound roles, until Boaz cut in.

"You realize we're doin' grown folks' jobs wit'out gettin' paid?" He popped another mushroom in his mouth.

Naomi and Elime exchanged looks.

"But don't worry," Boaz added. "My parents already peeped game. They're handlin' it."

The others laughed. Boaz always had the next step ready; that's why he was a beast in the kitchen.

"Well, excuse me." Naomi tapped her Praise, and her food vanished. "I got some Home Eco inventions to run by my teacher. I'll show y'all later. Bye!" She whisked away like a girl on a mission.

Boaz leaned back wit' relief. "I'm glad you finally talked to her. It's not awkward anymore when we all hang out, which is every day."

"You're right," Elime admitted. "I made things awkward, but that's the past."

Boaz chewed, eyein' him. "So how'd you get over it? Talkin' to her, I mean?"

"I just remembered Yah didn't give us a spirit of fear but of power, love, and a sound mind. Once that revelation kicked in, talkin' to her became easy the next time we saw each other." Elime sipped his water. "But… has she ever said anything about me bein' quiet before?"

Boaz snorted. "Dude, of course. She asked me every day when you'd start talkin' to her. There's only so many times I can say, 'He's shy,' before she digs deeper."

Elime froze. "You didn't tell her I was in love wit' her, did you?"

"Now you know I'd never do that," Boaz said. "But you need to tell her yourself. Keepin' secrets from Naomi never ends well, you know this."

"Bro, we're ten," Elime groaned. "I got time."

They both burst out laughin', loud enough for the whole cafeteria to stare. They quickly calmed, still grinnin'.

"Fine, you got time," Boaz said. "It's not like you'll die from keepin' it a secret."

"Yeah, dyin' over a secret? That ain't me. I love Yah too much." BUZZ! BUZZ! Their Praises vibrated.

"Back to our elementary school lives," Elime chuckled. "Crazy, right?"

"You should still tell her," Boaz pressed. "Everyone loves a love story at this age."

"Maybe," Elime dodged, changin' the subject. "But hey, aren't you glad we're still ten and get recess wit' our peers?"

"Yes, but don't think you're off the hook. You can confess at any age." They crossed campus toward the elementary playground, blendin' back in wit' kids their size.

"Fine," Elime said, climbin' after Boaz onto the jungle gym. "I'll tell her before I turn eighteen."

Boaz grinned from the top, sittin' like the king of the playground. "So I can hold you to that?"

"Yeah. Before eighteen, for sure." They shook hands.

Right then, Naomi climbed up wit' a dazzlin' smile.

"Hey guys, what'd I miss?"

CHAPTER 3

When Boaz and Naomi were 14

DROP! DROP!

A soft rain filled the city as Boaz and Naomi walked through the wide streets. The tall glass towers reflected hazy lights, blurred from the drizzle, makin' the whole city shimmer like it was alive. They had just recently graduated from high school and, before steppin' into their roles as innovators and inventors, they decided to spend a little more time bein' kids. There was somethin' 'bout the rain that slowed the pace of life, made them feel like they could stretch out this season before responsibility claimed it all.

"Where's Elime?" Naomi asked, steppin' into a puddle. A faint hum flickered from the prototype around her ankles. She had designed it to keep shoes dry, no matter the weather. The water rippled, slid off, and left her boots spotless. She pointed down, half-proud, half-playful. "Look at Yah. Won't He do it!"

"Won't He will!" Boaz jumped in right on beat, finishing her thought.

They both laughed. It was the kind of laugh that always bubbled up whenever one finished the other's sentence. It wasn't planned, just how their friendship worked, an unspoken rhythm. Boaz and Naomi had a bond, and there was no denyin' it.

"I guess your prototype worked," Boaz said, raising his brows. "I can definitely see this flyin' off the shelves."

"Thank you," Naomi said softly.

She smiled, but her humility weighed down her pride. She didn't care about riches or fame. She just wanted to make homemakers' lives easier to build inventions that gave people, especially mothers, more time for love and joy. She often dreamed about the kind of mother she might be one day, and the tools she built now were little gifts for her future self.

They walked on, rain drippin' from neon signs overhead, until they reached the park. There, children ran wild, splashin' through puddles, stompin' in the mud while their parents half-heartedly tried to stop them, half-amused to let them be kids. The air was filled wit' shrieks, laughter, and the squelch of waterlogged grass.

Boaz and Naomi came to a soaked wooden bench. Naomi whispered 'Hallelujah' into her Praise when a gust of wind burst from the band, dryin' the wood instantly. They sat, sheltered as Naomi's magnetic umbrella unfurled, growin' fivefold until it covered them both like a great dome.

"Cookie?" Boaz offered, producing a napkin-wrapped bundle.

"Did you make it?" Naomi asked.

"You already know." His grin widened. Naomi took one, bit into it, savorin' the chewy sweetness.

"So, Naomi," Boaz leaned back, his tone turning curious. "Why'd you drag me out of my warm bed into the cold rain?"

Naomi froze. Her fingers toyed wit' the edge of the cookie as she looked left, right, then back at Boaz. The rain tapped the umbrella like a thousand tiny drums.

"Well, there's somethin' I have to tell you, and only you."

"I figured," Boaz said wit' a smirk. "You didn't invite Elime. But lucky for you, he had an appointment today, so he won't be none the wiser."

"Yeah… well, the reason we're here is 'bout him. I didn't want him to know."

Boaz leaned in closer, intrigued. Naomi, hiding somethin' from Elime? That wasn't like her. The three of them had done everything together since they were seven. If one was missin', it always felt incomplete. For Naomi to want a secret? That was new.

"So, what is it? C'mon, spill it. You got me invested."

Naomi sat upright, her breath heavy, tryin' to push out air that wasn't even there. Her heart thumped loud, louder than the rain.

"I'm in love wit' Elime."

"Girl, I knew that!" Boaz burst into laughter so hard it nearly knocked him off the bench. "I thought you were gonna tell me you had a new invention." He snorted, clutchin' his stomach.

Naomi's glare snapped sharp enough to cut steel. "Okay, I get it. But was I really that obvious?"

"Yes." Boaz's answer landed flat, no hesitation. Then his tone shifted, serious. "So, when are you gonna tell him?"

"Tell him!?" Naomi shouted before catchin' herself, lowering her voice. "I can't tell him. It would ruin the friendship. I love him too much to lose him as my friend." Her gaze dropped to the cookie in her hands before lifting back to Boaz.

"That's sweet and all," Boaz said, "but don't you love yourself too much to risk missin' what could happen?"

Naomi bit into the cookie again, stalling for time. The sugar melted across her tongue but couldn't mask the weight in her chest.

"Okay, I see your point. But we're just kids. Didn't we just graduate high school? Ain't this love stuff meant to wait?"

"Naomi," Boaz shook his head slowly, "love doesn't care about a timeline. It's limitless. You can have it whenever, from whoever."

Naomi couldn't respond. His words settled in her chest as heavy as the rain. She let her mind wander wit' the drizzle, back to the beginnin'. Their friendship meant everything, Elime told her that himself. And she remembered, clear as lightnin', the very first time he ever spoke to her.

She had been sittin' alone at recess, watchin' other kids chase balls and jump ropes. Out of the corner of her eye, she saw Elime and Boaz walking toward her. Her heart leapt;those two were her whole world. She jumped up, runnin' to meet them, only to trip over a stray ball. She tumbled, landing right on Elime.

Mortified, she scrambled to her feet, brushing dust and grass off her dress. She reached down, hand trembling, to help him up. "Are you okay?"

"Yes, I'm fine. Are you?" he asked.

They froze. That was the first time Elime had ever spoken to her. For a moment the whole playground felt brighter. Like kids do, they celebrated the milestone wit' pure joy, laughing for no reason except that it happened. Boaz, confused but loyal, joined in, sharing their laughter wit'out needing an explanation.

Naomi had been a genius all her life, but moments like that reminded her she also had a childhood worth rememberin', one filled wit' innocence, clumsiness, and discovery.

SPLASH!

A child nearby stomped into a puddle, sendin' muddy water flying. Naomi blinked back into the present. Across from her, Boaz was lost in thought too, eyes glazed wit' memory. She nudged him wit' her shoulder.

"I guess we both daydreamed?" she said.

"It worked," Boaz smirked.

"What worked?"

"My cookies. Secret ingredient makes folks reminisce on happy memories. I designed it so the effect builds slowly, and doesn't hit right away. And it worked perfectly."

Naomi's jaw dropped. "So my whole daydream, Elime, the playground, that was your cookie?"

"Not just the cookie," Boaz explained. "The rain, the mood, the umbrella, all of it. Right environment speeds up the effect. Makes the memory more intense."

Naomi laughed, shakin' her head. "Well, you nailed it. Felt so real, like I was there."

"Good," Boaz grinned, chest swellin' wit' pride. "That means it's a success. Can't wait to tell my parents… and Elime." His grin faltered at the name. "Speakin' of Elime, when you gonna tell him how you feel?"

The memory dissolved fully, leavin' Naomi bare in reality. "Soon," she said, forcin' a smile.

"How soon?" Boaz pressed. "I need somethin' more concrete than that."

"Before I'm eighteen."

Boaz leaned back, studying her face. Then he nodded slowly and stuck out his hand. "I can dig it."

Naomi laughed and shook his hand, sealing the promise wit' a grip stronger than the rain around them.

CHAPTER 4

When Elime was 17

Sweat dripped from Elime's hands like a leaky faucet. He was enterin' his seventh inventors' competition this year. He had won each time but every single time he got nervous. He didn't live in fear 'cause Yah didn't give him that but what Yah did give him was humility. He was humbled that he had won every time. It really affirmed that Theology and Technology really went hand in hand.

He stood in the room that each participant received, attemptin' to calm himself down. He always psyched himself up for these events, and it sometimes almost caused him to lose. Today, he was gonna do somethin' different. He wasn't gonna play in his head but, instead of doin' his usual prep work, he was gonna pray.

"Dear Yah, thank You for this gift that You gave me. Thank You for telling my ancestors what to do and to keep You first in everything we do, not only tech, but life in general. I am grateful that since graduatin', my inventions have taken off and I have been able to take care of myself. I'm now in the position where I want a wife so, if you could just send her that would be awesome. Haha! No, but seriously, I'm ready. Let your will be done at this event. Bless all those who are in attendance and those competin'! Amen!"

"Amen!" I echoed. Elime, frightened, looked around wonderin' where that voice, My voice came from. "Who's there?"

"I AM!" My voice vibrated throughout his entire spirit, soul, and body. He instantly knew who I was and dropped down to his knees.

"Holy Spirit, I'm not worthy."

He bowed in My presence. One attribute I love 'bout Elime is his willin'ness to serve so openly and so freely. I wish more people in Neo-Eden were like him.

"Elime, stand up!"

He stood up to see a man that was equally as tall as him, dressed in all black wit' skin just as equally black.

"How are you my child?"

I hugged him. Yes, I AM a hugger and comforter. He knows that. He instantly hugged me back and didn't want to let go. He knew he was safe in My arms. I broke the hug. I wanted him to see My face. I also wanted to see his face.

"How are you, my child?"

I plopped down on the floor, motionin' him to sit. He was still in awe. He had wanted to see Me in My physical form since birth, and now he had his wish.

"Elime, you have to talk to Me. That is why I AM here."

"Uh yeah," he stammered, "sorry 'bout that. It's just that I always wanted to meet You, and now that I have, I'm at a loss for words."

"I get it. People who love Me imagine this day and what it would be like. I let their imagination run wild. Why? 'Cause I gave it to them to use it." Elime still stared at Me. I can tell that this was a dream come true; however, I did have business to take care of. "So, how are you feelin'?"

"A little nervous," he said, his honesty all over his face.

"That's understandable. You have a big day today. You've been 7/7 and now you are goin' for your 8/8. I AM proud of you."

"You are?" He spoke like a kid desirin' his father's approval.

"Yes, you are gonna do great today. I promise you that."

"Will I win?"

"Nice try," I smiled, "you know I can't say yes or no cause things are changin' all the time. Granted, I can see every possible outcome ever, but there's no way of truly knowin'. Now that was a word salad, but I have divine order and protection to keep here. What I can tell you is that today, Yah's Will, will be done. His Will will make you an extremely happy person. Guaranteed."

I tried not to give it all away cause I enjoyed watchin' the human experience. I enjoyed leadin' and guidin' and not makin' them do it. It kept balance.

"Well, I guess it is time for me to start walkin' out," he said, shaking his head as he tried to proceed out the door.

"Before you go, I have a question," I stopped him. He quickly turned around as he couldn't get enough of My presence. "Do you love me?"

"Of cou-," Elime caught his words before utterin'the wrong thing. "Ruach, you know the answer."

"Smart answer."

I had to give it to him. He did cook wit' that answer like Jeremiah didn't many nanobytes ago.

"Elime, if I gave you a task to complete, you would complete it, no matter what?"

"Ruach, You know the answer," he smiled.

"You would never keep a secret from the ones you love?"

"Ruach, you know the answer," he continued, smilin'.

He's right, I do know the answer, although sometimes I wish I didn't. I gave him another hug and he embraced me before he turned around headin' towards the door.

"Where you goin'? I questioned him.

"I'm goin' to my competition. This is a room they give all competitors to relax and get focus."

"No silly," I laughed, "you need to load out there."

"Load?" his eyes widened. "Isn't that dangerous? It's been tested but not tested-tested yet."

I gave the blankest stare that I could give before I leaned over and tapped his Praise, uploadin' him center stage of the competition.

Gasp! The entire audience breathed heavily as Elime downloaded into the event. The whispers filled the place faster than My presence. It had never been done by anyone other than a J.U.D.G.E. Elime was the first to successfully do it without the body ripping into shreds

He looked out in the crowd wit' a smile on his face. He knew this day was really in Yah's hands. The other contestants slowly walked on stage, lookin' at Elime wit' a new pair of eyes. He couldn't see all of them because there was quite a few, but the ones that he saw were intimidated. He liked the feel of that.

"Ladies and Gentlemen," the drone flew down, "welcome to the annual competition, Tech-on-Tech. Today, we have some of the best and brightest in Neo-Eden to compete for a chance to win 10k logs of Myrrh.

"Ohhhh!" The crowd was intrigued by the grand prize.

"Today, we have a special guest judge." The audience looked at each other as whispers filled the air like the many droids. "Yes, we have Prince Eglon, all the way from Moabolis."

The crowd roared as Prince Eglon suddenly appeared in a throne hovering above the people. The crowned prince of Moabolis was extremely popular in Neo-Eden. Everyone was obsessed wit' The Royal.

Elime watched as the contestants were tremblin' at the sight of Prince Eglon. Elime smiled as he knew he had this in the bag. He made inventions for Yah, who's the King of Kings and Lord of Lords. No one was greater than Him.

"Hello, contestants," Prince Eglon said, "I trust that you will bring your A game as I will judge what it is you create. Be safe and fun." The crowd applauded. "Contestants, are you ready?" The crowd grew in their applause. "Get set, go!"

Elime grabbed the tools and immediately started creating. He didn't even look at the competition; he knew that he had Yah on side and only His opinion mattered. Sparks flew, wires crossed, and metal clanked as he and the rest of the contestants invented alongside of him. Sweat felt like coolant leakin' from an overheated android. He didn't stop; he kept goin' until he knew he had something worth bein' proud of, not only by Yah, but by himself as well. He put his tools down satisfied wit' what he accomplished. The other contestants were still profusely workin' towards their invention. He looked out in the crowd and saw Boaz and his parents standin' there givin' him the thumbs up. He smiled as he gave it back.

"Time's Up!" Prince Eglon stated, "Contestants, put your tools down."

A mixture of noises left their mouths at the command of Prince Eglon. Some were happy most sounded disappointed. All Elime knew was that Yah's will must be done. Elime smiled as he knew he invented somethin' that the prince would like. He watched as Prince Eglon floated down the line and examined each invention meticulously. He finally made his way to Elime where he glanced down at the contraption. 'Push Here' was written on top of the contraption and Prince Eglon did just that. Instantly, a warm chocolate chip materialized in his mouth. Out of instinct, he bit it and caught it before it fell. As if the contraption was readin' his mind, a glass of oatmilk appeared and Prince Eglon gulped it down.

"Thank you!" He smiled before he made his way down to the other contestants.

Elime smiled as he was the only contestant that heard those words. He felt like he had it in the bag. He looked around at the lowly faces of the other contestants and prayed that they would feel better.

"Ladies and gentlemen," Prince Eglon spoke, "I would like to announce that for the first time in this competition, we will have a runner up. That runner up will receive 5k logs of Myrrh. The crowd roared wit' applause as this had never been done before but, wit' Prince Eglon judgin', he could do whatever he wanted. "Okay, our runner up is…Elime Efrathat wit' his instant cookie and oat milk machine.

Elime watched as silence waved over the crowd like a quantum veil, bending every soundwave into nothingness as if the universe itself had hit "mute." They had no idea how to respond. Elime had never lost before today.

"Thank you everyone, I am extremely honored," he smiled as the 5k of Myrrh was deposited into his Hallelujah.

The crowd slowly started to clap until they roared. Elime gestured to them to relax so they could hear who won this competition.

"The winner of this year's Tech-on-Tech competition is Naomi Judah for her instant bottlemaker. Me and Princess Lani will definitely be usin' this real soon."

Everyone except Elime roared in excitement for the new winner of the tech competition. He quickly snapped out of it and began to cheer and shout for her the loudest. He watched as Prince Eglon awarded her the 10k of Myrrh and the gold medal.

After the ceremony, Elime rushed back to his room, a little hurt.

"Hey bro, you okay?" Boaz came in checkin' on him.

"Yeah bro, why wouldn't I be?" Elime smiled.

"You didn't win and you're extremely competitive," Boaz smiled.

"Yeah," Elime nodded his head, "I would be bummed out, but Naomi won, and she's my best friend. And, what kind of friend would I be if I didn't support her? Now, I am upset that I didn't know that she was enterin'. I will tell her that when I see her."

As if his words were a signal, Naomi walked in wit' her medal around her neck. Elime smiled at her and she returned it.

"Well, you two, I'm gonna go this way out the door." Boaz hurried out the door, leavin' Elime and Naomi alone.

"Congrats!"

"Elime, let me explain. I know you're angry wit' me. Wait, did you just say congrats?"

"Yes, I did." Elime smiled at her.

"Oh, wow. Thank you and congrats on makin' him give you runner up." She hugged him, standin' on her tippy toes. Gone are the days of them bein' at eye level. Elime hit a growth spurt at 14, right along wit' Boaz and now they towered over the 5'3" Naomi. Elime enjoyed havin' short friends and this was one of those times. She had no choice but to return it, his arms drawn to her as if pulled by some irresistible gravitational field. "I was sure you were gonna win. You were the only person that he said 'thank you' to."

"I thought so too, but your automatic baby-bottle maker came in and swooped it away." He broke the hug. "That is one thing that I always loved 'bout you. You always use your tech to make not only the homemaker's, but the woman's life in general easier."

"Well, one thing I love 'bout you is that you always want to use technology, to bridge the gap between science and sanctification. Wait!" She stopped herself. "Did you say that you loved me?"

"Well, I mean there are things that I love 'bout you. But didn't you say that you loved me?"

"Yes, I did," Naomi smiled.

Elime glitched a bit, "Yeah, I mean I know like a friend."

"Did I say like a friend?" Naomi smiled.

"No," Elime returned her smile, "I love you too."

"Oh," Her voice became playful. "You mean like a friend?" Her voice turned flirty.

"No, I mean like this," He pulled her into a deep, passionate kiss.

CHAPTER 5

When Naomi was 17

Naomi paced back and forth in the room that was given to her for the competition. This was her first time enterin', and nerves rattled her whole body. She had never done anythin' like this before. Her genius had always gone into creatin' things for homemakin', inventions that made bein' a woman easier. She never imagined usin' her skills in a tech competition, especially the same one Elime always entered. He was humble but competitive, and winnin' meant the world to him. Doin' this could cost me my friendship, she thought.

"Naomi?" Boaz stepped through the door. "How are you?"

The look on her face nearly frightened him. "I'm not doin' fine. I'm scared."

"Why?"

"'Cause I know how Elime is wit' tech. He's so competitive. I'm nervous he won't like me anymore."

"Hahaha!" Boaz laughed. "Naomi, trust me. Elime will never stop likin' you. You're his best friend, just like me. We're a team."

"Easy for you to say. You don't compete." She snapped, then softened. "Sorry. I just care so much 'bout what he thinks of me."

Boaz grinned. "You think 'bout him a lot. I bet if he asked you to marry him, you would."

Her silence said everythin'. Naomi had dreamt of marryin' Elime since she was a girl. It was one reason she turned to Home Eco in the first place. Her inventions made that dream feel more possible. But competin' behind his back? That turned her dream into a nightmare.

"Just pray 'bout it," Boaz said as he left. "I'm sure Yah will come through, like He always does."

Naomi smiled, closed her eyes, and prayed:

"Dear Yah, thank You for this gift that You've given me. Thank You for guidin' my ancestors and showin' us to keep You first in everythin', not only tech, but life. I'm grateful that since graduatin', my homemaker inventions have taken off, and I've been able to care for myself. But now…I want a husband to share it wit'. If You could just send him, that would be awesome. Haha! No, but seriously, I'm ready. Let Your will be done at this event. Bless everyone competin'. Amen!"

"Amen!" I echoed.

Naomi startled, lookin' around. "Who's there?"

"I AM."

My voice shook her spirit, soul, and body. She instantly knew and dropped to her knees.

"Master, I'm not worthy."

One thing I love 'bout Naomi, I thought, is how open she is to serve Me, freely and humbly. I wish more Neo-Edens were like her.

"Naomi, stand up!"

She rose, seein' Me, a tall man in all black, skin as black as the night.

"How are you, My daughter?" I hugged her. Yes, I AM a hugger and comforter. She clung to Me, safe in My arms, until I pulled away so she could see My face.

"I never thought this day would come," she whispered, eyes shinin'.

"Naomi, I AM always near when you need Me. And now, you need Me. So, what's up?"

She hesitated. "I entered this competition behind my best friend's back, and…"

"You're afraid he'll be angry or stop bein' your friend."

"Exactly."

"Naomi, have you thought that maybe, just maybe, he'd be proud of you for competin'?"

She frowned. "But Elime is competitive. Competin' makes us rivals, and I don't want that."

"I know." I smiled. "You don't want to be his rival. You want to be his wife."

She froze, then turned away wit' a shy smile.

"Let Me be honest wit' you. It's not that you're afraid to compete. It's that you're afraid to win."

Her silence spoke volumes.

"You're the only one who can beat Elime. That's why you're afraid. But if he's truly your friend, don't you think he already knows, and still wants the best for you?"

Naomi nodded slowly.

"Good. Then go out there, do your best, and let Yah's will be done."

I stood, walked toward the door, and disappeared.

Naomi lifted her chin and stepped into the arena. She whispered to herself: "She who dwelleth in the secret place of the Most High shall abide in the shadow of the Almighty."

Her spirit steadied. It was time.

Naomi pushed through the crowd, movin' past contestants and onlookers. When she reached the stage, she took her place on the far left, half-hidden.

She glanced at the screen above them. A verse glowed at the bottom: "Now faith is the substance of things hoped for, the evidence of things not seen." Naomi smiled, takin' it as a sign Yah was wit' her.

Suddenly, Elime downloaded into the arena. The crowd gasped. Loadin' was dangerous, many had failed, but, of course, not Elime. He was the first to perfect it. Naomi chuckled, glancin' down at the pieces given to her.

"Ladies and gentlemen," a drone announced, "welcome to Tech-on-Tech! Today, the brightest of Neo-Eden will compete for a chance to win 10,000 logs of Myrrh!"

The audience roared.

"And today we have a special guest judge, Prince Eglon of Moabolis!"

The prince appeared on a hoverin' throne, smilin' wider than his slender frame. His popularity in Neo-Eden was unmatched; he was everywhere on social media. Contestants shifted nervously, but Naomi only grew calmer.

"Hello, Contestants," Prince Eglon said warmly. "Bring your Sunday's best. Be safe. Have fun." The crowd cheered. "Contestants, are you ready? Get set… go!"

Around her, inventors scrambled frantically. Naomi didn't rush. She watched, then whispered to herself: I make tech that makes bein' a homemaker, and a woman, easier. Simple but revolutionary.

"Hallelujah," she spoke as her Praise moved pieces together, formin' a sleek new device. She smiled. Maybe this feels so easy 'cause I've practiced my whole life, she thought, as the others panicked like beginners.

"Time's up!" Prince Eglon announced.

Contestants laid down their gadgets. Some grinned; most groaned. Naomi stayed calm. Whatever happened, Yah's will would be done.

Prince Eglon floated down the line, examin' each invention. He stopped at Naomi's first, pickin' up what looked like a bottle.

"What is this?" he asked.

"It's an automated baby bottle," Naomi explained. "Shake it, and the right measurement of formula and water is dispensed at the perfect temperature. It connects to the Praise and runs on the Upgrade. And if you don't have a Praise, it syncs to the S.O.U.L. Kitchen device."

"What if my child ages?"

"Each bottle is designed to adapt and follow that child throughout infancy."

Eglon nodded thoughtfully and moved down the line. Naomi watched as he reached Elime, who had built an instant cookie-and-oat milk machine. It was clever; she wanted one herself. Naomi heard the prince murmur a rare "Thank you."

Her heart twisted. Surely Elime had won.

"Ladies and gentlemen," Prince Eglon said, "I'm doin' somethin' new. Today, we will have a runner-up prize of 5,000 logs of Myrrh."

The crowd erupted in shock and excitement.

"Our runner-up is… Elime Ephrathat, for his instant cookie-and-oat milk machine!"

Silence rippled through the crowd, bendin' every soundwave into nothin'. Naomi herself froze. If Elime was runner-up… who had won?

Elime accepted wit' a smile so radiant Naomi almost melted. The crowd slowly built into applause, roarin' his name.

Then the arena hushed again.

"And the winner is," Prince Eglon declared, "Naomi Judah, for her instant baby bottle maker! My wife, Princess Lani, and I will be usin' this very soon."

The crowd screamed for joy. Naomi's chest heaved as the camera swung to her. A gold medal appeared around her neck, and Prince Eglon hovered down beside her.

"You did great," he said, pullin' her close for a photo. "This invention will bless not only my wife and me, but parents everywhere. Don't ever stop bein' you."

He hugged her, then flew off as the crowd thundered.

Naomi looked around at the mix of smilin' faces, some congratulatin', others hatin'. She decided to try somethin' a little risky. She tapped her Praise and downloaded back to her room.

She laughed softly. That was easier than I thought. Look at Yah.

"Naomi, you okay?"

She turned and saw Boaz comin' through the door.

"Yeah, I am."

She sank onto the couch, and he joined her.

"Naomi, you won. How does it feel?"

He reached over for a quick hug she didn't know she needed.

"I honestly feel good. I didn't think I was goin' to win," she laughed.

"Well, you did. You should feel great." Boaz leaned back, grinnin'. "Actually, you should go talk to Elime."

Naomi's eyes widened more than Neo-Eden's borders durin' the Great Exodus from Egypt.

"I do need to… but I don't know what to say."

"We've been friends since the third grade. You'll know."

Boaz tapped his Praise, sendin' himself to Elime's door.

Naomi sat back, breathin' it all in. She had just won. Some people had competed for years wit'out even placin', and here she was, victorious on her first try. Look at Yah, she thought.

Ping!

A message from Boaz lit up her Hallelujah: Come. Now.

She tapped her device and reappeared in front of Elime's door. Slowly, she walked in, catchin' 'em mid-conversation. The gleam of her medal spoke before she did. Each step toward 'em was a prayer that Yah would give her the right words.

"Well, you two, I'll go this way," Boaz said quickly, slipping out and leavin' 'em alone.

"Congrats," Elime said.

Naomi blinked. "Elime, let me explain. I know you're angry wit'...wait. Did you just say congrats?"

"Yes." He smiled softly.

"Oh. Well, thank you. And congrats on being runner-up." She hugged him, standing' on her tiptoes. Gone were the days they were eye level; his growth spurt had left her lookin' up. She didn't mind, not when his arms wrapped around her like they belonged there.

"I was sure you were going to win," she said, pullin' back just enough to meet his eyes. "You were the only person Prince Eglon said 'thank you' to."

"I thought so too," Elime admitted. "But your automatic baby bottle maker swept it away. That's one of the many things I've always loved about you. You use tech to make life easier, especially for women."

Naomi's breath caught. "Well, one thing I love about you is that you always find ways to bridge the gap between science and sanctification." She froze. "Wait, did you say you loved me?"

"Well, I mean… there are things I love about you." He rubbed the back of his neck. "But didn't you say you loved me?"

"Yes, I did." Naomi smiled, her heart racin'.

Elime glitched, fumblin' for words. "Yeah, but like… as a friend."

"Did I say like a friend?" she teased, refusin' to let the moment slip away.

He grinned. "No. And I love you too."

Her voice softened, playful and tremblin' all at once. "Oh, you mean like a friend?"

He laughed, shakin' his head. "No. I mean like this."

And then she leaned in, sealin' it wit' a deep, lingerin' kiss that said everything words couldn't.

CHAPTER 6

When Elime was 19

Elime lifted his head as Boaz fixed his tie for his weddin'. He was gonna use one of his gadgets for this occasion, but wanted the inimacy that came wit' havin' a brotha-cousin to help you.

"You ready?" Boaz questioned as he finished up the knot.

"Yes, I am. I couldn't be more ready for anythin' in my life."

Elime loved Naomi and had been dreamin' 'bout this day since he first laid eyes on her. He knew she was the one and wanted to make sure the whole world knew.

"Aren't you glad that you listened to me when I told you to marry her?" Boaz grinned, as he been tellin' Elime to propose to Naomi since they were kids.

He knew Elime wanted Naomi, and Naomi wanted Elime. It was hard for him to keep the secret, so he played into it so that they could finally get married.

"Yes, I am. I'm makin' the greatest decision of my life, and it is all thanks to you and Yah."

"It is," Boaz laughed. "I'm so glad to see my two best friends marryin' one another. This will be amazin'."

He shook his Hallelujah, and a glass of water appeared. The glow of his band flickered before stabilizin'. Boaz laughed it off, sippin' deep, but

Elime caught the stutter and frowned for half a second. Then he pushed it away. Today was too good for glitches. He gave Elime the bottle, but he refused.

"Okay well, if you will excuse me, I have to make sure the food is perfect."

Elime chuckled as Boaz left to check on the menu. Boaz was caterin', and he wanted the food to be perfect for this day. He remembered askin' Boaz to cater, and before the words could finish leavin' his lips, Boaz stopped them wit' a "Yes!"

Elime checked the time, realizin' that he didn't have any left and that it was time to marry his best friend and start their lives together.

Now, I thought 'bout showin' up in flesh, but I chose instead to be Spirit. I let my presence ride through the room heavy, but I won't linger too long 'cause this day belongs to them.

Elime walked over to a mirror, lookin' at his face once more. He realized that everything was 'bout to change, and he was ready for it.

He tapped a spot on the mirror. Then he was downloaded to the front of the church. The same murmurs that filled the space at the competition, years ago, were the same that filled the church. Elime still couldn't believe that folks were afraid of loadin' after he had done it for years since that one day.

He smiled at the Hallegraphic projection of his late parents showin' in the front row. His parents died when he was young, and he only had the memories of them that he kept in his Praise. Boaz's parents raised him ever since and tried their hardest to keep the memory of his parents alive. That's why they sat right next to the Hallegraphic projection. Elime shed a tear for them, as he never really had a chance to know them, nor did he know why they died. It happened when he was a baby and he didn't even have memories of them, only Hallegrams. It was a sad occasion, but what Elime didn't realize was their death had been 100% preventable; however, if he kept followin' in their footsteps, like I saw him doin', he'd end up just like them.

"La la la la la!"

Elime heard a voice, comin' from behind him and saw a Hallegram of a chocolate lady, wearin' green dress wit' blond hair, singin' a melody. Elime turned his head, when he saw a variety of people walkin' down the aisle to fill both the his side and his soon-to-be bride's. A chip fell from the sky, and a minister-droid built right in front. Everyone, includin' the Hallegrams, stood in anticipation for the bride.

Naomi downloaded right in the front of church, and was met wit' confusion and awe. She smiled as the guests looked surprised that she downloaded.

"Yes, I did upload. I wanted to add some razzle dazzle to my weddin'." she thought

Naomi gave her flowers to her bridesmaid and grabbed Elime's hands, sealin' her fate for a lifetime.

"Good afternoon! The bride and groom asked that we skip to the vows and the 'I do's' cause as they put it, they have been waitin' their whole lives for this moment," said the minister-droid, soundin' regal and seasoned. "Elime."

"My love for you is patient; my love for you is kind. I will not envy. I will not boast. I won't let pride ever stand between us. I will never dishonor you, nor keep a ledger of wrongs. I will not delight in evil, but will rejoice in truth. I will protect you, trust you, hope wit' you, and endure wit' you. My love will never fail." Elime stared into Naomi's eyes and saw his reflection in her soul.

Naomi wiped her tears. "My love for you is also patient and kind. I won't envy or boast, nor let anger burn between us. I will always rejoice wit' you in Yah's truth. I will protect you, trust you, hope wit' you, and endure wit' you. My love will never fail." She looked into Elime's eyes and found her forever home.

Tears fell down like ⅓ of the angels. There wasn't a dry eye. Their love was felt through the entire chapel. Cyborgs and humans alike were wipin' tears in an attempt to keep their composure. Elime and Naomi never took their eyes off each other.

"Now, we will have the exchangin' of the Hallelujahs to signify the love," the minister-droid spoke. "Elime and Naomi."

Elime and Naomi removed their Praises and placed 'em on each other's wrist. They both inhaled deeply at the sudden rush of feelin' another person's Praise.

"Do you Elime Ef—,"

"I do," Elime interrupted, making the entire place laugh.

"Okay, and do y—,"

"I do," Naomi said, doin' the same, causin' the chapel to laugh even harder.

The minister-droid even laughed. "Okay," he said. "By the power given to me by the Most High Yah, and M.O.E.E, I now pronounce you husband and wife. Elime, you may kiss your bride."

Elime pulled Naomi close to lock their lips into a passionate kiss that sealed not only their vows and the weddin' but also their love they had for each. Their kiss was joined wit' a loud roar from the crowd. They finally unlocked their lips long enough for people to cheer.

Boaz walked to the front of the chapel.

"Hello everyone,"he said. "Now, it is time for the reception."

He clapped twice, causin' the chapel to shift to a lounge filled wit' an AI DJ and copious amounts of food at different stations. The pews morphed into reserved seatin', and tables appeared for the guests to eat their food.

Elime and Naomi walked to the center and began slow dancin'. She rested her head on his chest, takin' this whole moment in. He followed by restin' his head on top of hers. They wished they could stay like this forever, but they knew life had other plans. They both were becomin' one before they even had the chance to truly become one.

After the song, folks ate like their lives depended on it. No dish was left unturned. When the food was gone, they tried to rise and dance, but the itis caught 'em quick. So they let the children spin on the floor while the grown folk sat heavy in their seats, laughin' and rubbin' their bellies.

They felt they couldn't eat another bite until they saw the carrot cake cupcake tower. Elime and Naomi looked at each other, then glanced at the crowd, and everyone just made their way to the cupcakes and ate them whole. They did save some for the kids.

"Can I have everyone's attention?" Boaz requested.

Everyone sat down wit' many other desserts that came out after the cupcakes to listen.

"I just want to say that I'm so happy that my two best friends got married. I remember us bein' in Mrs. Wires' class and we makin' a promise that we would always be best friends and always be there, except for if one of y'all die. I ain't comin' to the funeral, but I will pay and cater."

Everyone laughed at Boaz. He was charmin' and charismatic.

"I would like to toast to you both. I can't wait to see what your love brings to the world. I can't wait to see how your love glorifies Yah. I can't wait to see what your love brings to me. I just have a feelin' that it will."

Everyone raised their glass and took a drink. The crowd cheered for the newlyweds.

"Now, go on to your honeymoon!"

Elime and Naomi laughed as they were uploaded out of the venue on their way to their newfound destiny.

CHAPTER 7

When Elime was 22

Elime and Naomi were down in their lab, racin' against the clock, tryin' to create somethin' new. For Elime, he did this to keep his mind sharp, his tech sharper, and his love for Naomi the sharpest. She always brought the best out of him, like sunshine after a rainstorm. It was 'cause of this that he made a personal vow to make her life easier and safer, and he was doin' just that. What he didn't realize was Naomi also made a similar vow, and she was holdin' to it as if her life depended on it.

This caused many inventions to be made at one time, and the Neo-Edens and surroundin' countries were thankful for their minds. Well, more for Naomi, as her inventions would always be the better out of the two. Ever since she won the competition some macrobytes back, everyone who had a tech company or money wanted to invest and work wit' her, and she would always agree to it. Her only rule was that they had to bring Elime on. This made him extremely happy, as he was the same way when companies wanted to work wit' him. He always invited his wife, Naomi.

Because they did this, it led both of them to invent tech that revolutionized the world. Each day, they would compete wit' each other to see who made the better version or the fastest of a blueprint they both drew.

"Looks like I beat you again," Naomi said, leaning her head into Elime's chest. They were workin' on an equation that would optimize the AI in their house.

"I guess you did." Elime hugged her back. "You are one of the smartest people I know, and what you come up wit' can be attributed to the power of Yah."

"To Yah be the glory."

She faced him before restin' her head against his chest. Elime hugged her back when he noticed some scattered blueprints he hadn't seen before. He reached over her, causin' her head to follow his hands.

"What is this?" He examined the blueprint wit' a look of admiration on his face. "You been holdin' out on me." He smiled as he studied them intensely.

"Oh, these!" She grabbed his hand, placin' her finished work on top. "Those are a gift for Boaz, a thank you for introducin' me to you and bein' the best friend anyone could ask for." Her finger traced up his chest, almost makin' him forget what he wanted to say. Almost.

"Nice try." He grabbed her hands, sealin' 'em wit' a kiss. "It won't work today. I want details."

Her eyes rolled wit' a playful look.

"Fine. I designed Boaz, a diner-by-day, lounge-by-night restaurant. The entire system will be built off the Word of Yah, through the power of the Upgrade, and can be utilized and controlled by our Praise."

Naomi's voice grew happier and happier wit' each word. Elime picked up the design, lookin' at it wit' a fresh pair of eyes. He couldn't believe someone invented somethin' so genius.

"I didn't think I could love you more than I already do, but you never cease to amaze me." He wrapped his arms around her waist, pullin' her in for a passionate kiss. "I am so thankful to Yah that I listened to Boaz when he said, 'Marry her."

"I am thankful as well." She held onto his waist. "I was skeptical, but from the moment I met you, you made me feel safe."

Elime's head tilted in response to her statement. "Why were you skeptical?"

Naomi smiled. "Elime, you are extremely competitive when it comes to bein' an inventor. That is what I admire the most and what I fell in love wit'." Naomi placed her head on his chest. "But the very thing I fell in love wit' made me skeptical 'cause I didn't want to spend my entire marriage competin' wit' my husband."

"You really think I would have been competitive wit' you?"

"Elime, it's not like you would've gone out of your way to compete wit' me. It would've been in your subconscious to always outdo me. I didn't want that, so I prayed on it, and Yah came through."

"He sure did." Elime squeezed her body a little tighter for extra comfort.

"He did, which is why I made a decision." She pulled away from Elime, lookin' directly into his soul wit' those big brown eyes. "After I finish the blueprint for Boaz's restaurant, I will be shiftin' my focus to other areas of my life."

"What does that mean?" Elime questioned.

"I will be usin' my intelligence to help my family." She smiled.

"Family? It's just you and I." Elime smiled. Naomi rolled her eyes, then focused them right on Elime. "Wait!" He tilted his head, then the revelation hit him like the flood did the people durin' the days of Noah. "Naomi, you pregnant?!" He screamed from the depths of his soul. She just smiled as he picked her up from the ground, givin' her a spin. He couldn't believe he was gonna be a dad, and that his amazin' wife was gonna be a mom.

"Well, there is another surprise." He placed her hand on the table, disregardin' the papers and blueprints. "We havin' twins!"

Elime passed clean out from the news. Naomi sat on the table for a minute before whisperin, 'Hallelujah'. The AI voice glitched for a split breath before correctin' itself: "Water, provided." She threw it on his face, wakin' him up slowly in the process. She straddled him, layin' her soft afro on his rapidly beatin' chest. He wrapped his arms around her in disbelief. I'm gonna be a dad to twins, he thought.

"We are gonna be parents to twins," he whispered to Naomi.

"Yes, we are." Naomi closed her eyes, wantin' to savor this moment for life.

Elime sat up, causin' her to lift her head wit' him. He looked at her differently than he ever did. Naomi wasn't just the girl he'd been in love wit' since he was a child. She was now his wife and the mother of his twins. He loved her so much more that he didn't think his love for her could grow to this magnitude.

"Naomi, hear me when I tell you this," he spoke. "I vow to take care of and love you and my twins forever." He held her like he never did before. "I vow to love you the way Yah loves us."

"And I vow to do the same," she replied. He just held her, not wantin' to end this moment. He knew that if he trusted Yah, he could have this moment forever.

CHAPTER 8

When Elime was 25

WAHHH! WAHHH!

The wailin' sounds of crying filled the air as Elime and Naomi tried to console their twins.

"It will be alright, Chillion. Daddy loves you." Elime reached down pickin' up Chillion's Praise teethin' ring. For a brief moment, the Praise band on his arm flickered, just a faint glitch in the glow, so quick he almost thought he imagined it. He slipped the ring into his son's mouth, which calmed him down instantly. Still, the flicker left a whisper of unease sittin' heavy in Elime's chest. He placed Chillion back into his hovercrib, that his mom invented to keep them together as they roam 'round the house. The crib hovered smoothly for a second, then gave the slightest stutter before glidin' forward. Elime forced a smile at Mahlon, who was bitin' on his wit' no care in the world. Why do the little things suddenly feel like warnings? he thought, shakin' it off.

He tapped the hovercrib ever so gently, causin' it to glide across the room. This usually kept the kids occupied easily. Elime tied his locs up, makin' his way toward the kitchen.

"How was Chillion?" Naomi asked as she sipped her juice.

"How did you know it was Chillion?" he questioned.

"A mother knows," she answered, leanin' back in her chair. "That, and Chillion has a special place in your heart. Mahlon has mine."

Elime scrunched his face.

"And before you say anything," she continued, "there's nothin' wrong wit' havin' a special place in your heart for one of your kids. Everyone leans toward somethin' they love over somethin' they also love. It's human."

Elime relaxed his face in agreement. He truly enjoyed his wife when she spoke. She was the smartest person he knew, always makin' life sound clear and simple. "You're right." He reached over, pullin' her into his lap. "I love you wit' the love of Yah."

"I love you wit' the love of Yah." They kissed. Naomi gave him a look, and then it hit him.

"I know I need a retwist. It's a struggle wit' kids." He let his hair down, watchin' Naomi's fingers dance through his locs. He loved when she played wit' his hair; it made him feel grounded.

"Don't worry, I already got that covered." She whispered into her Praise, Hallelujah, and a small gadget zipped from the ceilin', dartin' from room to room before stoppin' in front of them.

"Naomi," Elime said, eyebrows raised, "what's that?"

"This," she pointed proudly, "is Glamzmo. One of my greatest creations." Restin' her head on his chest, she explained, "This bot scans you and gives you anything hair-related. If you need a wash, a dry, even a retwist, Glamzmo handles it. Watch. Hello Glamzmo."

"Hello," the robotic voice responded. "How can I assist you today?"

"Glamzmo, give my husband a wash and retwist. Can you do that?"

"Affirmative," Glamzmo replied as it got to work.

Elime kept his head steady as nanocode-charged water poured over his crown. His locs unraveled while Glamzmo massaged his scalp, hummin' in sacred frequency. From the ceilin' descended another Glamzmo for Naomi, silver fingers orbitin' like celestial rings, partin', twistin', and alignin' each root wit' precision. Oils infused wit' ancestral algorithms seeped into both their hair, sealin' the coils wit' memory and promise. When the final clip locked in place, their dreadlocks glowed faintly, recalibrated like antennae tuned to Yah's eternal signal.

The second Glamzmo flew back into the ceilin' as the first displayed a photo of their finished style. They smiled in satisfaction.

"Thank you," Naomi said warmly.

"You're welcome," Glamzmo replied before vanishin' into the ceilin'.

"Naomi," Elime touched his fresh retwist, "when did you find the time, wit' two twin boys under three, to invent such a masterpiece?"

"Well, durin' my prayer time," She held his neck gently. "Yah speaks to me and tells me what to invent, and I just obey. I'm just like you."

"Well, since you're just like me, then you need to release this item to the general public." He wrapped his arms around her waist. "It is written: 'Each one should use whatever gift he or she has received to serve others, faithfully administerin' Yah's grace in its various forms.'"

Naomi rolled her eyes. "You're right. I should share Glamzmo, but didn't I tell you I wanted to keep my tech just for the family?"

Elime hugged her tighter. "It is written: 'No longer strangers and foreigners, but fellow citizens wit' the saints and members of the household of Yah.'"

"Fine," she huffed, pulling away. "I'll do it."

Splat! A Hallegram screen appeared. Across it read: Glamzmo: Send or Keep. Elime just smiled at her as she pressed Sent.

"Good. Now how do you feel?" he asked, still smilin'.

"I feel good."

Splat! Another Hallegram appeared, this one flashin': Hovercrib: Sent or Keep and Instabottle: Sent or Keep.

Naomi glanced sideways at her husband, noticin' his grin stretch even wider. "Fine," she sighed, tappin' Sent for both. Then she rested her head against his chest again.

He held her close, makin' her feel safe. "You know I love you and only want what's best."

"I know."

Wahhh! Wahhh!

Chillion's cries echoed through the house like an alarm. Elime closed his eyes, hopin' he'd stop, and he did. When they opened, they froze. A silhouette stood over the hovercrib, holdin' Chillion. Their Praise glowed in defense until the man turned around.

"There you go," Boaz said, poppin' the teethin' ring back into Chillion's mouth. He smiled. "Hello."

They sighed in relief, realizin' they weren't 'bout to catch a case.

"Hey Boaz, how are you?" Elime asked.

"I'm good. How are y'all?"

They shrugged in unison.

"Well, at least your hair is did," Boaz joked, gesturin' at their fresh updos.

"Naomi created Glamzmo," Elime said proudly, "and it handled everything."

"Really?" Boaz raised his brows.

"Yes, but this one," Naomi thumbed at Elime, "made me share it wit' the world." She rolled her eyes again.

Boaz chuckled, settin' Chillion back beside Mahlon. "I'm glad he did. There's nothin' wrong wit' sharin' what Yah gave you. That's what bein' Neo-Eden is all about."

"I know," Naomi admitted, sittin' back on Elime's lap. "So, what brings you here?"

"I came to give y'all a break. Twins are a lot, so I'm babysittin'. Go out on a date."

Elime and Naomi exchanged looks. "Boaz, you don't have to—"

"Thank you, we'll get ready," Elime interrupted, tappin' his Praise to uploadin' 'em upstairs.

He rushed to Naomi's vanity, swipin' for outfits.

"Elime, what are you doin'?" she asked.

"I'm choosin' our outfits," he said, still scrollin'. "And before you argue, we're goin' out. The babies will be fine. You'll be fine."

Naomi's face said otherwise, but instead she helped Elime pick something to wear. They decided on all black, Elime's go-to. After showerin', they tapped the vanity, watchin' the clothes materialize before their eyes. Keepin' their updos from earlier, they downloaded to Boaz.

"How do we look?" they asked in unison.

Boaz looked up from playin' wit' the boys, eyes wide. "Amazin'! Spin around!" They twirled, then bowed. "Have fun."

"Oh, we will!" Elime grinned, whisperin' Hallelujah to download them to their sanctuary: the Threshin' Floor. The lounge glowed in warm browns and deep blacks, hummin' to the soulful Lofi AI singer, Luna Moon. The place buzzed, full of earthbound and celestial patrons alike. Off to the side, the Manager, a sentient android, oversaw the room, keepin' things in order whether or not Boaz was there. Elime and Naomi slipped into their private VIP sectional, sound-proofed and shaded for privacy. Elime whispered Hallelujah, callin' up a menu. He ordered frozen hot chocolate wit' cookies and cream for them both. Cups materialized, and they downed them quickly, laughin' as refills appeared.

"I love you," Elime whispered, pullin' Naomi onto his lap.

"I love you, too." She rested her head against his chest, listenin' to his heartbeat. It calmed her every time.

"Naomi, I never wanna stop datin' you. I love you more every second we're together."

She lifted her head, eyes shinin'. "I've loved you since we were kids. You still prove why I do." She hugged him, meltin' into his arms. "You miss the kids, don't you?" she asked softly.

Elime nodded. He wanted time wit' her, but he longed for his babies too. She felt the same. Hallelujah, wit' a whisper towards his Praise, they uploaded back home. Boaz snored on the couch while the twins climbed him like a jungle gym. Elime and Naomi laughed, scoopin' up their boys. Boaz startled awake, eyes wide.

"Havin' fun?" Elime teased.

Boaz rubbed his face. "They wore me out. They were fine in the crib; then I played wit' 'em, fed them, put them back. But… there was an accident."

Naomi's brows furrowed. "What happened?"

Boaz sighed. "The hovercrib crashed into your vanity. I'm so sorry, Naomi. I'll replace it!"

Naomi hugged him. "It's fine. I'm just grateful the kids weren't hurt. Nothin' means more to me than them, and you."

"Absolutely," Elime added, huggin' him. "You're my brother. Don't worry about the vanity. If it takes a lifetime, I'll restore it. That's the least I can do."

Boaz relaxed. "Love y'all. But I need sleep." He whispered Hallelujah into his Praise and uploaded home.

Elime checked the twins through his Praise. "They're asleep. You know what that means?" He grinned.

"Yes, I do." Naomi clapped her hands, summonin' pajamas. They uploaded upstairs, layin' the babies in their crib before crawlin' into bed themselves, driftin' off to sleep.

CHAPTER 9

When Elime was 33

"Look, kids," Elime spoke as he held a gadget in his hand. His sons, Mahlon and Chillion, gazed as they saw the gizmo just lyin' dormant.

"How does it work, papa?" Mahlon asked.

"It's voice-activated, like our faith in Yah. You have to say 'Hallelujah'." He smiled at his sons. Elime enjoyed bein' a father. It was a lifelong dream that he was thankful for each and every day.

"Hallelujah," the boys spoke together. The gadget turned on, and immediately began soarin' out the door.

"Race you to get it!" Chillion took off runnin'.

"Not so fast," Mahlon followed behind.

"Hey, y'all! Be careful." Elime gave his best dad voice. He had been working on it ever since they were young and felt like he'd perfected it. However, what he is havin' a real trouble perfectin' was childproofin' a lab. He never imagined that he'd have to childproof his lab, but he and Naomi both agreed that they wanted both of their boys to be inventors and innovators like they are. So, that meant makin' sure everything was child safe so the boys could spend more time in the lab.

He always had a checklist and would hear either a soft ping or a loud ring, dependin' on if he did it, and so far, he had. He decided to return to a project that he had been secretly workin' on, tryin' to fix Naomi's vanity that was destroyed many macrobytes ago when the kids were little. He dabbled at it piece by piece since then but never really jumped in full throttle. He tried, but it always seemed like somethin' was blockin' him. Wit' Naomi out wit' Boaz and the boys busy chasin' the gadgets he purposely made to occupy 'em, he figured now was the time to try and get to this vanity.

He would have gone real far wit' it but I had other plans.

"Hello, Elime," I popped next to him. In true Elime fashion, he dropped to the floor.

"I'm not worthy." His words muffled through the floor.

I sat down next to him, "Elime, you can get up now and face Me." I slightly chuckled. I do enjoy seein' him as he does have a great reverence for me. I just hope that after today, he still does.

Elime sat up, facin' me wit' a slight sense of nervousness. "Hello," his words shook.

"Hello," I reached over for a hug. He hugged me back kinda nervously. I told him I was a hugger he must have forgotten. "So, I AM gonna cut to the chase. I have been tryin' to get your attention in hopes you would come to Me."

Elime stared at me peculiarly, "Tryna get my attention? How?"

"Wit' the tech glitchin'." I usually love havin' the witty banter wit' you, but, maybe after we could.

Elime stared at me like I had five heads, which in some universes I do. "Yes, I did that in hope you would come to Me, but I guess I have to come to you and be direct."

"Direct 'bout what?"

Why I AM here which I AM here to talk 'bout your parents."

Elime leaned so far that he almost fell. His parents died when he was young so he doesn't really remember them. He had seen home videos of their life, so that brought him somewhat closer..

"What 'bout my parents?" He questioned. He always wanted to know more, outside of videos and stories he heard from Boaz's parents.

"Well, we need to discuss how they died."

Silence filled the room and left space for the beepin' and doopin' from the machines surroundin' us.

"Tell me how you are feelin'!"

Elime stared at Me as if I had ten heads this time which, I do in certain universes. "I don't know how to feel 'bout that information. I guess I'm indifferent 'bout it."

"Fair," I nodded, "well, it's important that you know 'bout their death."

"Ah, man!" Elime heard his boys, as their feet began to chase the gadgets through the house.

"I knew they were comin' and didn't want to be interrupted." I smiled at Elime. I want this to go well. "So, Elime. Your mom and dad died when you were little and you were sent to live wit' your aunt and uncle, Boaz's parents. You follow?" Elime nodded. "Okay, so here's the thing. Your mother was never meant to die, only your father."

"Huh?" Elime was confused by My statement and I don't blame him.

"Your father was supposed to be the only one that died but your mother bein' 'round him caused her to catch a stray."

"So, let me get this straight," Elime was tryin' to wrap his mind around this information, "my father was supposed to die, but not my mom. The only reason she did was 'cause she was 'round my dad?"

"Yes," My voice crescendoed. "She should be here, but she isn't. Now, on to your father." Elime's body tensed immediately. "Elime, relax."

"I know. It's just a lot right now," He was tryin' to find the words but couldn't. I know it is tough to speak 'bout death to humans but, it's a part of their experience.

"Well, many macrobytes ago, I spoke wit' your father, and told him 'bout this family secret that no one ever told him. I told him that he needs to tell his wife sooner rather than later. He never told her so he died 'cause of it."

A single tear ran down Elime's cheek. "So, my dad, my parent's death was preventable?" I hugged him just in time for the tears to fall and man, did they fall. I allowed him to take as much time as he needed to feel how he wanted to feel. I enjoy creatin' space for Yah's people to feel vulnerable and safe. It's why I'm here, amongst other things. He finally pulled away.

"I don't want you to view your parents' death as whether or not it was preventable. I want you to view it as a chance to learn from them so you can change your fate."

"My fate," his words startled out, "what do you mean?"

I took a deep breath, "His fate could become yours."

The noises from the machines filled the air, yet the silence felt heavy. Elime couldn't believe what he was bein' told. He began playin' it in his mind, and wit' each time, it became more real. "Umm, one more time?"

"You heard me the first time. His fate could become your fate." I readjusted my body. "Now, what I will tell you is this: Everything that I say or someone from M.O.E.E says, unless a revelation, is conditional. You have the power to change it but that's up to you."

He nodded his head. Elime, above all else, loved me wit' his soul. "So, wit' all that bein' said, the big family secret is......."

I saw Elime tilt his head before focusin' his eyes on me. "That's it?" Elime knew it sounded ridiculous, as I did too but, he needed to know. "I thought you were gonna tell me somethin' dark and sinister." He chuckled

"First off," I had to interrupt, "nothin' I do or say is dark and sinister. It is good 'cause it comes from Yah and Yah is good." Our laughter filled the air like my Presence on a Sunday mornin'.

"So, what do I have to do?"

"You have to tell Naomi what I told you," I smiled.

"That's it?" He questioned.

"Would you like a post-apocalyptic prophecy? I have tons of those to give."

He shook his head profusely.

"I thought so," I smiled. I knew very well how much Neo-Edens despise my post-apocalyptic prophecies. Little did they know that those would be few and far between if they just listened to Yah, the first time. I stood to my feet on my way to leave. He followed my motions and I reached over for a hug, which we shared. I looked him in his eyes "Before you go, I have a question," I stopped him. He quickly turned around as he couldn't get enough of my presence. He quickly returned in front before even I could blink. "Do you love me?"

"Of cou-," Elime caught his words before utterin' wrong thing. "Ruach, you know the answer."

Same response he gave Me, just like before. I AM sure I did know the answer and I was gonna make sure he knew it too.

CHAPTER 10

When Elime was 37

Elime worked diligently in his lab on his latest project: the restoration of his wife's vanity. Drops of sweat glided down his face, as passion and exhaustion pushed him forward. This project was more than a gift; it was a tribute. Naomi had sacrificed a part of who she was just to pour it into her family. Though Elime would nudge her to share her genius wit' the world, she always chose to give it to those closest to her. She had stood by him through thick and thin, whether it was the annual tech competition they both entered at 17 or the time an investor sought her out but she insisted Elime be included.

Wit' all the inventions they had released across the multiverse, it would be easy to assume Elime had already built somethin' just for Naomi. But one day he realized he hadn't. His twins were their shared legacy, yes, but he wanted to create somethin' that honored only her, somethin' that reflected her steadfast love and faith. He knew he was a great inventor because he was connected to Yah. His Praise gave him access to divine inspiration. And wit' that guidance, he would craft a genuine "thank you" for the woman who had supported his life.

Elime could've restored the vanity in the traditional way, but technology was his language, his art. And this was no ordinary gift. Addin' the Word of Yah to her vanity would link Naomi to both the outside world and the cyber realm.. No one had ever attempted such a feat, but Elime had faith. He trusted in Yah, who guided his hands and eyes. That belief carried him through an exhaustin' week until the final screw slid into place.

Leanin' against the wall, Elime gazed at his creation in awe. The old wooden, makeup-stained counter had become the VXT 2000, a futuristic, three-mirror vanity system wit' glowin' interfaces. It wasn't just furniture; it was the first of its kind, a machine designed to give the user direct access to Yah and His A.N.G.E.Ls (Augmented Neural Guidance and Enlightenment Links).

But there was a problem: the Word of Yah wouldn't configure wit' the vanity.

The blueprints looked perfect, yet the system remained lifeless. Elime rewired, reconstructed, and redesigned, but nothin' worked. Frustration mounted as the days blurred together. His fingertips were burned from solderin', his eyes bloodshot from lack of rest, but still he pressed on. He was close to givin' up when, in the stillness of his lab, I whispered in his mind:

"Hello. Return to the original design."

Wit'out hesitation, he grabbed the Word of Yah module, wiped the sweat from his brow, and followed the guidance he'd received. He stripped away the unnecessary, simplified the connections, and restored the system to its purest form. By the time he finished, exhaustion weighed on him like a heavy cloak, but peace settled deep in his chest. The VXT 2000 wasn't yet functionin', but he felt relief in obeyin' the voice. Starin' at his reflection in the sleek glass, he allowed himself a rare moment of pride.

Hungry and worn out, Elime decided to take a break. As he walked away, a faint hum stopped him in his tracks. He froze, listenin' intently. A flicker of light danced across the vanity's surface. His heart leapt as he rushed back, nearly trippin' in his haste. "It flickered," he thought, hope surgin' through him. Yet, when he reached the console, the machine was silent again. Disappointment threatened, but he brushed it aside wit' a deep breath, much like Naomi brushing her hair in front of the vanity.

BOOM.

The explosion hurled him across the room, slammin' him into the wall. Dazed, Elime blinked, tryin' to process what had just happened. Smoke curled through the air, burnin' his lungs as he coughed. The acrid tang of melted wires stung his nose. As his vision cleared, his jaw dropped. The VXT 2000 was alive. Sparks of electricity danced along its frame as the vanity settled into a glowin', ethereal state. The mirrors shimmered wit' vibrant colors, displayin' dynamic scripture and celestial visuals. The Word of Yah had infused the vanity wit' divine brilliance, exceedin' anythin' Elime could have imagined.

He wanted to leap up and rejoice, but the twenty-foot throw had other plans. His ribs ached, and his hands trembled from the shock. Instead, he leaned back against the wall and raised his hands in gratitude. Tears streamed down his face as he praised Yah for guidin' his work and bringin' his vision to life. The burden he had carried all week lifted from his shoulders, leavin' only peace.

For the first time in days, Elime allowed himself to rest. He knew Naomi would love it, not just for its technological marvel, but for the love and faith woven into every wire and every screw.

Naomi knelt in intense prayer, her brow furrowed as she sought a revelation from Yah. A gentle tap on her back broke the quiet hum of her thoughts. Startled, she whipped around, her irritation evident.

"WHAT?!!" she snapped, her voice sharper than she intended.

Elime's smile, radiant and warm, melted her frustration in an instant. If there was one person she could never stay mad at, it was him. Naomi leapt into his arms, her joy evident in the wide smile that spread across her face.

"I know you hate havin' your time wit' Yah interrupted," Elime said, his tone soft but teasin', "but I've got a surprise for you."

Naomi spun out of his arms, curiosity piqued. She did like surprises. Closin' her eyes and openin' her palms in eager anticipation, she grinned.

"No peekin'," Elime said as he guided her to her desk. Naomi couldn't resist crackin' one eye open slightly. When she saw the surprise, her scream echoed through the room like a pinball machine.

"AHHH!"

There it was: the VXT 2000, a limited-edition vanity wit' a Praise connection. Naomi's grin stretched from ear to ear. She had given up hope that it could ever be fixed. She remembered the terror she felt that night when Boaz said there was an accident involvin' her babies. Relief had rushed over her when she realized it was only her vanity. Her heart still fluttered remembering the way her knees nearly buckled that night, the fear latching on before being ripped away by relief.

"Do you love it?" Elime asked, his heart swellin' at her delight.

"Elime, it's perfect! I love it!"

Elime knew she would. Her joy made the hours of preparation, and the slight concussion he'd gotten from a mishap durin' setup, worth it. He smiled, realizin' that Naomi was more than capable of fixin' her vanity herself. Why did Yah have me do it? he thought. But before he could dwell on it, or she could dive into explorin' its features, Elime wrapped an arm around her shoulders and leaned close.

"Naomi?" he said, his voice lowerin'. "Please, don't tell anyone 'bout the VXT 2000. I know we always encourage each other to share our inventions wit' the world, but this is somethin' specially for you. Okay?"

Naomi nodded absentmindedly, already engrossed in the intricate design. She typically listened to Elime, but today felt different. She didn't want to go against her husband, yet she felt her family would benefit tremendously from sharin' this invention. Elime sighed, knowin' full well his wife's tendency to share excitin' news. He repeated himself for emphasis, but deep down, he knew she wasn't truly listenin'. What he didn't realize was the magnitude of her not listenin', not until it was too late.

From the moment Elime left Naomi alone, he felt in his spirit that she was itchin' to tell everyone about her new vanity. He could never blame Naomi for wantin' to express her love. She was deeply in love wit' Elime and extremely proud of the work he did each day. She was her husband's biggest support system, which often turned into his biggest advertisement. No matter what Elime made, whether flawless or needin' some work, Naomi spread the word.

Spread the word she did. Wit'in three days, Elime's latest invention had ended up on the web, in magazines, across social media, and even in the newspaper. Elime sat on the sofa, his head in his hands, chucklin' despite himself. He knew his wife couldn't hold water; what he didn't realize was just how heavy the bucket was. Naomi had told Boaz, who told a patron at his restaurant, who told everyone. Now the whole dimension knew about the VXT 2000. Deep down, Elime couldn't be mad. He knew his wife, knew who he married. And truthfully, he wanted the word to spread, because this invention felt like somethin' that would change his life.

Requests flooded in faster than he could process them. Every woman in the dimension seemed to want the limited-edition vanity wit' Praise connection. The console in the corner blinked incessantly wit' incomin' messages, its glow fillin' the room like a digital sunrise.

Elime exhaled deeply, frustration and resignation tangled in his voice. He couldn't stay mad at Naomi. He had always pushed her to share her inventions, so it was only right she did the same. Her excitement was part of why he loved her. Still, this wasn't how he'd planned to unveil his creation. He knew eventually it would reach the world, Naomi would have made sure of it. She always wanted the best not for herself but for her family.

What he didn't anticipate was the passion she carried when spreadin' the news. That fire was one of the many reasons he loved her, but now it had him drownin' in orders. He wasn't ready for mass production, yet the numbers were the best he'd seen in years. Her passion had become a blessin' in disguise.

Ignorin' most of the messages, he slouched back on the sofa until the console's glow shifted, brighter now, more urgent.

SPAT!

A Hallegram materialized before him, the divine signature unmistakable. He straightened, recognizin' Yah's hand in it. "Do you wish to have the VXT 2000 manufactured and distributed to all those who ordered?" The message floated in midair, accompanied by a simple voice request: If "Yes" say "Hallelujah." If "No" say "Ouch."

Elime hesitated, then exhaled deeply, starin' at the "Yes" option. "If this is Yah's will… Hallelujah," he muttered, pressing it.

Instantly, the Praise console hummed to life, processin' the orders wit' divine efficiency. The glow illuminated the room, and Elime leaned back, knowin' he'd need Yah's help to keep up wit' the demand.

"Lord, I know there is a reason You wanted me to say yes, but can You please tell me why?" Elime whispered as he rose from the couch.

"You already know why," I whispered into his spirit.

He stumbled, bowing his head in reverence. He was taught to stay out of his feelin's, but this time it was easier said than done. Sometimes it was difficult to trust Yah, though Yah had always led him down the path of righteousness. His thoughts warred wit' his emotions as he walked down the hall. Halfway to his bedroom, another Hallegram flashed before him.

"Moabolis? If 'Yes' say 'Hallelujah.' If 'No' say 'Ouch.'"

"Baby! Mahlon! Chillion! Come here!" Elime's family rushed to meet him starin' blankly at the screen.

"Yes, dear?" Naomi creased her brow in concern. Elime pointed at the floatin' words. He'd never seen anythin' like it. Messages usually came through his Hallelujah console, but this one appeared out of nowhere. He wanted to be fearful, but he knew Yah never gave that spirit.

"Why's it askin' if we wanna go to Moabolis?" Mahlon asked.

"I dunno, but I don't wanna say no." Elime paced before the text, then shook his head. Stressin' each syllable, he declared, "This! Is! Yah!"

"Well," Chillion asked, "can we know why we have to go to Moabolis?"

The Hallegram went black, replaced by a single word: 'Famine.'

Elime knew of the famine. People hadn't heard from Yah in many macrobytes, except for the J.U.D.G.Es and a chosen few. It must be digital, since we're already in a cyber famine, Elime thought.

"So, what we doin'?" Naomi's voice trembled, fear creeping in.

"I guess the answer is yes." Elime spoke "Hallelujah," and the screen disappeared. The house screamed in silence. Everyone stared at him until he chuckled nervously. "Well, I guess we start packin' for Moabolis!"

He tried to walk forward but hit an invisible wall. Stumblin' back, confusion raced through him. He tried again and was thrown back harder. Frustrated, he charged at it, bumpin' his head and fallin' to the ground. Naomi crouched beside him as he rubbed his head.

"Dad," Mahlon asked, "what's happenin'?"

"I dunno…" Elime muttered as Naomi helped him to his feet.

"Hello," said a digital voice from the heavens. "Thank you for allowin' Yah to lead your life."

The phrase struck him, words from his earliest memories. He was always taught to allow Yah to lead, but this was the first time his faith grew weary. Still, he didn't want his family to see that weakness. Faith was all they had; it shaped everythin', from breathin' to buildin' a mainframe. But his family's faces were covered wit' panic.

"You selected to move to Moabolis. Since you have received the upgrade of the Holy Spirit, you will be downloaded to Moabolis in five seconds."

"Downloaded?" Chillion whispered. "You mean?"

"I mean," the voice continued, "you all will be uploaded into the cyber realm and downloaded straight to Moabolis."

Elime's spine tingled. He tried to stay calm, feelin' his family's eyes on him.

"Thank You for allowin' Yah to lead your life," the voice concluded. "Keep believin'."

The lights flicked off. A Hallegram number five appeared in the air, flashin' like a taunt. Then the beeps began.

'5'
"Dad, I am scared," Mahlon said.

'4'
"Do somethin'!" Naomi screamed.

'3'
"There's nothin' I can do," Elime answered. "This is the will of Yah."

'2'
"Will of Yah?!" Naomi grabbed his shoulders, pleadin'. "So there's nothin' we can do?"

'1'
"Actually, there is." Elime grabbed his family close, eyes shut. "We can believe!"

They were digitally uploaded, their screams dissolvin' into rushing data streams. Elime opened his eyes mid-scream, stunned by the surreal beauty—streams of data, music downloads, shoppin' carts, even stray viruses whizzin' past. It felt like a dream. He remembered his first time being uploaded into the competition, but never imagined it wit' his family, shot across the galaxy.

When they finally landed, the family staggered, disoriented but unharmed. They were in Moabolis, a city defyin' logic. Towerin' skyscrapers of stone and wire hovered in the air, ancient craftsmanship fused wit' futuristic tech. Hover cars zipped overhead; on the streets, humans and androids mingled. A group lounged outside a cybercafé, sippin' grape drink. Cyborgs patrolled the skies, glowin' eyes scannin' the crowd.

Elime's breath caught.

"What is this place?" Naomi whispered.

"This is Moabolis," Elime answered, equally mesmerized. "We're here for a reason. Yah doesn't make mistakes." Excitement stirred in him; he'd followed Prince Eglon on social media, amazed at the prince's life and city.

The silence broke when Chillion asked sharply, "What do we do now?"

Elime took a deep breath. "The only thing we can do, son. We ask Yah for help."

As if on cue, a Hallegram appeared: "Follow Me." The words morphed into a pulsatin' arrow floatin' down the street.

The Efrathats exchanged glances, then followed. It led them through the bustle—androids, cyborgs, vendors hawkin' gadgets—until they reached a massive warehouse. The Hallegram flickered one last word: "Home."

"This must be it," Elime said firmly.

Chillion frowned. "How you know?"

Elime turned to his sons. "What have I always told you about Yah? What must we do, always?"

The boys exchanged a look, then answered together: "We must believe!"

"Exactly." Elime smiled, then stepped forward. As he neared, the doors slid open wit' a hiss.

"Look at Yah!" he whispered in awe, beckonin' them forward.

Inside, the warehouse transformed. Lights flickered, curtains drew open, soft music played. Plates of steamin' food hovered on trays, fillin' the room wit' comfortin' aromas. Everythin' seemed alive, as though the house had scanned them and knew what they needed.

"Welcome to the home of The Efrathats," a cheerful digital voice announced.

The family was wide-eyed as the house morphed into an upgraded version of their Neo-Eden home. Hoverin' furniture drifted into place, sweepers zipped across the floor, and a plush carpet hovered above the ground. They burst into laughter when a sweeper zipped under their feet.

"So, Dad, is this why we believe?" Mahlon smiled.

Elime's eyes softened. "Yes, my child. This is why we always believe."

The family explored their new digital home, their laughter echoin' through the space. For Elime, it had been a strange, miraculous journey. Settlin' onto the floatin' couch, he felt peace wash over him. Yah had brought them here for a reason, and for now, that was enough.

CHAPTER 11

When Elime was 40

It didn't take long for Elime and his family to adapt to bein' in this new city. Growin' up, he always wanted to visit Moabolis and dreamt of the day he could. It always seemed like everyone was havin' a good time and not in constant disobedience like the Neo-Edens were. The biggest discrepancy that he did have was their unbelief in Yah. Belief was a cornerstone of not only Elime, but the people where he came from, for the most part. He always found it strange that the people in his nation turned their noses up towards others who did not worship Yah and Yah only. Mind you, they would worship strange gods, and then when it didn't work out always turned to Yah for help. Yah, bein' Yah, always would rescue them and save them every single time. These were always the thoughts that danced around in Elime's mind almost every day since he moved to Moabolis wit' his family.

Elime was loungin' on the sofa when he noticed his family movin' 'round the house. His sons were no longer listenin' to the rhythm and blues of their city. Now it was the all popular Moabolis group, Alice's Escape. The house would literally ping every time, TheMoMa, a popular vlog throughout the universe, would post. From his wife's cookin' to havin' automatic Moabolis meals prepared by his kitchen just from her sayin' it out loud; he learned that was common in this city. It was extremely evident in the family's new choice of fashion. Wit' the KE3's, a luxury gym shoe worn exclusively by Moabolians, marked wit' the signature balsam flower on the side, the people of Moabolis showed off their pride. They loved the Balsam, since it symbolized their country and grew naturally in their land. Elime never imagined he'd be counted among 'em, but stranger things had happened.

He whispered Hallelujah into his Praise, promptin' a Hallegram to appear. He placed the Hallegram on the coffee table and began workin'. Checkin' logistics and day-to-day operations of his business was how he spent some mornin's. His VXT, the vanity he made for his wife, was sellin' daily which allowed him to spend time wit' his family and monitor his progress. Naomi curled next to him as he was doin' his work. He kissed her forehead while checkin' the analytics. The day-to-day workin's of his business wasn't glamorous. He was grateful to Yah that he was able to have access to his lab through his Praise. He was even more grateful that this house came wit' a lab as well. This extra lab helped in many ways as he was able to increase his production wit' less effort.

He was so grateful for all the help that Yah provided. It made life much easier when you can put your business into the all-knowin', all-powerful bein' and allow Him to have his way. Elime was thankful that he was able to work from home and be fruitful in his labor. He did not have a care in the world. He thought there was nothin' that could ruin this moment. He thought wrong.

A message popped across the display. He was 'bout to swipe ignore 'cause he received 1000s of emails throughout the day. There was always somethin' or someone tryin' to get somethin' from him. He even had people that he never talked to when he was a kid from Neo-Eden wantin' to be friends now that his invention is sellin' every day. He ignored them and blocked them as any Believer should. However, this subject line caught his attention: King Eglon Summons you.' Elime and Naomi took off laughin'. They knew this must be spam for they hadn't heard from, or seen, the King since he was a prince judgin' their competition. There's no way that he could have remembered Elime and Naomi. Elime tried to delete the message, but it would not delete.

"That's odd?" Elime muttered. "It won't delete."

"Maybe you should open it?" Naomi shrugged. Elime, skeptical at the suggestion, knew nothin' sinister could happen. He had the upgrade, Holy Spirit, throughout the firewalls and mainframe. No virus was comin' in here. With one tap, the message opened and a video began playin' of King Eglon.

"Elime Efrathat, you and your family are cordially invited to a private dinner wit' King Eglon, Queen Lani, Princess Orpah & Princess Ruth. The dinner will be tonight at 7:00 p.m. A royal car will arrive at 6:50 p.m. to pick you and your family up and bring them to the castle. If you have any questions, please respond to this message. Finally, attendance is mandatory."

The message went blank as Elime and Naomi stared at each for what felt like forever. Elime was first to break the silence. "AHHHHHHHHHHHH!"

"AHHHHHHHHHHHHH!" Naomi screamed back. They hadn't screamed like that in years. Last time they did, they were graduatin' high school and felt like they had the world ahead of them. That day was engraved in Elime and Naomi's minds forever. This day would be engraved right next to it.

Their sons ran into the room "What's wrong?" Mahlon asked. Elime and Naomi pointed to the video message from the king. Chillion stepped forward and hit play.

"AHHHHHHHHHHH!" the brothers yelled.

"Now, you know how we feel." Naomi smiled.

"So what does this mean?" Chillion asked, puzzled.

"This means," said the king as if he was listenin' to the conversation , "that y'all have to be ready by 6:50 p.m. for dinner wit' the king." Mahlon and Chillion read the clock at 5:50 p.m. and ran to their respective rooms so that they could find somethin' to wear. Naomi and Elime followed their lead. The entire family frantically tried to look their best. His family had the same sentiment because they were vigorously tryin' to get ready.

After Naomi showered, she whispered Hallelujah and a Hallegram appeared. She swiped through it vigorously tryin' to find somethin' elegant to wear. She could not find anythin'. Frustrated, she walked toward her husband who was takin' a nap.

"Elime! Baby, wake up!" Elime was peacefully dreamin' about how he was wowin' the king, a second time, wit' his words, how the king was so fascinated 'bout his invention, and what he was sayin'. It was a great dream that he didn't want to let go of. He was havin' an amazin' time until he heard somethin' familiar, somethin' real.

Elime jumped out of his sleep in a panic. He thought he missed the dinner but it was just his wife.

"What is it?" Elime shook his head to regain his composure.

"First, you are not dressed. Second, we don't have anythin' to wear." Naomi could not hide her frustration any longer. This event needed to go perfect and Elime did not seem worried in the slightest.

"Honey, I have that all taken care of!" He smiled. Naomi gave him a careful side-eye. They had nothin' elegant for dinner wit' King Eglon and he was takin' a nap like everythin' was fine.

"Naomi, Yah does not give us the spirit of fear but…." Elime's voice faded.

"Of power, love, and sound mind ." Elime stood up and engulfed her in muscular arms and as always Naomi smiled. Elime held her in such a way that made her feel loved and protected. It was why she married, and remained married, to him. He released her and headed toward his closet. He kneeled down, grabbin' boxes of shoes.

"Mahlon! Chillion!" Elime yelled. "Come here. His sons quickly ran to their parents' room in a panic. "You all need somethin' to wear, correct?" Everyone nodded. "Well, I have that all taken care of. Look at Yah!" He began to give them each a box of shoes. They started at Elime confused but he nudged them to open their boxes. When they did they saw the most stunnin' and mesmerizin' pair of black shoes. Naomi received a pair of onyx spiked stilettos. Mahlon received a pair of jet-black spiked loafers. Chillion received a pair of obsidian spiked chukka boots. While Elime had a pair of classic jet-black spiked dress shoes. Elime's family stared at him oddly.

"Bae?" Naomi said, tryin' not to make eye contact. "So, we just gonna wear shoes and no clothes?"

The boys began to chuckle.

Elime shook his head wit' a smile, "Oh, you of little faith. Try them on."

Naomi and the boys stared at each other skeptically before tryin' on the shoes. Elime smiled each step of the way.

"Okay, so what now!" Naomi threw Elime a puzzled look before she felt somethin' crawlin' at her feet. She wasn't the only one as she noticed her children were starin' at each other. They looked down, frozen solid as somethin' like pixels crawled up their body. The pixels began to form the most elegant and stylish clothes for an evenin' wit' a king. Mahlon's jet-black spiked loafers engulfed him wit' cuffed pants, cashmere sweater, and shades, all black. Chillion's obsidian chukka boots covered him wit' black skinny jeans, a T-shirt, a leather jacket, and shades, all obsidian. Naomi's onyx spiked stilettos pixelated an Star of David ball gown, matchin' pocketbook, and shades, all onyx.

When it was over, they each took a look at each other wit' amazement. They stared at Elime, now in a tailor-made suit, bowtie, and shades, all black.

"Bae? What did you do?" Naomi found words to speak.

"I believed Yah and He came through!" Elime wrapped his arms around her. "The shoes were an invention for several years in the makin'. I had to wait for just the right time to try them out. Tonight seemed to be the right time."

They were all still amazed that Elime created a powerful and stylish invention. He'd been doin' it all his life but somethin' 'bout today felt unique. "Basically, the shoes run a cerebral scan and determine your personality. Then, create an outfit based on personality and the event for that day. As you can see, we are goin' somewhere classy, so the clothes matched." Elime proceeded towards the door. "Y'all, I would love to go into details but, the car will be here any minute." The family understood and went outside to wait for him.

The Efrathats went outside and a blindin' light greeted them from above. "Elime Efrathat and family." A voice from above grabbed their attention and they looked up. "Please continue to stare up for facial recognition." The infrared light blinded Elime and he looked around to see the rest of the family also blinded through squinted eyes. All he saw was the car scannin' to verify their identities. "Identity confirmed," The AI voice from the car spoke. Suddenly, the light centered on Elime and his family and they instantly uploaded into the car. Elime looked around as the king picked them up in the HR 1804, the fastest, smartest, and gravity-defyin' car to date. They all kept quiet as the car flew them to the center of the city where the king was waitin' for them to arrive.

CHAPTER 12

When Elime was still 40

The HR 1804 downloaded the Efrathats down right into the magnificent ballroom. Everything 'round them was crafted out of the finest marble, limestone, and, strangely enough, salt.

"Mahlon! Chillion!" Elime glanced over to his sons. "Don't touch nothin'," he scolded them, he noticed out of the corner of his eyes that Naomi was happily touchin' stuff. "Now, I just told them to not touch, and here you go!" Naomi froze wit' a playful expression on her face.

Elime shook his head. "That not working today. Don't touch!" Naomi threw her hands up and walked towards Elime. He welcomed her hug and gazed into her eyes wit' a grin.

"Hello there!"

The kiss was cut short by a servant-droid. "I'm Cami. I am the head droid here at the palace. I will be showin' you where you will be havin' dinner."

Cami turned around and walked in the opposite direction. Elime and his family followed. They admired the art and statues that decorated the hallway, which was long. Finally, they came to the center of the dinin' room, which had a giant crystal ball defyin' gravity. Off to the side, was a long table that had a buffet-style setup.

"You will wait here." Cami motioned them to stop. "The Royal Family will greet you here. Then you will sit at that table wit' the food and eat."

The amount of food displayed could rival that of a Sunday. "Umm, that's a lot of food? Who's eatin' all that!?" Mahlon asked. It seemed quite excessive for only eight people.

Cami chuckled, "You'll see."

Lofi music began to play as the lights went off and the crystal ball lit up. A moment later, The Royal Family, the De Moabs, appeared ten feet away in all white. It startled Elime and his family for many reasons. The main reason was the king.

King Eglon was a fat, borderline-obsessed man. As he started walkin', Elime noticed that he was slower than his family and had to take breaks. By the time he approached them, he was short-winded. Elime didn't remember King Eglon bein' this big the first time they met. Then again, they were kids.

"Your Majesty!" Elime bowed, and his family followed suit.

"Please. Call me K.E.!"

"This is my family," King Eglon announced. "My wife, Queen Lani. My daughters, Princess Ruth and Princess Orpah." The Royal Family bowed their heads.

Elime froze in shock. "Your Mag—" Elime stopped himself. "K.E., why did your family bow to us? We're the guests and you guys are royalty."

"It's like I always say. If you want to be treated like royalty then…" King Eglon paused,

"You have to treat others like royalty." His family finished.

Elime was not expectin' that. It was refreshin' to hear him believe that everyone is royal. Elime noticed the king walkin' towards the dinner table and everyone followed. As Elime approached the table he realized that it was a round table. He didn't know where to sit 'til Queen Lani motioned down where he saw his name on a place mat. He sat down and the family joined.

The king knew how to entertain guests. What he lacked in physical appearance, he made up wit' charisma and charm. Everyone was as happy as the king was hungry. Elime and his family watched as the king became a human garbage disposal. While the Efrathats had one plate each of food, King Eglon had several. What was even more shockin' was that his family's eatin' behavior was identical to his. These three petite women ate like they were tryin' to win an eatin' contest. They shoveled food into their mouths frantically and swallowed as if they evolved from chewin'. They gulped down water and belched loudly, leavin' the Efrathats starin' in amazement and disgust. It was a disturbin' scene that left a lastin' impression.

"Y'all ain't hungry?" King Eglon looked concerned at his guests' empty plates.

"No, we had enough." The Efrathats shook their heads. "Gotta save room for dessert."

King Eglon froze, "You are right. Honey! Girls! Stop eatin'!" Queen Lani and her daughters placed their forks down and wiped their mouths. King Eglon clapped and the food vanished. Suddenly, every type of cake, cookie, brownie, pie, and ice cream, materialized before them. Elime and his family each took a slice of pie and one scoop of ice cream. King Eglon and his family grabbed every treat the eye could see and began wolfin' at it. No cake was safe and no cookie was sound when the De Moabs were near them. Once again, the Efrathats watched in horror as the De Moabs were viciously inhalin' the treats like wolves on the hunt for prey. Those treats didn't stand a chance against the De Moabs. Elime almost felt sorry for the desserts as if they were innocent victims, brought to the slaughter.

Elime, unable to stomach the lack of etiquette displayed at dinner, decided to break the silence to move forward. "K.E.?" King Eglon and his family stop mid-bite and stare directly at him. "As much as me and my family are enjoyin' your royal company, I do have a question. Why did you request me to come and have dinner wit' you?"

King Eglon swallowed his food and wiped his hands off. His family does the same.

"Uh, yes! Give me one second!" King Eglon turned to his wife and began to whisper somethin' that was incoherent. He turned back to Elime, smiles, and clapped his hands on the side of his head. Suddenly, King Eglon and Elime vanished from the dining hall.

CHAPTER 13

When Elime was still 40

The cyber-assistant, Cami, was sittin' off to the side in the giant office. She was accompanied by a desk, several bookshelves, and the green metal that accented the trim. Two color-changin' couches mirrored each other in the center of the office. King Eglon and Elime teleported into the office, each arrivin' on a sofa. Today, the couches were black.

"I can tell you loaded before!" King Eglon was jolly, to say the least.

"How do you think I got here to Moabolis?"

King Eglon's mouth matched his round face in certainty. "I knew that was you. It took you long enough."

Elime sat up in confusion. "Wait, what?"

King Eglon rolled around like Humpty-Dumpty on the great wall and laughed. He motioned for Elime to come sit next to him. He leaned in and gave Elime a big hug that was almost as big as he was. "How have you been, Elime? It's been a minute since I saw you."

Elime's eyes widened. "K.E., you remember me?"

King Eglon laughed. "I do. And Naomi." He calmed down. "I never could forget my first and only competition that I judged in Neo-Eden. I even used Naomi's bottle for my girls." He reached behind him and pulled out a replica of the bottle Naomi made to win the competition. "Although, she did say that you invented it."

"She did?" Elime was confused.

"Yes," King Eglon said.

Elime couldn't believe what he was hearin'. King Eglon remembered who he was and even had his wife's invention next to him, or that his wife put his name on her invention. "I don't know what to say."

"Don't worry, you'll find the words." King Eglon wobbled toward the end of the couch, which was now a light blue. "I will say that I was most pleased to see you accept my dinner invite. I assumed you remembered me."

"Really? You're the king. How could I forget? And," Elime added, "you invited us? Attendance was mandatory."

King Eglon chuckled. "You and your wife are famous inventors specifically of the VXT 2000, for you. My wife and daughters love that vanity. I figured you might be too busy to come, so I made attendance mandatory."

Elime smiled widely and felt himself blush. "Thank you!"

"You are welcome!"

Elime relaxed onto a now-green sofa and leaned into the cushions. "So, what brings me and my family here?"

King Eglon jumped to his feet, then held out his arms to steady himself, like that was the fastest he had moved in a long time.

"Yes! Why are you here? Yes, that is important." Already out of breath and sweatin', King Eglon sat back down. "I need your help." A glass of water appeared floatin' next to him wit' a towel.

"My help? For what?"

King Eglon took the towel and wiped his face. "As you clearly see, I am fat and not what you are used to seein' of me since you saw me when I was younger. I need help gettin' around. My last hover-scooter broke down. I want you to invent a new one."

"Me? Sure, I can do that." Elime gave the king a knowin' smile. "What's the catch?"

King Eglon returned the devilish grin and sat up on the sofa.

"Catch? There's no catch!"

Elime raised a brow as if to say, *Really?*, which sparked another laugh from the king.

"Okay! There is one giant catch! Maybe!"

Elime leaned forward. "What is it?"

King Eglon sat up and stared eye-to-eye wit' Elime. "I want your sons to marry my daughters!"

Those words shot Elime into a daze. He did not expect K.E. to ask this. He expected an exclusive contract on inventions or upgradin' the city's power mainframe. Those requests would've made him more at ease but marriage? He could not possibly have imagined that.

"ELIME!" the king's voice boomed, bringin' the inventor back to the office.

Elime shook his head, regainin' all his thoughts. Gatherin' his composure, he stood up. "Um, K.E... I don't know what to say!"

"Say yes!"

Elime started walkin' to the window that had a view of the entire country of Moabolis. He knew Yah had sent him here for a reason. The reason was always 'yes' and 'amen' no matter the situation. He was just tryin' to wrap his mind around how his world went from buildin' vanities to securin' his sons' future as princes of Moabolis.

"I can make you a hover-scooter that's no biggie but how do I tell my sons that I've found them wives?"

King Eglon waddled over to the window and stood right beside him. "Simple. Just say, 'You're marryin' princesses and have a chance at a comfortable life.'"

"My sons aren't royal, though!"

"They're rich. Close enough!" Elime and King Eglon turned to each other, paused, then laughed.

"So, what do you say?" the king asked.

Elime pondered. "Why my sons, though?"

"Elime, I knew your kids inherited you and Naomi's brains. I want that around my daughters and future grandkids."

Elime grinned. He understood what the king meant. His sons were literally followin' in their parents' footsteps, even down to finishin' high school at fourteen. He decided to take a leap of faith like he preached. "I'm gonna say yes!"

The reaction on King Eglon's face was met wit' a smile from Elime. Elime knew there was a reason, a Yah reason on why his family was downloaded to Moabolis. The question followed him like a Believer followin' Yah. He knew for certain this was the reason he was here.

King Eglon clapped a meaty hand on Elime's shoulder. "Just like that, huh? Thought it'd take a couple of days to wear you down."

"I'm a Believer!"

King Eglon's eyes widened to show solidarity wit' Elime's response. He knew the choice he made was goin' to secure his kingdom for generations to come.

Elime noticed the clock on the wall and realized his family was probably wonderin' where he was.

"K.E., it's gettin' late. I have to go and tell the family the good news, marriage, hover-rounds. I can't wait to see their reactions."

"Me too!"

King Eglon turned to speak to Cami.

"Cam—"

"Yes, Your Majesty!" she answered, cuttin' him off.

Elime noticed that K.E. was startled by Cami's response. "Um, yes. Send Elime and his family home!"

"Yes, Your Majesty."

Elime began to feel himself bein' pixelated in front of the smilin' King Eglon. Moments later, he was standin' in front of his own home. His mind was racin'. Dinner wit' the King's family, a marriage proposal, and a hover-scooter. These were the moments that were goin' to change his destiny.

"So," Naomi said, placin' her hand in his. "What did y'all talk 'bout?"

CHAPTER 14

When Elime was 42

The cleanin'-droid that usually fixed the bed and cleaned the room was overshadowed by Mahlon and Chillion pacin' back and forth. Their umBlaselo swished to the rhythm of their excitement, the fabric hissin' like restless waves against their sides.

"I can't believe we gettin' married!" Mahlon passed by Chillion in motion, his feet tappin' against the polished floor like a drumline.

"I can't believe that we agreed to it!" Chillion replied, his eyes wide but his grin stretchin' ear to ear.

"I mean, why not? We may not know 'em per se, but they are royalty, and we are children of the King of Kings."

"Yes, but these folk don't believe in Him."

"I kinda agree wit' that, but…"

"But what?"

They realized they had been pacin' back and forth and decided to sit on the freshly made bed. The cleanin'-droid froze, its round head twitchin', red sensors blinkin' like fury before stormin' off in metallic stomps.

"Maybe Ruth will start to worship Yah!" Mahlon blurted. He had been thinkin' about it for some time, fingers nervously drummin' against his knees, eyes dartin' toward the ceilin'. He knew you could change a situation wit' your words.

"You know, it's probable! I hope Orpah will as well." Chillion's voice rose wit' a lilt, his optimism spillin' out like sunlight after rain. He knew words could justify or condemn a person, so it was always best to stay positive.

"What will life be like when we married?" Mahlon whispered, his voice suddenly small, like a boy starin' at the unknown.

"I dunno, but I am kinda excited."

"Me too."

Elime passed the cleanin'-droid wit' fumes spoutin' from her head. He caught the faint scent of burnt wires, and his stomach sank. H knew his sons must've sat on their freshly made bed. It was the cleanin'-droid's pet peeve, one he had programmed himself. He walked into the room wit' a concerned look, and his sons quickly stopped talkin', their shoulders stiffenin' like kids caught stealin' figs. He knew the new news would send them over the edge.

"Hey, Dad! You okay?"

"I have some surprisin' news, boys."

Mahlon and Chillion's faces froze between surprise and fear. The last time Elime told them he had a surprise was a couple of nanobytes ago, when they found out they were goin' to be married to the princesses of Moabolis. They'd been on edge ever since. Elime wanted to take this news slowly, but he was on a time limit. His voice wavered as though he was choosin' which word might sting less.

"So, y'all know how y'all gettin' married in two months?"

"Yeah! What happened? Are we still gettin' married?"

"Yeah, yeah!" Elime assured, holdin' his hands out to calm their nerves. "Nothin' happened—it's just that the weddin's been moved."

Mahlon and Chillion's faces dropped, their mouths hangin' open as if the floor itself had betrayed them. Elime knew this was goin' to happen, but he'd been expectin' it. He decided to let them process the words before movin' forward. Luckily, Chillion was the brave one to speak.

"Mo—moved? To when?"

Elime grinned, though it barely reached his eyes. "Today."

Mahlon and Chillion screamed for their lives! The sound rattled the room, bouncin' off the metal walls, their lungs pourin' out terror until their voices cracked. Elime closed his eyes and allowed them to scream for what felt like a lifetime.

"WHHHAAATTTTT?!"

"Yes. King Eglon messaged me and said he wants y'all married today."

"Why?"

"Well, King Eglon discovered he won't get his new hover-scooter until after the marriage."

"You mean the one wit' the automatic fountain drink dispenser and chocolate chip cookie maker?"

"Yep, that's the one!" Elime smiled as he thought of his invention for the king. He lowkey wanted the scooter for himself. That chocolate chip cookie dispenser was one of his proudest moments to date. I guess Boaz was right 'bout food. However, it was a dowry to K.E., and he had to keep his word.

"So, when do we leave?"

Elime was so wrapped up in his fantasy, he didn't notice his sons both fall back on the bed, their arms flung out like warriors struck down.

"Oh yeah! Actually, right now!"

The boys shot up from the bed as a glowin' light started to upload them. Their eyes darted back and forth, tryin' to grab one last glimpse of their childhood room before the shimmer swallowed 'em.

Elime turned around, enterin' the hallways. The long corridor, lined wit' ever-changin' photos of Elime and his family, seemed to shift more rapidly as he entered. The walls hummed, whisperin' wit' memories. Elime turned down the next hallway, only to bump into his wife, Naomi, already dressed for the weddin'. She stared at him oddly, since the ceremony was only an hour away and he wasn't even dressed. He'd made sure to tell her first, 'cause sometimes it took Naomi a while to get ready.

"Honey, why ain't you dressed? We have a weddin' to go to."

"I'm gettin' ready in my lab so I can check the hover-scooter."

"Your lab?"

Elime knew those weren't the words his wife wanted to hear. He'd been spendin' more time in the lab recently, but K.E.'s hover-scooter was the reason this weddin' was even happenin'. He did have to be dressed for their sons' double weddin', but he also had to make sure the hover-scooter was workin'. His chest tightened under Naomi's eyes, guilt pressin' heavier than his robes.

"Yeah. I just wanna wipe down the hover-scooter and tweak my shoes for the weddin'."

"O-okay!"

Naomi walked down the hallway in disbelief, her footsteps echoing sharp like a metronome of doubt. Elime shook his wrist, and a portal to his lab materialized in front of him. He hurried inside, seekin' comfort in the familiar hum of circuits and code. He glided to his desk quickly, sat down, and put his face in his hands.

I appeared as a dark silhouette on his desk.

"You need to tell her," it said.

"No!" Elime snapped. "I have time!"

"No, you don't!"

"Why not, Ruach?"

"Elime! I gave you more than enough time to tell your wife and kids your secret; the one you want buried. But instead, it seems like it'll bury you!" I had planted the seed a while back at his competition and even sat down and told him what to do explicitly. Now, he was in disobedience, and it was eatin' him alive 'cause he'd never been disobedient before. He was always willin' and obedient to do Yah's will. I just don't know why this moment was different.

My face showed the empathy I felt for Elime, but my nerves were wearin' thin. My tone said it, and Elime heard it. He was stunned by my words as he stared at me. His lips trembled as though they wanted to shape excuses but couldn't. I sat sternly in my explanation. Elime didn't want to look at me for long. After all, I was a constant reminder of his mortality.

"Why can't this just pass me?!"

"I have my reasons."

Elime stood up and stared at me as I remained seated. I knew he was petrified. Sweat trickled down his temples, drippin' onto the metal desk wit' soft plinks. He was fidgetin', twistin' the hem of his sleeve. He was afraid of me, but had no reason to be.

"I prayed, fasted, and gave alms. Surely this can pass me, Ruach?"

"Elime, you actin' like I told you somethin' that could shatter space and time. This is tame compared to what I've told others. Maybe you should tell her."

"I can't. I just don't wanna break her heart."

"Her heart will break even more when your secret becomes your sons' secret."

Elime's eyes widened wit' fear and anger. His breath came ragged, and his fists clenched until his knuckles turned pale. I kept my composure. I am the rational one in these conversations. I always am. Elime's fidgetin' eyes screamed that he wanted to lose control but couldn't, out of respect.

"Elime, calm down. I told you it was generational, and you even thought it was silly, but I can see you ain't gonna tell her. So, your time is up."

"Up?! You mean—?"

"Yes. You're gonna die."

Elime began to cry at the sound of his own death so soon. He placed his hands over his face. The sobs shook through his shoulders, raw and jagged like torn wires. I got up from the desk and held him. I knew that death wasn't easy for no one, especially the mortals. I tried my best to comfort him for the small time he had left.

"Remember, I love you and your family. Also remember that I am much more than the Upgrade. I AM THAT I AM."

I was gone, and Elime was left cryin' alone in his lab. He whispered through his tears, "Hallelujah," and a cup of water appeared floatin'. He threw the water on his face in an attempt to calm down. He materialized a towel to wipe his face when Naomi appeared on a Hallegram.

"Bae, you good? 'Cause we gotta go!"

"I'm good, Bae. I'm comin' out right now!"

Elime ended the video call and stepped into his shoes. The shoes placed him in traditional Soulaan attire for the weddin', and he kept walkin' wit'out missin' a beat. A portal of white light appeared, and Elime walked through it in sync, his head held down.

CHAPTER 15

When Elime was still 42

Elime sat in the front row, sweat runnin' down his face as the brides walked down the aisle. His discomfort was palpable, like a thousand tiny, invisible hands pressin' down on him. His sweat glistened, mirrorin' the slow, graceful procession of the two brides, Orpah and Ruth, daughters of King Eglon, princesses of Moabolis. The weight of it all was suffocatin'. He wiped his face, careful not to let Naomi see, not wantin' her to worry.

But what could he really hide from her? She had already seen the strain on him, the sleepless nights, the distractions, the faraway look in his eyes. It wasn't the weddin' that troubled him. No, this was somethin' much deeper, somethin' darker.

Elime's sons, his pride, stood there in the front row, their fake smiles just as bright and carefully placed as their father's. They had learned well, these two, how to hide pain and nerves behind a grin so dazzlin' that even the most perceptive observer would believe everything was fine.

Their anxiety was palpable, hoverin' around them like a cloud. Their nerves tightened, the beads of sweat gatherin' just as Elime's had. The weddin' march swelled, the sound of the B3 organ fillin' the space, and the collective tension rose as the brides moved forward, their presence heraldin' the beginnin' of a new chapter.

"Elime," I whispered to him, though I knew it sounded like a scream. "Your time is up. You know this, don't you? You've known it for weeks. It will come to pass."

But he shook his head, tryin' to ignore me, as he always did. It was easier to focus on the ceremony, on the joy of this moment, than face the inevitable. He couldn't deny it much longer. He had made his choice, and he would never tell Naomi the truth.

King Eglon, weary and slow, escorted his daughters to the altar. His movements were heavy, his breath labored. A mechanical hum filled the air as his augmented limbs struggled wit' the weight of his years. Everyone in the room felt his struggle but pretended not to notice, maintainin' their decorum.

He leaned forward, his breath ragged, and kissed both brides on the forehead. Then the minister-droid, the sterile officiant of this age, spoke.

"Who gives these two brides away?"

"I do," King Eglon wheezed, the words comin' out in strained gasps as he took his seat.

Elime shifted uncomfortably in his chair, his mind elsewhere, caught in a storm of memories. His gaze was fixed on his sons, yet his heart was miles away, tangled in the web of his own death. His lab, the experiments, the diagnosis, none of it was meant to unfold this way.

"You are gonna die," I had told him. My voice was not kind nor cruel. It simply was. "It's generational, Elime. It's in your blood, your very cells. You cannot outrun it."

The words echoed in Elime's mind, each repetition louder, more insistent. He could not escape the truth. His hands trembled as he reached for a tissue from Naomi. She saw his tears, mistakin' them for a father's emotion, a father's pride. She did not know that it wasn't his sons' weddin' that brought him to this point.

"Stop cryin', Elime," I urged, watchin' him, watchin' Naomi comfort him wit' her touch. "You cannot hide from this, no matter how hard you try. You knew this moment would come. You chose not to tell her. Now, it's too late."

Naomi pressed her hand gently against his arm, her own eyes glistenin' wit' tears, misreadin' the source of his pain. She thought it was the weddin' that had moved him, his sons growin' up, becomin' men. She didn't know, could never know, that the man beside her was already mournin' his own death.

I saw it all, their future unspoolin' in front of them. Elime's legacy, his quiet sufferin', his refusal to share the truth. His tears fell one by one, just like the delicate petals from the flower girl's basket. A soft rain of sorrow, unnoticed by the world around him, yet heavy and crushin' in his chest.

And then they kissed, the two sons now married to the princesses of Moabolis. They sealed their vows, and Elime's heart broke. His tears fell like microchips thrown by the guests at the bride and grooms' departure, abundant and uncontrollable.

"This is the end of a chapter," I whispered again, my voice vibratin' through the ether. "But not your end, Elime. Your end is yet to come."

Naomi noticed his tears more closely now. She thought she understood, thought she knew what moved him. But in this, she was mistaken. Elime would never tell her. The truth flickered in his eyes, and it filled me wit' sadness, not for him, but for her.

The weddin' concluded, and the guests filed out. But Elime remained seated, his soul heavy wit' grief, his body fightin' the inevitable. Naomi wrapped her arm around him, guidin' him through the exit, never knowin' the truth that clung to his every breath.

I followed, silent as always, watchin' as the future unfolded for them all. Elime's time was runnin' out, but he would never speak of it. I could only watch and wait.

CHAPTER 16

When Elime was 45

The Efrathats sat at the park filled wit' music, games, and art. Children rode hover-bikes past them while surroundin' families held virtual cookouts. Sounds of birds chirpin' and kids laughin' made this day perfect. Elime and Naomi watched Mahlon, Ruth, Chillion, and Orpah havin' a picnic to celebrate their three-year anniversary. They were sittin' on a hoverin' park bench wit' a table and chairs, laughin' and eatin' like tomorrow ain't promised.

"I love you!" was said between the newlyweds after three years of bein' together. The honeymoon phase was still in full effect, and Elime's sons and K.E.'s daughters were madly in love. The constant kissin' reminded Elime of how Naomi and he behaved all them moons ago. Elime and Naomi couldn't help but smile. It had been one year since their sons married King Eglon's daughters, and they could not be happier parents. They watched their sons smile a new kind of smile as the girls took sips of their water and bites of veggie burgers.

"Mama! Papa! Y'all hungry?" Ruth yelled.

"No, dear," Naomi smiled. "We good."

Elime knew how much Naomi wanted daughters of her own. He knew Naomi bein' called "Mama" by Ruth was the best thing to come from this marriage. Her smile proved it.

I appeared next to Elime, but no one could see me. "Elime, your time is up!" Elime's eyes widened. He thought I had forgotten since it had been some years. Sike! I remembered the judgment that was due to him. Naomi had been prayin' for him somethin' heavy, and I had to honor My daughter. Her prayers only held off Yah's judgment; they didn't stop it.

He tried to hide it, but it was too late. Naomi noticed. He hasn't been actin' like himself since the weddin', she thought. She then decided to change her prayer to, "Let Yah's will be done." It was one of the most dangerous prayers to pray, but it's what you pray when you don't know what else to say, she thought.

"Honey, you good?"

"Yeah, I'm good. I'm just exhausted for some reason."

Elime had looked tired since the day I came to talk to him. He couldn't sleep or eat. It had been a nightmare tryin' to shake the feelin' that he would die soon.

"You been complainin' for many macrobytes. You been fastin', prayin', and givin' alms to get healed?"

"Yes. I think I just need to lie down!"

Suddenly, a screen appeared from his Praise. Elime knew this was Me rushin' him home. His wife also found it peculiar that his Praise wanted him then. She knew not to ask questions, since it was a message from Yah. Naturally, Elime whispered, "Hallelujah," and turned to kiss Naomi as he started to upload. Elime turned to his family and screamed at the top of his lungs so the whole park could hear, "I LOVE you all, Naomi, Mahlon, Ruth, Chillion, and Orpah! Nothin' will ever change that!"

"We love you too!"

Everyone exchanged an eerie look. Naomi gazed at her kids in confusion. That kind of expression wasn't Elime's character at all. His family knew he was laid-back and chill. He never wanted to be the center of attention. So why now did he scream "I love you" in a park full of strangers?

"Somethin' felt off 'bout dat," Chillion said.

"True!" Ruth agreed.

"What should we do?"

"We should do what we always do when somethin' doesn't seem right. We pray!"

The four of them grabbed hands as Chillion began. "Dear Yah, whatever my dad is goin' thru, please let this test be over peacefully. Amen!"

"Amen!" everyone said.

Elime downloaded onto his modern, round bed in his bedroom. He and I were starin' at each other as he began to lay down. His body language screamed exhaustion mixed wit' anger, while I stood in front of him, happy as happy could be.

I broke the silence. "Well, this is it."

"No!" Elime screamed.

"You had years to tell her your secret. You decided not to, and these are the consequences."

"Gimme more time!" Elime turned frantic. He started cryin' hysterically. Everyone has to die one day, but he couldn't believe he was goin' to die wit'out even tellin' his family goodbye.

"You had enough. My judgment is set!" Ruach's voice boomed, steady as a metronome.

"Three."

Elime tryin' fight it, his voice crackin'. "Please, let me live! I'm beggin' you!"

"Two."

He shook his head wildly, tears streamin' down to his pillow. "No, no, no. This can't be happenin'. Not like this!"

"One."

CHAPTER 17

When Naomi was 45

Naomi stared happily wit' her sons and new in-laws while they were prayin'. She enjoyed prayin' and made sure to teach her kids the joys of prayer and how effective it could be. Watchin' them pray always brought joy to her heart.

"Yes and Amen!" she spoke as her kids concluded their prayer. She was certain that they were prayin' for their father, Elime.

She had been sayin' her silent prayers for him every time she was 'round him. His behavior had become unpleasant ever since the weddin', and she began to feel that it was a mistake for their sons to marry the princesses of Moabolis. That was until she personally met the two princesses and instantly fell in love. She was finally happy that she had daughters of her own. Bein' in a house of men could be overwhelmin' at times, and havin' the two princesses made her life more fulfilled.

Naomi and the rest of the kids locked eyes in silent confirmation of their prayer. It had been about Elime. She smiled in their direction, accompanied by a nod to assure them that she was in agreement wit' what they prayed.

"Hmm." She turned her head fast as the most serious expression crept across her face. She felt somethin' was off. She would get these feelin's more frequently because of her husband, Elime.

Her sons and their wives noticed her expression, gathered their belongin's, and made their way to her bench.

"Mama, what's wrong?" Chillion sat down slowly, placin' his arm on her shoulder like she used to do when he was upset.

"Somethin's wrong." Naomi slowly lifted her head to meet his gaze before turnin' her head in the other direction.

"What do you mean?" Chillion questioned, tryin' to gain her focus.

Naomi turned back toward him swiftly. "I mean, there is somethin' wrong, and I do believe that it's your father."

"Why you say that, Mama?"

"Because," Naomi motioned for the group to come closer, "your father and I are one. We know when somethin's wrong wit' each other. It's been that way since the day we got married. We can't hide it from each other, either."

"So what's wrong wit' Dad? He's been actin' strange for quite some time." Chillion was always the voice. He said how he felt, and he did it wit' the power of Yah behind him.

"Baby, I don't know." Naomi inhaled sharply. Recently, every time she began to think 'bout her husband, Elime, she was brought to tears. It wasn't that he wanted to keep somethin' from her. She felt he had his reasons and might be obeyin' Yah. Obeyin' Yah had always been the greatest time of their lives; she knew that. However, there were also times when it wasn't so great, and right now she felt that more than ever, like when the Holy Spirit rests upon the body.

"He never used to keep secrets from me, but for a while now, he hasn't told me what's happenin' to him." Naomi's hands clenched and shook profusely, but her sons and their wives rallied behind her and comforted her the only way people connected to Yah know how. They prayed.

"Dear Yah," Chillion began, "whatever is happenin' wit' my father, please heal him and take the sufferin' away. We want him healed and whole. Amen."

"Amen," they all said in unison.

Naomi relaxed her hand long enough to start typin' into her Praise so she could upload home. She finished puttin' in the final coordinates, but nothin' happened. Usually, when she did it, they were instantly taken home, but this time nothin'.

"Hmmm." She reentered the coordinates, meticulously as always, while prayin' for a breakthrough in the situation. "Hallelujah," she said, but still nothin' happened. She looked at her sons, then around. Nothin'.

"Chillion," she spoke, "enter the coordinates to the house. My Praise seems off."

"It isn't workin'?" Disgust washed over his face like a rag durin' shower time. "You okay?"

"I'm fine, I promise," Naomi assured her son. She had taught them that if your Praise seems off, it's a personal problem wit' yourself and doesn't have anythin' to do wit' Yah.

Chillion typed precisely the coordinates needed to upload, but nothin' happened. One by one, each of the others tried enterin' the coordinates, but nothin' came of it.

"Okay," Naomi said, unsure of what happened, "I guess we're walkin'." She stood up and began walkin' as her sons and their wives followed suit.

"Somethin' life-changin' is 'bout to happen!" Naomi yelled across the park. Eyes fell on her, so she hid behind her hat. She walked past people wit' her family and began walkin' home.

"Why you say that?" Chillion questioned.

"The last time we walked home," Naomi smiled, "was the first day we arrived in Moabolis."

Naomi began to remember that day, walkin' around the city of Moabolis to arrive at her new home. It had been quite an adventure, one she would be sure to tell her future generations. "If Yah has us walkin' home, and only He could block the downloadin', then it must be somethin' big." Naomi picked up her pace as the park faded behind her.

Yes, I had to not allow her request to go through to get to her house. Naomi is one of those Believers that if she prayed, or more specifically utilized her Praise, then I would have to answer quickly. She spent a tremendous amount of time in prayer, fastin', and almsgivin'. She deserved her request to be answered, not because she did those things, but because she loved Me enough to show Me that she could handle what I had for her.

Now she was on the busy street of downtown Moabolis. She never realized how alive and thrivin' the downtown area was. She mostly would download everywhere, so it was no surprise she never took the time to live and love in this moment.

She came to a stop and waited wit' her kids for the light to change. When it did, she started to walk, and for the first time in a while, felt immense joy, like everything was goin' to be fine. She turned to her family around her and noticed all of them were smilin' too. What she didn't know was that feelin' was the calm before the storm.

They had only taken a few steps when Naomi suddenly realized she didn't have a clue how to get to their house on foot. She had become so used to loadin' that it was the only way she traveled. It was said to be dangerous and even life-threatenin' if not done properly. She didn't care; she trusted Yah, and He always saw fit for her to travel that way.

Her walk came to an abrupt stop, and she stared ahead. "How do we get home?" she started to laugh. Everyone turned toward each other in sheer confusion. They didn't know how to get home either. Like Naomi, they were used to downloadin' around the city. They looked Naomi in the eye and laughed right along wit' her.

"This feels amazin'," she thought. She hadn't laughed like that in ages, not since Elime's sudden change in behavior, especially wit' her family right there.

Wit' all that joy, the family didn't realize a giant arrow was pulsin' nearby. Naomi smiled. She remembered the last time an arrow came and led them home. She knew they were safe and that Yah was wit' them. The arrow took them through the city, but this time she paid attention to her surroundin's. She admired the beautiful architecture of the buildings, the citizens in their tracksuits that everyone wore. She truly enjoyed herself. Yah made sure that the Believers enjoyed the life He provided.

They all arrived home; however, somethin' felt different. The joy they had felt moments before subdued. Naomi entered the house first, and her family followed.

"Elime! Baby!" she yelled throughout the house. Naomi became worried. Her husband always responded to her, no matter how busy he was. He even did it in his sleep.

"I'm gonna go check on your father." Naomi proceeded to her bedroom. She left her family to their own devices.

She walked into their shared bedroom. He appeared to be asleep wit' a smile on his face. Typically, Naomi would talk to him until he woke up, but today somethin' was off. She sat next to him, caressin' his face.

"Honey, can you wake up?" He said nothin'. Naomi started to shake his body, yet he did not move at all.

Sheer panic engulfed her body. Naomi began to freak out. She sat on top of him and started beatin' his chest like a drum durin' praise and worship.

Tears poured out of her eyes like the flood from Noah, each one representin' a different emotion: fear, anger, and a sharp grief that tasted like iron on her tongue. Her breath hitched, then rushed, like wind through a cracked window. The words fought to leave her throat, clawin' their way out. She released a huge wail that shook the house to its core, a sound that was part prayer and part wounded cry.

Naomi didn't even feel her kids run into the room as she let out a soul-piercin' scream.

"Nooooo!"

CHAPTER 18

When Naomi was still 45

Low, mournful rhythms drifted from the organ, minglin' wit' the tears of Naomi and her family. A hallegraphic video of Elime wit' friends and family played in sync wit' the rhythms. Naomi sat in an array of emotions, tryin' to understand what events led her life to this moment.

"How could I ignore the signs?" she thought, playin' the final moments of her husband's life over and over again like a sad song. She desperately tried to find anything she missed that would explain his death. She knew her husband wasn't the same as he used to be, but she never thought what was botherin' him would bury him.

Wipin' the tears from her face, she turned, watchin' her sons bein' held by their wives. Since Elime's death, their wives had stepped up and really showed what it meant to be a wife. They were there for their husbands and for Naomi as well. She could not have asked for better wives for her sons, and she thanked Yah for that every single day.

"Mama," Ruth said, sittin' next to her and embracin' her wit' a hug. Naomi hugged her back, weepin' on her shoulder. Ruth squeezed her tight, causin' Naomi to cry harder, as if she were a rag bein' wrung dry. Before she released her, Naomi began to silently pray for Ruth.

"Yah, thank You for her. Please never leave her side." Naomi finally let her go, long enough to look at her.

"It will be okay, I promise you. I will always be here for you," Ruth smiled. Naomi felt the words of Ruth wrap around her like a rod and a staff that comfort. Those words were accompanied wit' an influx of hugs from the rest of her family. They held each other as tears fell harder than a third of the A.N.G.E.L.S. Naomi never realized how hard and long someone could cry.

She finally let them go when the minister-droid tapped her on the shoulder. "We will start in a few minutes." Ruth nodded her head, allowin' the minister-droid to scurry off. Naomi stood up to move her legs before sittin' back down. Watchin' all the memories and relivin' some of hers was interestin'. On one hand, it helped her; on the other hand, it harmed her.

"Mama," Mahlon said, wipin' snot from his nose. "Where is everyone?"

"Well, Mahlon," Naomi inhaled. "This is almost everyone." She motioned to her sons and their wives. "Your dad always told me that if he were to ever die, it could only be y'all, your wives, me, and, if married, your in-laws. He didn't want everyone, 'cause your father hated funerals and I do mean hated."

They looked at each other, then glanced around. "Does that explain why it's in our backyard and not a church?"

"Yes. Your father wanted to have his celebration of life at his house." Naomi let a genuine smile spread across her face. "Elime wanted y'all to be comfortable, and what better way to be comfortable than to be at home?" Everyone nodded in agreement. "Besides, this was free, and your father loved a good deal. How you think we got these two lovely ladies?"

Everyone laughed. Mahlon and Chillion hugged their wives as if sayin' a quiet thank-you to their father.

Naomi smiled when she felt a light tap on her shoulder. She turned around and saw King Eglon on his hover-scooter and Queen Lani dressed in all-black tracksuits wit' matchin' black sneakers. Naomi laughed under her breath. She commended King Eglon and Queen Lani for their commitment to the tracksuit; no matter the occasion, they were wearin' one. She laughed a little harder when she remembered the only reason Ruth and Orpah didn't wear tracksuits was 'cause they didn't wanna offend their new family.

"Naomi," Queen Lani hugged her tightly, then stepped aside to let King Eglon hug her. Naomi tried her best, but she could only wrap her arms around his neck on account of how large he was.

"How you holdin' up?"

Naomi shrugged her shoulders. She didn't know how to respond. It ain't every day you lose the love of your life out the blue. She still hadn't processed what happened or how to work through it. "I am here for them," Naomi said, pointin' at her sons and their wives. "Yah put them in my life to keep me goin', and I intend to."

The King and Queen smiled.

Ruth and Orpah came over, huggin' their parents. "Mom! Dad!" Ruth said. Orpah motioned for Mahlon and Chillion, and they came over to hug their in-laws.

"Thank you for comin'," Chillion smiled.

"Of course," King Eglon said. "We wouldn't miss this for anything. We loved Elime too. He's been a blessin' ever since we first met him. It is an honor and a privilege." The entire royal family bowed as a sign of respect. Naomi remembered the first time she met the Royals wit' her husband, and how they bowed then too. She was always pleasantly surprised by the way they treated others.

The King and Queen smiled, but then Queen Lani looked at her daughter strangely.

"Mom, I know what you thinkin'," Orpah began. "We wanted to dress like this out of respect for our new family."

"I told them they could wear tracksuits and sneakers," Naomi interjected, "but they said they wanted to dress like how we dress."

Queen Lani chuckled. "Well, as long as you're happy, then I'm happy."

The minister-droid motioned for everyone to sit down as it stood before the small, quaint family. "Good morning," the minister-droid began. "I won't be before you long." Naomi and her sons rolled their eyes at that statement. They were used to ministers, both human and AI, sayin' those words then preachin' for two hours minimum.

"Mom, do somethin'!"

Before the minister-droid could synthesize a prayer to begin, Naomi made her way to the front.

"Hello," Naomi interjected, "as stated before, he won't be before you long." She nudged her way to the front where the minister-droid stood. "Thank you, I appreciate it." The minister-droid just stared at her.

"So, this is how this is gonna go. First, the minister-droid will do a prayer." Naomi gave it a bump as a signal to start.

"Uh, yes. Everyone close your eyes and bow your heads." The whole group followed suit. "Dear Yah, thank You for this day, and thank You for wakin' us up. I pray this service goes well and You remain wit' the family in their tryin' times. Amen!"

The whole room echoed, "Amen!"

"Now," she began, "I will say a few words 'bout my husband." Naomi took a deep breath before she spoke. The tears were tryin' to form, but she kept them down the best she could. "Um, hi. Y'all know who I am. My name is Naomi, and I am the wife of Elime Efrathat." She took another deep breath, pacin' herself, tryin' to keep the tears out of this conversation.

"I loved my husband like all of you did. The best thing I loved about him was his love of Yah. He taught me what it meant to be a Believer, and I will cherish that, as well as the members of his family. I could go on and on, but I won't—for the sake of time." Naomi inhaled, maintainin' her composure.

"Now my son, Mahlon, will bless the food so we can eat. Before we begin, I would like to thank my best friend and brother-in-love, Boaz, for caterin' the food." She started clappin', causin' the others to join in. Confused faces started formin' as no one saw another person outside of those here.

"Boaz was Elime's brother. When we were younger, we all agreed to never go to the homegoin' of one another. Boaz kept his word but says he loves each and every one of you and will be in touch." The confusion began to die down slowly.

She motioned for Mahlon to come up quickly to finish the service. She wanted this to be over like everyone else did.

"Hello, my name is Mahlon, and Elime was my dad." Naomi placed her hand on his back to reassure him that he had her support. "Dear Yah, thank You for the life my dad had. I'm glad to call him my dad. Bless the food and bless the hands that prepared it. Amen."

"Amen!" the rest said. Mahlon went to sit down next to his wife, Ruth.

Naomi clapped her hands together, causin' the outdoor settin' of chairs and hallegraphic images of Elime to disappear, makin' room for the food. She clapped again, and copious amounts of food materialized on a long table wit' chairs, silverware, and plates set in place. Naomi knew one thing for sure: the Royal Family loved food and lots of it. She wanted her family to have the option to eat their pain away. It might not have been holy, but it felt good. Right now, all she wanted was to feel good.

"Let's eat!" Naomi called, watchin' as the Royal Family dove in like they were in a food-eatin' contest. One thing was certain: no matter the occasion, the Royal Family was gonna eat. She let out a chuckle as she saw her sons and the minister-droid starin' in sheer terror while the Royals inhaled food.

"Y'all aren't hungry?" Naomi asked.

"Not anymore," Mahlon responded.

"Yeh, we lost our appetite," Chillion added.

Naomi laughed, not thinkin' too much of it. It reminded her of the first time she met the Royal Family, and again she smiled. In the midst of her smile, she noticed that, outside of water, there weren't any beverages.

"Mahlon, where are the drinks? I told you to go get 'em."

Before Mahlon could answer, he grabbed some food and immediately started eatin' like he was tryin' to beat King Eglon in a food-eatin' contest. He nudged Chillion to join so Naomi wouldn't fuss at him.

"Fine, I'll get it." Annoyance colored Naomi's words as she pushed herself from the table, makin' her way toward the door. She moved through the house, ready to cross the street for the drinks.

Ruth finished her bite and noticed her mother-in-law about to leave. She swallowed quickly. "Mama, where you goin'?"

Naomi halted in her steps, stumblin' a bit.

"You okay, Mama?"

"Yes, I am." Naomi composed herself. "I'm on my way to get those drinks that someone forgot to do!" she said, projectin' her voice in Mahlon's direction.

"You need some help? You know you can download those right over."

"Nah," Naomi shook her head. "I'm okay. I need this time to be alone. Thank you, though."

Naomi mazed her way through her home, eventually steppin' out the door. She took a deep breath in, holdin' on to it like she did the promises of Yah. She finally exhaled, then looked both ways before crossin' the street to the coffee shop.

Walkin' had become therapeutic for Naomi. Ever since the day she walked home and saw her husband's dead body lyin' in the bed, she walked more and more. It took some time to get used to, 'cause she was so used to loadin' every single day that she forgot Yah gave her two legs to walk and enjoy Him and the world around her. Yah was everywhere and everything, she thought as she stepped into the coffee shop.

She waited in line patiently, takin' in the ambient scenery. She was glad to be out of the house. Everything back home reminded her of Elime;

from the gadgets and gizmos to her very own sons who looked and acted just like him. She needed a break from a place that felt so full of him.

When she got to the front, the service droid handed her a Hot Frozen, frozen hot chocolate wit' cookies and cream. Perplexity flushed across her face, 'cause Naomi hadn't placed no order, and neither had her son. That was the whole reason she came.

"It's on the house," the service droid said. "We heard what happened to our favorite customer, Elime." The droid glanced over her shoulder, revealin' a Hallegraphic video of her husband smilin' and sippin' on his favorite drink: the Hot Frozen.

Suddenly, confetti poured from the sky as upbeat hip-hop music shook the room. A tall man dressed in a hunter-green suit came around holdin' a plaque. "On behalf of me and all my service-droids, we would like to officially change the name of the Hot Frozen to Elime's Drink!"

The whole coffee shop erupted into cheerin' and celebration as the hallegram changed the name of the drink right in front of Naomi. She forced a smile through the noise. It wasn't that she wasn't glad they honored her husband. She just wasn't expectin' it, and it knocked her off balance.

The owner gave her a hug before slippin' to the back. Eventually, the sound faded, leavin' Naomi standin' there, lost in the middle of the shop. She never thought fetchin' her husband's favorite drink would turn into a celebration of life. But then again, that was what Elime always preached: Yah was, is, and will always be life.

Naomi carried her drinks and emotions to the table to gather them accordingly. She whispered, "Hallelujah," causin' the drinks to halleport back to her house. She kept one for herself, findin' a small table in the corner to relax and process it all. She took a sip of the drink when I decided to join her.

"Hello, Naomi!"

"Ruach," she said my name wit' more frost than her drink. It wasn't just that she was mad, she was in pain.

"Talk to me. You know I love it when you share wit' me."

Naomi took a few more sips before respondin'. Each audible gulp was her contemplatin' her next words. "I am in pain that the love of my life is gone. I am hurt that my sons do not have a father, especially since they just got married. I am angry at You for not bein' a healer, after I grew up hearin' that all my life."

I leaned back in my chair, smilin'. I love when my Believers are honest wit' me. It helps 'em heal a whole lot quicker. "You angry at Me? Tell me more."

Naomi startled at my response, then leaned closer. "Yes, I am angry that You did not heal my husband from whatever it was he was goin' through. I know I ain't supposed to be angry at You, but I am."

"Who told you that you ain't allowed to be angry wit' Me?" I squinted. Naomi froze. She never thought I was gonna question that. "I'm serious. Tell me, who told you that you can't be angry wit' Me?"

"Umm," she began to stammer, "it was what was passed on to me that I was just supposed to accept what Yah allows, even if I don't understand, 'cause it's workin' for my good."

"Well, Naomi," I began, "I don't agree wit' that at all. You're allowed to be angry wit' Me, and you're allowed to ask questions 'bout why I let things happen the way I do. You're allowed to question Me. I'm okay wit' that."

Naomi let her eyes do the talkin', 'cause she had no words to speak. She never would've imagined Ruach would allow her to question what He does or His actions. She was taught that obedience was better than sacrifice but, she never thought that, in her obedience, she'd be allowed to question.

"Naomi," I began. "I want you to get to know Me on a personal level. That ain't possible unless you spend time wit' Me and get to know Me. Now, how does one get to know somebody?"

Naomi shook her head, wakin' herself up from the revelation I was givin' her. "You ask questions?" Her words weren't confident, and her body language showed it.

"Yes," My voice accented. I tapped on the table a few times, and Elime's Drink appeared before Me. I took a sip of the soon-to-be most popular drink in all of Moabolis. I looked at Naomi. The emotions sittin' heavy on her face couldn't be swallowed down wit' no sip of her drink. They were still there.

"Naomi, you grew up hearin', 'study to show thyself approved' and 'test the spirit.' But wit' all that studyin' and testin', how you think you gon' do it wit'out askin' questions? Testin' and studyin' is literally based on askin' questions."

The revelation hit Naomi like the flood did many nanobytes ago. She had vivid memories of sittin' on her nana's lap, hearin' her speak those truths but, back then she never questioned. Relief filled her chest like oxygen in her lungs. At that moment, she didn't feel angry or sad anymore, but relieved. I sat across from her, watchin' her receive understandin' like a father watchin' his child code their first program. I was proud of her. She was proud of herself.

I stood up wit' My arms open, motionin' for a hug. She stood up and hugged Me so tight—like two friends who hadn't seen each other in years.

"I love you, Naomi!"

"I love you too," she said, lettin' me go and reachin' down to grab her drink but, I had already vanished. Still, My presence was wit' her.

She walked wit' a new smile through the coffee shop, receivin' genius waves and good-byes from staff and patrons. She pushed through the door, lookin' both ways before crossin' the street.

Back at her house, she saw her family in the distance, sippin' their drinks. As she stepped through the door leadin' to the backyard, they raised their glasses to her. She lifted hers in return, then sat down beside her sons.

Naomi knew this next chapter of her life was gonna be different but, at least she knew one thing for sure: she wasn't alone.

CHAPTER 19

When Mahlon and Chillion were 26

It had been many macrobytes since Elime's passin', and Naomi and her family were growin' accustomed to the new normal. Some days were better than others, but today wasn't one of those days. Naomi had been avoidin' readin' her husband's will, but today she realized she couldn't avoid it any longer.

The kitchen self-cleaned as Naomi sat at the table in her house clothes, readin' The Will of Elime. Takin' a sip of her orange juice, she continued to read, swipin' left to make sure her husband's final affairs were in order. Naomi's sons, Mahlon and Chillion, and their wives, Ruth and Orpah, entered the kitchen and saw their mother sittin' there, readin'.

"Hey, Mama!"

"Hello, Mahlon!" Naomi replied, not liftin' her head from the hallegraphic projection.

Everyone sat around her, watchin' as she swiped her finger from left to right on the hallegraphic screen of the will. The tension was suffocatin' as the children watched their mama robotically scan through the document like a magazine. With each swipe, they could tell she was growin' colder and colder. Someone had to change the scene.

"How are you?" Chillion asked.

"Fine. It's just weird that he isn't here wit' us. I miss him dearly."

"I know. We all do."

Naomi leaned back in the chair, glancin' up and noticin' her kids smilin' at her with comfort. Mahlon, Ruth, Chillion, and Orpah were starin' at her with compassion. Naomi, wearin' a stern look, began to speak 'bout why she had called them there. She knew she had to force a smile, not for herself, but for her kids, who needed her more than anythin'.

"Ma? Why'd you call us here?" Mahlon asked.

"Your father's will. He left y'all his company. I'm trustin' you to make great decisions when it comes to your father's business."

"We will, Mama!" her sons said together.

"I know." Naomi rose from the table with no expression on her face. She forgot to fake a smile for her kids because the sight of them reminded her that her husband wasn't there. Naomi's children watched their once-vivacious mother slowly fade away, as their father did, with each step they heard her take.

"She's changed since Papa died. Some days she's good, and other days she isn't," Mahlon said, feelin' defeated. He watched his loud and vibrant mother turn into a quiet church mouse. It was a sight he knew he'd never get used to, no matter how much he prayed to make it normal.

"I'm worried," Ruth confessed.

"Don't worry! Let's pray."

They all grabbed hands and lifted their eyes upward.

"Dear Yah, please keep Your hand on our mother. Lord, I pray that You restore all she has lost. Lord, restore her happiness, for her name means happy. Lord, we know times like this cause a woman to lose her softness as she now has to handle business. Lord, we rebuke depression, heartache, and pain. Keep her happy, please. Amen."

"Amen."

Mahlon, Ruth, Chillion, and Orpah sat at the hoverin' kitchen table, lookin' at one another with worried expressions. Havin' their names on the business wasn't a surprise; Elime always said he wanted to leave a legacy of science and salvation through his sons. It was what both he and Naomi wanted for them. They just never thought their parents' wishes would come to pass so suddenly.

"What we gonna do 'bout Mama?" Orpah asked, concerned.

"We gonna let Yah deal wit' her," Chillion answered.

"Wow. I can't believe Papa trusts us to run the business," Mahlon said, side-eyein'.

"I can. We're smart," Chillion smiled.

"Yes, y'all are," I spoke.

Mahlon and Chillion looked at each other suspiciously. The familiar voice sent shivers down their spines. Their wives, Ruth and Orpah, noticed their sudden change in behavior. The boys could never hide their emotions. They were truly Naomi's children.

"Y'all good?" Ruth asked.

"We good," they both said quickly.

Ruth and Orpah calmed down slightly. Their husbands bein' twins and speakin' in sync was somethin' they usually found funny. It always lightened the mood but, this time it didn't. This time was too sensitive for jokes.

"We can't tell!" Orpah rolled her neck.

"We good. We just wanna read over the will. Actually, why don't y'all go find a movie on the TV, and we'll join you?"

Mahlon and Chillion kissed their wives in an effort to keep calm. Ruth and Orpah weren't buyin' the act, their sudden calm demeanor didn't fool them. But for the sake of keepin' emotions low, they decided to play along.

"Sure," Ruth said. "We'll do that. C'mon, Orpah."

"Right behind you!"

Mahlon and Chillion watched as their wives whispered "Hallelujah" and uploaded to their respective bedrooms. They quickly turned to each other with scared expressions. They couldn't hide their concern and fear any longer. Fear rushed up their spines like demons fleein' from the presence of Yah. They searched the room, tryin' to locate the voice they'd both heard.

"Who was that?" Mahlon asked.

"I dunno," Chillion answered.

"Y'all know who I AM," I declared.

Mahlon and Chillion froze, fallin' to the floor in fear. They were speechless as I, the One who commanded the room with My presence, stood before them smilin'. They couldn't find words to express what they felt, but their faces said it all.

"That's the same expression your father gave Me when he first saw Me," I smiled and began to do what I always did—change the atmosphere.

"You human?"

"Well… I can become one."

"WHOA!"

Mahlon and Chillion rose from the floor and quickly moved to the table, starin' at Me and My fresh fade. They turned for a split second, and I was already seated at the table waitin' for them. Elime's sons hadn't experienced Me the way their father did, so I knew I had to take things slowly.

"Y'all look like you seen a ghost," I chuckled.

Mahlon and Chillion had a million thoughts runnin' through their heads, but their mouths couldn't form a word. I was dripped in all black, standin' before them, waitin' for a reaction. They wanted to speak but couldn't move their lips. Still, they knew I was familiar. They just didn't know from where. That was, until I spoke and then everything made sense.

"Well, I AM Ruach HaKodesh. I AM the Upgrade to Praise. I AM the reason Neo-Eden's been killin' the tech game for centuries. I AM also your father's best friend."

Mahlon and Chillion stared at Me as a rush of emotions overflowed into tears. I was the Being their father had told them about all the time. Elime had so many stories—how we used to hang out, shoot lazers, and build androids for fun. They'd always assumed he was jokin' when he called Me the Upgrade to his life.

"You remind us of our papa," Mahlon said through his tears.

"I know," I smiled as the only the Upgrade would. "We did act a lot alike."

Mahlon and Chillion kept cryin' until I brushed their tears away. The moment I did, their sadness lifted. My white smile gleamed against My ebony skin as they finally saw and thought clearly again.

"Thank You," Mahlon said. "We haven't felt this good in a long time."

"You're welcome," I assured. "Remember, it is written: 'I will wipe every tear from your eyes.'"

They were grateful for the peace I brought. Not many can wipe away tears and calm emotions in one final swoop.

"So why are You here?" Mahlon asked.

"I'm here to encourage you and to tell you why your father died."

Mahlon and Chillion gasped. They'd never been told how their papa died. They only knew he hadn't been feelin' well, went home to rest, and was gone by the time they returned. Naomi had tried for hours to wake him before she finally accepted he was gone.

"Wh-What? Our papa?" Mahlon stammered.

"We thought he died in his sleep," Chillion added.

"He did. Maybe he knew he was goin' to die in his sleep. Maybe he didn't." I shrugged. Who doesn't love a little dramatic effect? I know I do. But when I looked into their eyes, I saw hope. Even as panic tried to creep in, they resisted it, hungry for the truth.

"Our father knew he was goin' to die?" Mahlon asked, puzzled.

"Yes."

"Why didn't he tell us?" Chillion pressed.

"He was supposed to but he didn't. He ain't wanna worry y'all."

Mahlon and Chillion exchanged perplexed looks. They trusted Me, but believin' was still hard.

"Well, can You tell us why our papa died?" Mahlon asked. Someone had to know the truth.

"Your pappy had a secret, a secret he wanted to bury. Instead, it buried him. Literally."

Mahlon and Chillion froze. They'd never known their father to keep secrets especially not from their mama. They always thought their parents' love was flawless, transparent, divine. Now they realized every relationship holds mysteries. But this mystery was one worth solv'n.

"Well, what's the secret?"

"Awe, the secret is…" I paused, grinnin'.

By the looks on their faces, I could tell they were realizin' they'd met Me for the first time. Their papa's death wasn't what they expected, and what came next wasn't either. I had to tell them they'd die soon too. They weren't too happy 'bout that, but I AM the messenger. Even I have rules to follow.

"Is there anythin' we can do?" Mahlon asked desperately.

"Just keep livin' life. Yes, y'all will die too, but your legacy will live on. Tellin' your family the secret won't change anything. Elime ruined that."

They clenched the tablecloth in frustration at the thought of their fate. I get it, nobody wants to die young. But Yah's will must be done. Their father taught them that well.

"I have a trained agent sent to make sure everything goes as planned."

"An agent? Like a spy?" Mahlon asked, brows furrowed.

"No… like for cleanin'. Yes, a spy," I laughed. "But you'll never guess who that agent is. So just keep livin' your life. Oh and that reminds Me!"

Just then, Mahlon and Chillion turned as Ruth and Orpah called them to watch a movie. When they looked back, I was gone, but they could still feel My presence lingerin'.

"Mahlon! C'mon!" Ruth yelled.

"Chillion! You too!" Orpah echoed.

They followed the voices to the media room. Ruth and Orpah sat with fresh popcorn, the movie paused. Mahlon and Chillion joined them, seein' the frustration on their wives' faces. Mahlon noticed Ruth's glare and braced himself. He knew she was about to speak her mind.

"Mahlon, what's wrong? You look like you saw a ghost!"

CHAPTER 20

When Mahlon and Chillion were 29

Some macrobytes had passed, and I occasionally visited the boys to get them prepared and make sure everything was in order. I am a God of decency and order. I wanted all My Believers to be a reflection of those qualities and those qualities, the twins had. I am so happy when My Believers actually listen. Mahlon and Chillion entered Elime's state-of-the-art lab like it was any other day, not realizin' this day would be their last one in that familiar space.

The lab itself was a wonder, a whole memory capsule of who their father was. Twisty do-dads and thingamajiggers labeled as such sat on shelves like museum pieces. A reflection of their father's sense of humor and his refusal to take life too seriously. Every corner of the lab was filled wit' pieces of his brilliance—gadgets that hummed, machines that blinked, and contraptions that looked like they came straight from a dream. Since gainin' ownership of their father's business, they worked in his lab constantly. It reminded them of the great times they had as a family, before Moabolis. There was even a 3-D portrait of all of them on the wall—Elime, Naomi, Mahlon, and Chillion—frozen in time, laughin' together. That picture had been there for years, but today it seemed to shine brighter, like even the portrait knew somethin' was about to change.

They decided to get to work because this was different from any other day. Mahlon and Chillion sat cross-legged across from each other on the floor of their father's lab. They both had three screens up, tappin' and watchin' them excessively. Mahlon wrote both their last wills and testaments, his fingers flyin' across the hallegraphic screen wit' precision. Chillion was runnin' their father's business from the other side, answerin' messages, reviewin' contracts, makin' sure everythin' was in line. They were steady in their tasks, yet there was a weight in the air that neither wanted to name.

And then, I appeared suddenly between them to make sure that all items were in order before their death. My sudden appearance had them jumpin' back, fallin' over like little boys again.

"Ruach! Why you do that?" Mahlon said, tryin' to sit up straight, brushin' dust from his shirt.

"Right, can't you warn us first?" Chillion followed his lead, eyes wide, hand on his chest like his heart was beatin' out his rib cage.

"That's no fun," I replied wit' a smile, though I knew the heaviness of the moment.

The brothers wiped away their hallegraphic screens to focus on Me. They wanted to protest but decided not to. They knew it wouldn't change the situation—and I knew that My judgment was set. Their father had resisted Me, but these boys, nah, they were different.

"Will it hurt?" Mahlon asked, his voice softer than usual but steady.

"Nah, you will go peacefully—just like your papa. Also, I know y'all been prayin' 'bout this. Naomi will be taken care of. We got an agent called a Believer that was sent by Yah to help Naomi."

Their eyes widened, sparks of curiosity flashin' in them. They wanted to know more—they wanted a name, a face, somethin' to hold on to. I wanted to tell them who the Believer was—it would've made everythin' easier, but when You have orders to carry out, You can't defy them.

"Now, you already know I can't say a thang 'bout it!" I said, smilin'.

We all laughed. Laughter was like medicine, and it has a great way of calmin' people and emotions down. And when discussin' death, the more they were at peace, the better. Still, there was always somethin' to be concerned wit'.

"We don't have children, which sucks, 'cause we been married for many macrobytes." Mahlon's voice cracked a bit. He was concerned wit' who was gonna run their father's business. No heir, no business.

However, I had that taken care of, like I always do.

"That will be taken care of. Trust Me!"

"Amen!" they both said together.

They carried the same silence their father had—a weight that lived in unspoken glances and unfinished sentences. Each of them believed they were shieldin' their families, not realizin' the quiet would one day feel louder than words. In the end, it wasn't just the early graves that tied them to their father, but the way they left their loved ones to face the unknown—unprepared and alone.

Elime had shaped their minds wit' care and purpose. If he could see them now—standin' tall, their actions echoin' the lessons he'd sown—his pride would rise like the sun breakin' through a clouded sky. I felt as if these were My sons, and I couldn't help but be happy.

I wanted to talk more, to linger in their presence, but it was that time.

"Three."

They didn't flinch. Their eyes locked on Me, steady, ready.

"Two."

Still calm, though their wives' names slipped through their lips in whispers.

"On—wait, y'all aren't gonna protest? Beg and plead for your life? Anythin'?"

Mahlon and Chillion looked confused. They accepted the will of Yah much better than their father did. I assumed, like most people, they would be askin' for mo' time.

"No," Mahlon said, his voice clear. "This is Yah's will, and we accept it. We're waitin' for what's next."

"True!" Chillion added. "Plus, we're kinda excited to see our papa!" They both smiled at that thought. "We do love our mom and wives. We do wanna stay here, but we have to go, and our papa is there." Still, there was that smile, hopeful, genuine, unshaken.

"Wow! I wish your papa was like this," I said wit' a laugh. Their father had panicked, begged, wrestled wit' the inevitability. But his sons, they leaned into faith like it was breathin' itself.

All he had to do was tell his family his secret. But he never did. That secret sat on his chest like a stone until the end. His sons, though, were free of that weight. Their trust in Yah made them lighter, even now.

I wanted to say somethin' else, to give them more comfort, but they started to laugh because I was laughin'. Man, did they laugh. Their laughter filled the lab, bouncin' off the walls, shakin' the dust off their father's machines. It was contagious and warm, a sound that made even death seem small.

So, since they were laughin', I had to do what I had to do.

"One."

The word fell heavy but also gentle, like the last note of a song sung long into the night.

And as the light filled the lab, I thought about how rare it is for Believers to walk into death wit' such peace. These two boys, My sons in spirit, had done what so many could not. They trusted fully, even when the end was near.

Their laughter faded into eternity, but their faith echoed on.

CHAPTER 21

•

When Ruth and Orpah were 33

Ruth and Orpah walked throughout their husbands' lab, each step makin' them feel more uncertain. The floor beneath them hummed wit' the faint vibration of machines that once needed their husbands' hands to stay alive. It wasn't too long ago that they discovered their husbands' bodies lyin' on the floor wit' the most pleasant smiles on their faces. The stillness of that moment kept replayin' in their minds like a broken Halletape. Their faces contrasted it wit' sheer horror and panic. They could not believe that not many nanobytes ago, they were buryin' their father-in-law, Elime. Now, they would be doin' the same wit' their husbands.

The sistahs grabbed and slowly touched the many gadgets, gizmos, and inventions their husbands had created since takin' over the company. The smell of burnt wires still lingered in the air, mixed wit' the faint musk of their husbands' cologne that somehow clung to the room.

"Ruth, look at this!" Orpah picked up a small mirror that had wires stickin' out of it, its cracked surface reflectin' her swollen eyes.

"Be careful, Orpah!" Ruth yelled, her voice shakin'. "One of those wires could stick your eye out." She rushed to Orpah, snatchin' the mirror from her hand like a mother pullin' a child from danger.

"Okay, Mom!" Orpah shot back sarcastically. But her sarcasm had no sting; it was just muscle memory of how they used to joke before grief came crashin' in. Ruth had always been a mother figure to Orpah, although Orpah was the older twin. Ruth felt it was her duty to protect her sistah, and Orpah was reminded of it every single day.

Ruth laughed a tired laugh that barely lifted the air. "Orpah, you know I only care."

"Yeah, I know!" Orpah softened, pressin' her lips against her sistah's cheek. The warmth lingered. They both took a seat on the cold lab floor, lookin' around wit' a fresh pair of eyes. Every contraption and gizmo felt alive, like the ghosts of their husbands lived inside the nuts, bolts, and wires. They wanted to be happy about what their husbands had accomplished, but at the same time, sorrow sat heavy on their chests 'cause the men weren't there to keep creatin'.

"What are we gonna do?" Orpah's voice cracked like glass under weight.

"That's a good question," Ruth whispered, her hands fiddlin' wit' the hem of her dress as if answers could be sewn there.

They just stared at each other in silence. Yet silence ain't never truly silent; it carried the echo of their heartbreak. The unspoken question of how to live on when the people you love most are gone.

And I knew I had to come and help process their pain.

"I may have an answer to that question."

The sistahs stood up immediately, spinnin' around tryin' to find the source of My voice. Their eyes darted from wall to wall, from gadget to gadget, searchin' like frightened children. They knew they'd heard somethin', but they had no idea where it came from. Once they didn't hear anything, I spoke again.

"Hello, I AM right here."

I instantly appeared next to 'em, sittin' on the floor. My presence bent the air itself; it grew warm, then cool, then steady as if the whole lab adjusted itself to Me.

The sistahs screamed and jumped back, tumblin' like dominoes.

"Cami, INTRUDERRRR!" Ruth hollered.

Cami was the security system that King Eglon gave to Elime when his daughters married his sons. Cami was his assistant, but they cloned her AI so the girls could always have a piece of her wit' 'em. Over time, she became more than a machine, she was a voice they trusted, a presence that reassured.

A gadget dropped from the ceiling like a hawk, beams of scarlet light scanin' every corner. "No threat detected!" the womanly voice rang, smooth as ever.

Ruth and Orpah's faces grew as red as that light. They inched back slowly, their breaths shallow.

"What do you mean, 'No threat'? He is right there!"

The gadget swooped again, sweepin' the lab faster than the blink of an eye. After a full scan, it reported the same: "No threat detected!"

"What!" Ruth shrieked. "NAOOMMMIIII!!! NAAOOMMMIIII!!!"

I tilted My head at 'em, confused for just a moment. Then it struck Me: they had heard of the Upgrade but never met Me in the flesh.

"Ruth! Orpah! Calm down! Let Me speak!"

Their breaths quickened, panic written across their faces.

"How do you know our names?"

"'Cause before you were in your mother's womb, I knew you!" I said softly, yet My words thundered in their souls.

Ruth froze mid-crawl, eyes wide, breath caught in her throat. Slowly, shakily, she rose, her body betrayin' the battle between fear and hope. Step by step she drew near, each one heavier yet lighter than the last. When she was just a foot away, the word left her lips in a trembling whisper:

"Ruach?"

"I AM," I answered.

Her smile broke like dawn over darkness. She threw herself into My arms, clutchin' Me like her soul depended on it. The grief that strangled her heart dissolved in the embrace, laughter spillin' out like a stream freed from a dam.

When she pulled away, her eyes glowed wit' somethin' brand new. She ran to Orpah, helpin' her up. "Orpah, this is Ruach. You remember what our husbands told us about the Upgrade?"

"Uhhh, yeah!" Orpah stammered, still stuck between disbelief and awe.

"Well, this is Him. He is the Upgrade!" Ruth's voice lifted, childlike in its wonder.

Orpah blinked, glanced at Me, then back at Ruth. "Wait… you mean this man standin' right here is the Upgrade?"

"Yes!" Ruth nodded wildly, joy spillin' everywhere.

"Oh my!" Orpah rushed into My arms, clingy as if she'd known Me her whole life. I held her just as firm, lettin' her grief melt into peace.

Finally, we all sat together on the floor, the three of us. The lab that once felt like a tomb now held somethin' more: hope.

"So tell Me, how you feelin' in this moment?" I asked, My voice soft but steady, shiftin' the air.

"I feel great," Ruth said quickly, her tone surprised at herself.

"Yeah, me too!" Orpah admitted.

"And how were you feelin' before I arrived?" I pressed gently, invitin' 'em to put words to their wounds.

Ruth swallowed. "I think I can speak for my sistah when I say we were in pain." Orpah nodded hard. "We just lost our father-in-law, who we loved, and now we lost our husbands."

Their eyes brimmed wit' tears again, water glistenin' like jewels ready to spill.

"I know losin' someone you love is terrible. But remember this, bein' able to love at all is a gift. A gift that can hurt, but also heal."

The words touched Orpah, but also ignited her ache.

"You get it?" she barked, her voice sharpened by sorrow. "What do you mean, you get it? You don't get it!"

She rose to her feet, every inch closin' the distance between us charged wit' pain.

"I am wit'out a husband, and so is my sistah and my mother-in-law. We are hurtin'. You let this happen. You let them die. You are the cause of all of this!"

Her tears finally poured out, wild and unstoppable. "They said, 'You heal,' but You didn't heal them! They said, 'You comfort,' but I feel broken! They said, 'You bring peace,' but I'm in pieces!"

She collapsed into My arms, the dam of her soul burstin'. Ruth followed, crashin' into the embrace. I held them both as their cries shook the room.

Only after their tears slowed did I ask, "Y'all feel better?"

They nodded faintly, like weary children.

"Good. Now let's talk."

We all sat back down on the floor, the cool steel beneath us remindin' them of the emptiness they felt. Ruth wiped her cheeks wit' the back of her hand, leavin' a wet streak across her face. Orpah sniffled, starin' at the ground like the answers to life itself were etched in the cracks of the tile.

"Now," I began, "let's talk." My voice carried no thunder this time, just a steady warmth that filled the space like a fire in winter.

They looked at Me like students waitin' on a teacher weary but hungry.

"You both said you heard I was a healer, a comforter, a bringer of peace, right?"

They nodded slow, as if noddin' too fast might shatter the fragile air around us.

"Okay." I leaned in closer, lookin' 'em in their eyes. "That's what you heard. But have you tried Me for yourself?"

The lab went quiet. Machines hummed in the corners, but even their noise bowed down to the silence that fell between us.

"That ain't rhetorical," I pressed. "I'm askin' y'all somethin'. Have you ever sought Me on your own? Not through your husbands. Not through Naomi. Not through the stories passed down. But you, Ruth? You, Orpah?"

Ruth chewed her lip, her hand tremblin' in her lap. Orpah finally broke the silence.

"Well," she muttered, "uhhh… no."

I turned to Ruth. She didn't say a word, just shook her head slow, eyes glassy.

"I thought so," I said — not wit' disappointment, but wit' the same truth a doctor brings when givin' a hard diagnosis. "And there lies the issue. There will always be an issue when people don't know Yah for themselves."

Their eyes lifted to Me, heavy wit' questions.

"You can't always rely on others for your relationship wit' Me," I continued. "You can't enter into the Kingdom ridin' on what others say or do. It gotta come from you. That's the only way you can truly say, 'I tried Him, and I know Him.'"

The words sat on 'em like weights, not crushin', but pressin', pressin' 'em to think, to wrestle, to breathe deeper.

Ruth leaned forward, voice barely above a whisper. "So you sayin'… all this time, we believed… but not really?"

I smiled softly, touchin' her hand. "I'm sayin' belief secondhand ain't the same as faith firsthand. You loved through your husbands, you prayed through Naomi, but you never tested for yourself. Now life has dragged you to this moment. Your husband is gone, your father-in-law is gone, and you're left asking why your heart feels hollow. It's 'cause your cup was filled by others. But now I'm askin' you to let Me pour into you directly."

Orpah let out a shaky breath, almost a laugh though it wasn't joy, it was exhaustion. "But Ruach… we don't even know where to start."

"Start here," I said, tappin' My chest. "Start wit' honesty. You already gave Me your tears, your anger, your questions. That's a start. Don't think I need polished prayers or perfect words. I want you. The raw, the real, the Ruth and Orpah sittin' right here. That's enough."

Ruth's eyes widened as if light finally cracked through the fog. She grabbed Orpah's hand, squeezin' it tight.

"So… if we walk wit' You ourselves," Ruth said slowly, "will it stop the pain?"

I shook My head gentle. "No. But it will change the pain. Pain won't be your master no more; it'll become your teacher. And in Me, pain don't get the final say. Love does."

The sisters looked at each other. Ruth's grip on Orpah's hand tightened again, this time not in fear but in somethin' like courage. Orpah nodded, small at first, then firmer.

"Then show us how," Orpah whispered, voice crackin' like a child askin' for guidance.

"That's all I been waitin' for." I stretched My arms out, invitin' 'em close again. They came, not runnin' this time, but walkin' steady like their feet finally found ground they could trust.

I wrapped 'em both in My arms, not to erase their grief, but to anchor 'em through it. And as they held on, the lab itself seemed different.

Machines still hummed, lights still flickered but hope had entered the room and sat down to stay.

CHAPTER 22

When Naomi was 53

It had been many macrobytes since her sons had passed, and Naomi was still processin' what had transpired. Some days were better than others, but this day was rough, as she was readin' the will of her two late sons, Mahlon and Chillion. The memory of their laughter still echoed faintly in the corners of her home, like programs runnin' in the background long after the mainframe had shut down.

Naomi sat in the same spot she had been many nanobytes ago, when her husband died, as she read his will—the table still bearin' faint scratches from all the nights Elime would tinker wit' his gadgets. Her daughters-in-law, Ruth and Orpah, looked sad and weary. They had been sittin' across from her, their hands interlocked as if lettin' go would cause 'em to fall apart completely. Ruth's knuckles were white from squeezin' Orpah's hand too hard.

Ruth and Orpah both looked and noticed Naomi's stone-cold, expressionless face. It was a look that hid the hurricane underneath. Naomi was a woman who had weathered storms before, but this one had stripped her skies bare. Naomi is so strong. I can't even imagine, Ruth thought, her chest tightenin' as she tried to steady her own breathin'.

Naomi used her finger, spinnin' the hallegraphic projection of her sons' will toward their wives. The light from the hallegram cast eerie shadows on her face, makin' her look both fragile and indestructible all at once.

"Ruth. Orpah. I love y'all like I gave birth to y'all." Her voice cracked in ways she didn't mean it to, but she steadied herself. "As you see here in the will, your husbands, my sons, left me fifty percent of the billion-dollar company. That doesn't mean much, since it's hard for women to do business at this time. I'm not sayin' it's impossible or unlikely. I've seen women take over certain sectors and do it better than men, but they always had to do way more than their male counterparts, and that can be exhaustin'. However, they did leave y'all some shares of the company, so y'all will be taken care of."

Ruth's lips trembled, her eyes floodin' wit' tears, but she blinked 'em back before they fell. "Mama, I want you to have my share," she said quickly, as if the words would vanish if she didn't release 'em fast enough.

"Me too! We're royalty. Our parents will take care of us!" Orpah added, her tone tryin' to sound firm, though her voice wavered at the edges.

Naomi was shocked by her daughters-in-law's willingness to sign over their shares. For a moment, she could only stare, the hallegram flickerin' between their faces as if it too couldn't comprehend their sacrifice. Ruth and Orpah smiled through the pain, their faces brave masks for hearts that quietly fractured. Each held tightly to the other, knowin' that shared grief was all they had left of the life they'd known. Behind their smiles lingered the unspoken truth: love had tethered them to this moment, but the paths ahead would soon diverge, unfamiliar yet inevitable.

Suddenly, a Hallescreen spat out of her Praise right next to the will. Its glow was urgent, commandin', as if heaven itself had interrupted their grief. The girls leaned in to read it.

HALLESCREEN: Neo-Eden? "Yes" or "No"

The room grew still, the only sound the low hum of the hallegram projectors. Naomi leaned back in her chair, and her daughters followed suit. The weight of those two words pressed heavy on the air.

Since the moment she found her sons in Elime's lab, dead wit' smiles on their faces, she knew she had run her course in Moabolis. She had replayed that sight countless times, how Mahlon's hand still rested on the console, how Chillion's head tilted like he'd only dozed off, both wearin' peace in a way that mocked her pain. She was grateful, in a twisted way, that she found 'em first and not their wives. She bore the scar so Ruth and Orpah wouldn't have to.

"Yes," she realized, "the sight of seein' your twin sons dead is one I wouldn't wish on my worst enemy." Naomi's throat closed as the memory surged. The only great moments to come from this were starin' her in the face now, forcin' a smile to keep from cryin'.

"What does this mean?" Orpah asked, her voice so small it almost disappeared into the hum.

"Yah wants me to come home," Naomi responded, her words soft but sharp as blades.

"Home?" Ruth questioned. "But you are home."

"To Neo-Eden. I guess my story doesn't end here, and Yah has plans for me there." Naomi said it like a woman resigned but not broken, a soldier waitin' for her next assignment.

"May we come wit' you?" Orpah's eyes widened, childlike and desperate. She really loved Naomi and did not want her to leave her life.

"No! No!" Naomi shook her head, the motion wild, as tears began threatenin' to spill. She didn't want to tell her daughters no, but she felt she had nothin' left to offer them. Ruth and Orpah's faces pleaded wit' Naomi to take them wit' her. Their eyes were two mirrors reflectin' her own emptiness.

Naomi knew her daughters meant well, but—

"There's nothin' I can do for y'all! I can't give y'all sons for husbands! Y'all should go back to your parents, they can take care of y'all!" Her voice grew louder, like each word built a wall between them. Naomi didn't want to send her daughters away. If anything, she wanted to run wit' them into the safety of the King and Queen's palace. But she knew she couldn't. Yah's will must be done.

"But we wanna go wit'chu." Ruth's words were barely more than a whisper, but they clung to the air like a sacred vow.

Naomi couldn't handle it. All the emotions she'd kept bottled up finally exploded into uncontrollable tears. She pressed her palms to her face, sobbin' until her shoulders shook. Tears for her husband, her sons, and her new life witout 'em. Ruth and Orpah couldn't help but start cryin' after seein' Naomi cry. Their tears mixed into one river of grief, streamin' down cheeks, fallin' into their laps, drownin' the silence.

Naomi had to fight through the tears as she faced some difficult decisions. Her voice was hoarse when she finally spoke. "Please, just sign your shares over and go back. Lookin' at y'all reminds me too much of my sons. I'm sorry."

Orpah's lip quivered as she reached out, her hand shakin', swipin' her finger over the Hallegraphic screen, givin' all her shares to Naomi. Orpah leaned in and gave Naomi and Ruth each a goodbye kiss—her lips lingerin' on Naomi's forehead longer than usual, as if tryin' to memorize the feel of her. Her Praise sensed her time wit' Naomi and Ruth was done and uploaded her back to her parents' castle in a shimmer of light.

Naomi waited for Ruth to follow suit. Her face, streaked wit' tears, turned toward her last daughter-in-law. "Girl, you might as well follow your sistah!"

Ruth's chest rose and fell, her breath uneven, but her eyes blazed steady. "No! I will not. You are my mom. Where you go, I go! Where you pray, I pray. Your God is now my God!"

The weight of those words broke Naomi's last defense. She saw herself in Ruth, young, stubborn, fearless in faith. Naomi knew not to argue wit' Ruth. She was the most like Naomi, especially when she was Ruth's age. She knew she had to take Ruth wit' her. Only a person who loved Yah would have said those kind words to her. Ruth knew she was a Believer.

"Well, I guess we should go," Naomi whispered, breathin' deep, gatherin' courage. And wit' that, Naomi pushed YES.

The room warped, the Hallegram flarin' like a star about to explode. Ruth and Naomi ended up at the entrance of Neo-Eden. Their feet touched new ground, soft and glowin', as if alive. They were confused, their eyes dartin' around, expectin' to see Naomi's mansion on the hills. Instead, they stood at gates carved from light, pulsatin' wit' Yah's presence.

Naomi clutched Ruth's hand. Her heart raced, half in fear and half in awe. If there was one thing Naomi knew not to do, because Elime reminded her every day, it was to not question what Yah allows.

But the silence of Neo-Eden begged for questions.

Naomi tilted her face upward, her tears dryin' against the warm glow.

"Naomi, why did Yah download us here?" Ruth asked, her voice filled wit' wonder and unease.

Naomi exhaled slowly, the weight of her life sittin' on her shoulders, yet lightened by the unknown promise before her. "That's a great question."

PART II:
THE BARLEY HARVEST

CHAPTER 23

The metropolitan city of Neo-Eden was lit up for the celebration of the Barley Harvest, a giant citywide festival rooted in an alternative and peculiar lens of Afro-expression. Every gizmo and gadget was on display, fully operatin' and flyin' around their respective store vendors. People were outside laughin', talkin', and sellin'.

Naomi felt sadness wit' every step she took through her city. Everyone was glad she came back and showed her mad love, but she felt terrible, 'cause her family wasn't there. To make matters worse, she and Ruth were wearin' matchin' red and white tracksuits. Naomi was in stilettos, and Ruth was in high tops. This was not what anyone would wear to the Barley Festival. Naomi not only knew this, but felt it wit' every stare she received.

"Wow! Someone is surely the hometown hero," Ruth smirked.
"What you talkin' 'bout, Ruth?" Naomi asked.
"Those people! They were showin' you mad love! Big-uppin' you! Are you a celebrity here or somethin'?"

Naomi kept walkin', not tryin' to catch anyone's attention, for she knew she was not properly dressed, and that was unlike her.
"Yes. I was. Elime was very successful and very popular."
"I can believe it. My father idolized him!"

Ruth and Naomi both laughed as they walked, finally comin' to the end of the road. Ruth looked at Naomi and noticed that she was in her element. She's on home court, and I'm the visitor, Ruth thought. She also noticed the pain on Naomi's face when people started callin' to her and sayin' hi. Ruth prayed that Naomi's pain would soon be taken away.

"Hallelujah," Naomi said boldly. "A car's comin' to get us." Ruth nodded as she waited next to her. They stood at the intersection, and Ruth stared ahead through the bustle of the city at the giant neon sign, Threshin' Floor. Naomi was lookin' around.

Suddenly, they both were beamed up into a black car and whisked away to their new home. Ruth wanted a quiet moment, but she had so much on her mind.

"Mama, what's the Threshin' Floor?"

"The Threshin' Floor? Oh… that's my best friend, my brotha-in-love's lounge. His name is Boaz. He's the reason why I'm married."

"Really? How so?"

"He's my husband's brotha-cousin and best friend, and mine too. He was the one that would listen to me and Elime talk 'bout each other and encourage us to marry, and we did."

"Wow, so he's really cool."

"Sure is. He catered the weddin', but had to leave soon after for an emergency. I wish you could've met him. He's a gem. He'll give you the shirt off his back. Anyone that needs help goes to him, and he helps them all."

"Why didn't he ever come visit us in Moabolis?" Ruth asked.

"'Cause Yah told him not to," Naomi responded. "We invited him plenty of times, but Yah spoke to him and said he had to stay in Neo-Eden. He was allowed for the weddin', but that was it."

"His devotion sounds a lot like Elime's," Ruth chuckled.

"Yes, they were two peas in a pod," Naomi laughed.

Ruth gazed out the window, captivated by the brightly colored festival that seemed to wrap the entire town in its embrace. Each twist and turn revealed a new fragment of her late husband's culture, vibrant and alive, offerin' her pieces of him she'd never fully understood. In every rhythm, every hue, she found a silent explanation for the man she had loved, as if the festival itself were tellin' his story.

Out of the corner of her eye, she noticed Naomi workin' on a hallegraphic projection of somethin' she'd never seen before. Ruth wanted to voice her concern, but just then they pulled up to a house larger than Naomi's in Moabolis.

Ruth and Naomi beamed down from the car wit' a ping behind them.
"Payment approved!" the car stated as it flew off for the next customer.

They walked toward the house, and immediately the double doors opened. It was dark, the only light comin' from the Praise they wore. Suddenly, every light, gadget, and gizmo turned on.
"AAAHHHH!" One almost hit Ruth as she ducked out the way. All Naomi could do was laugh and shake her head.

"Follow me." Naomi walked to the livin' room, and Ruth followed her. They sat down on the couch opposite each other.
"So, mama, why we here?"
"We here 'cause Yah sent us here. I just wish He sent us directly to the house. All that walkin' and havin' to call a car…"
"So what do you think He has planned for us?"
"Baby, I dunno. But knowin' Yah, it's somethin' powerful."
"I bet."
"We bettah get some sleep."

Naomi started down the hallway, and Ruth knew to follow. She was so enamored by the paintings on the wall that she almost ran into Naomi, who had stopped in front of a door.

"This is Mahlon's room. You can sleep here."

"Why are there two beds?"

"Mahlon and Chillion loved each other so much they shared a room, even when they were older."

Naomi always found that strange. She and Elime provided enough for everyone to have their own space, but instead, they always chose to stay around each other. She had to change her mind, 'cause the thought of those memories began to weigh on her heart, heavy. Ruth knew Naomi would embrace those memories wit' joy. She admired that 'bout her.

Ruth stepped into the room, her breath hitchin' as her eyes darted over the scattered remnants of Mahlon's life. Posters of distant galaxies clung to the walls, their edges curlin' wit' age. A half-filled mug sat abandoned on the desk, its rim smudged wit' dried coffee stains. The faint scent of cedar lingered in the air, minglin' wit' the sharp tang of metal from a dismantled robot restin' on the floor. She ran her fingers along the bookshelf, tracin' the spines of dog-eared sci-fi novels. It was as if time had paused the moment Mahlon left, and now, standin' here, Ruth felt like an intruder in a place that whispered his secrets.

The whole self-cleanin' house does come in handy when you move away for some macrobytes, she thought. She recognized the giant mirror in the room. It looked identical to the replica back in Moabolis. Ruth walked to the mirror and had to tap it. That was her favorite thing to do, since Mahlon's mirror in Moabolis did cool tricks. Surely, it was no surprise that this mirror was the same, as Ruth now had options to choose her pajamas. She swiped, mixed, and matched before decidin' on a pink silk pajama set. "Hallelujah," she spoke before noticin' the pajama set start to materialize over her body. That will always be cool to me, she thought.

"Ahhhh-hhaaaaaa." Ruth ain't realize how tired she was until that yawn left her body. She was walkin' to Mahlon's bed when she heard a voice comin' from the mirror.

"Hey, Ruth!" Quickly, she turned around and saw that it was Mahlon. She ran to the mirror faster than the prodigal son returnin' home. Sweatin' profusely, Ruth placed all her attention on Mahlon.

"Hey, Ruth, it's Mahlon. If you're watchin' this, then I died. I'm sorry, but there was nothin' I could do. Now you're alone, and it's all my fault. I'm sorry. One thing I can say is please learn from my mistakes. Do not let the Spirit of Fear control you. I rebuke it through the power of the Upgrade, the Holy Spirit. You are perfect, you are wonderful, and you will do great things in the digital world as well as the physical. Just always remember two things when it comes to Yah, Yes and Amen. I love you, from here until eternity."

The mirror returned to a regular mirror.

Ruth began tappin' it frantically to restart or replay the message. She savored every voice memory and video she had wit' Mahlon. It is what kept her sane through this whole ordeal. She wanted to replay this one over and over again, but it wouldn't allow her, which crushed her into tears. She ran to her bed, cryin' and wishin' she could see him, touch him, hold him one more time. She knew she couldn't do it now, but she knew one day she'd be wit' him again. She decided to pray her way through the tears. It was the only way she was gonna sleep.

"The Lord my Yah is in my midst,
a mighty one who will save;
He will rejoice over me wit' gladness;
He will quiet me by His love;"

CHAPTER 24

Naomi was surrounded by a whirlwind of noises from the coffee pot and juice machine. She enjoyed bein' awake early in the mornin'. It gave her time to pray and be alone wit' her thoughts. Once she finished prayin', orange juice appeared next to her as it had in the past. However, she lifted her Praise, whispered Hallelujah, and the orange juice was replaced wit' Elime's Drink. It was her little keepsake that Elime was always wit' her—as I was always wit' her. She took a sip just as Ruth walked into the kitchen, lookin' surprisin'ly refreshed.

"How did you sleep?"
"Surprisingly, I slept great. Got a message from an old friend." Mahlon's message still replayed in Ruth's mind, and it brought her joy now instead of heartache.
"Really? Anyone I know?"
"Yeah! You do!"

Ruth and Naomi traded smiles. It was easier to smile than to cry.
"What'chu got planned for today?"
"Well, I plan on goin' to the Barley Harvest to see what it's 'bout. I remember Mahlon tellin' me all 'bout it when he was alive and how he always wanted to take me."

Naomi smiled. She loved hearin' how Ruth always tried to honor Mahlon in everything she did.
"Okay, what else you plan on doin'?"
"Well, I'm always hungry," Ruth chuckled. "So, Imma try out that restaurant you talked 'bout—The Threshin' Floor."

"Yes, they got some great food. Bring me back somethin'!"

"Hahaha! I will. Love you."

Ruth went back to her room after stealin' a kiss from Naomi. She decided to catch a cab to the city. It didn't take long for an all-black van to arrive and upload her, whiskin' her away. She made sure to add coordinates that would drop her off right in the heart of the city. She remembered hearin' about the Barley Harvest from Mahlon and his family, but this was the first time she would be able to experience it herself.

The cab downloaded her right smack in the middle of the city, and she was instantly taken aback. Her jaw dropped as she spun in slow circles, tryin' to take it all in. Gadgets zipped overhead like tiny rockets, and metallic droids bumped past her wit' trays of steamin' food that smelled like roasted barley and sweet fruit. Vendors shouted from every corner, their voices mixin' wit' the clang of machines and the hum of neon signs. They wore vibrant, peculiar, and loud clothin', jackets that glowed and pants that changed color every few seconds, makin' Ruth feel like she stepped into a dream she wasn't dressed for.

She glanced down at her Moabolian tracksuit, red and white wit' KE-3's, and sighed. She realized she stood out worse than a 2 in binary code: obvious, awkward, and impossible to hide. A few folks gave her curious looks, but Ruth straightened her back, remindin' herself who she was.

She lifted her Praise close, whisperin' Hallelujah. Her voice was soft, almost shaky, but she meant it from the pit of her soul. Like an answer to her prayer, the Praise responded. A light burst forth, so bright she had to shield her eyes. Nobody else seemed to notice, though. The crowd moved on, laughin' and hagglin', blind to what was happenin'. Ruth blinked hard as the light dimmed and reshaped itself into a giant arrow. It hovered in front of her for only a breath before dartin' into the crowd like the gizmo that nearly smacked her earlier.

Before she could even think, her feet shot forward. She weaved through strangers, nearly knockin' folks over as she twisted, ran, slowed, then darted again, never lettin' the arrow out of her sight. Her chest burned, but she pushed on until finally it stopped.

It hovered in front of a vendor booth unlike any other. Dresses swayed in the artificial breeze, and Ruth froze in her tracks. Her breath caught in her throat. These weren't just dresses, they were covered in delicate patterns of balsam flowers. Some designs even bloomed across the fabric as if alive.

A tear slid down her cheek before she even realized she was cryin'. She pressed her hand to her chest and whispered a thank-you. "Yah, you led me here," she breathed. In the middle of a city that felt like another world, she had stumbled onto a piece of home.

"How may I help you?" a woman's voice called from the back.

An old lady appeared, short and petite, wit' glasses and salt-and-pepper microlocs. She was eccentric and eclectic, at least that's how Ruth saw her. Ruth stepped forward, introduced herself, and pointed to a two-piece black-and-yellow balsam-flower set. From the moment she touched it, she knew she had to have it.

"Uh, hello!" Ruth said wit' uncertainty.
"Yes?" The old lady looked up from behind the booth, covered in flowers and carryin' fabric. Ruth stepped forward slowly to introduce herself, though the older woman kept glancin' around her booth, searchin' for somethin' while still tryin' to pay attention.

"Hi, how are you?" Ruth smiled. "I'm interested in your two-piece black-and-yellow balsam-flower set right here."

Ruth slowly raised the outfit off the table to show her. From the moment she grabbed it, it instantly felt like her, somethin' she missed every day.

"Sure, dear, one moment," the lady said, pickin' somethin' up off the ground.

"Ah-hah! I found it, my lucky pen." The lady held her pen in victory as if she'd won a medal. "I been lookin' for this all day. It's my favorite."

Wit'out lookin' at Ruth, she took the clothes from her and bagged them up slowly.
"Thank you so much," Ruth began. "When I saw it, I knew I had to have it. It reminded me of home."

Suddenly, the lady stopped mid-packin'. "Did you say home?" Her frail voice lingered in the air.
"Yes," Ruth smiled. "You see, I'm from Moabolis, and the balsam flower is one of our pride and joys. Anytime I see it, I instantly feel like I'm a little girl again, spendin' time wit' my family."

The old woman lifted her hands slowly and turned even slower. She fixed her glasses as she walked back to the front of the booth to get a better look at who she was speakin' wit'. Before she could even get a few steps closer, she stumbled back in shock.
"Princess Ruth!" she screamed, louder than the lo-fi music in the background.

Random people from all around began to turn their heads toward Ruth and whisper. Ruth noticed but didn't break her gaze from the old woman.

"Yes," Ruth said calmly, not tryin' to draw attention to herself. "Oh my! It's you!" The older woman came from behind the booth and gave her a big hug.

Suddenly, Ruth was bein' dragged inside the booth by the old woman's aged hand. Her grip was firmer than Ruth expected, like someone who carried fabric bolts and sewing machines. The woman pulled two chairs from the side and set them down wit' a surprising snap of strength. Ruth barely had time to settle before the old woman shuffled to the front, flipped the sign to Closed, and yanked the curtains together, shuttin' out the noisy festival.

The difference was immediate. Outside, the city roared wit' hover carts, voices, and music, but in here it was quiet, just the faint hum of a cooling unit and the scent of fabric dye mixed wit' citrus oils.

Ruth sat motionless until the old woman reemerged wit' two cups of orange juice. The cups floated at her fingertips like they were lighter than cloth. She slid one toward Ruth, then sipped her own while starin' straight into Ruth's eyes. Ruth lifted the cup politely, but her hand trembled slightly. She took a careful sip, the sweet tang floodin' her tongue, and forced a smile to ease the mood.

"Princess Ruth," the old woman said at last, placin' her drink aside to float in mid-air. She leaned closer, her voice softer now and heavy wit' meanin'. "What are you doin' here?"

Ruth squinted, uneasy at the question. The title Princess was a name she hadn't heard since Moabolis. It cut through her like a reminder of who she used to be and who she was tryin' to be now.

"I'm sorry, but who are you? And how do you know I'm a princess?" She placed her cup in the air, lettin' it hover beside the woman's.

"My heavens!" the old woman cried out, throwin' her hands up. "Please forgive my rudeness. My name is Mosh. It's nice to finally meet you." She stretched her hand out, waitin' for Ruth to shake it.

Ruth's eyes widened wider than her first steps in Neo-Eden. Wit'out thinkin', she threw her arms around the woman, huggin' her tight. She pulled back just as quick, realizin' what she'd done.

"Sorry, but I know that name anywhere. You're Mosh, the legendary designer from Moabolis. I love your work. I'm wearin' you right now." She stood and twirled, the red-and-white tracksuit shimmerin' under the booth's lights.

"Me and my sistah even wore weddin' dresses from your collection, House of Che."

"Hallelujah." Ruth's Praise flicked, projectin' a carousel of weddin' photos. She and Orpah stood in mutated fabric of vibrant reds, blues, and golds. Beadwork glittered in motifs of flowers and birds. Their sheer, beaded capes caught the sunlight, scatterin' it like tiny rainbows. Headwraps framed their faces, while jewelry sparkled like they'd been dipped in starlight.

Mosh pressed her hand to her mouth, overwhelmed.

"Wow, Princess Ruth, I'm honored. I had no idea I designed your weddin' dress." She reached for her floatin' drink, took a sip, and set it back. "I remember gettin' those instructions, measurements, notes, and a mountain of money. I worked day and night, stitchin' every bead by hand. When they picked 'em up, they left even more money and a thank-you card." She laughed, shaky but proud. "Wit' that much, I packed up and moved to Neo-Eden. I still run the shop in Moabolis, but here nobody knows me. I can breathe."

Ruth smiled knowingly. Bein' a princess had perks, sure, rich clothes, respect, every door open. But it also meant no freedom. Everywhere she went, eyes followed. Guards shadowed her. Even laughin' felt like a performance. Wit' Naomi, she had space. Space to grieve, space to breathe, space to remember Mahlon wit'out cameras snappin'.

"I totally understand," Ruth said, her voice softer now. "That's why I came wit' Naomi. I needed a place where I could just… be."

Mosh leaned back, crossin' her legs, her salt-and-pepper locs slippin' from behind her ear. "Princess Ruth, why are you really here?"

The question settled heavy in the room. Ruth reached for her cup, clutchin' it like it might give her courage. She downed the rest in one long gulp, the juice cold against her throat. She set the cup on the ground, drew in a deep breath, countin' to five, then let it out slow.

"My sistah and I… we married two amazin' men." Her voice cracked. She swallowed and pushed on. "We were happy for some macrobytes. We had joy. We had dreams. But then, they died, both of 'em. Their father had already passed many nanobytes before that. So it left Orpah, Naomi, and me. Orpah stayed in Moabolis, but I couldn't. Everythin' reminds me of Mahlon, every street, every song, even the smell of the city. It was suffocatin' me. So when Naomi asked, I left wit' her. We just… we got along so well. She feels like my own mama sometimes. Plus, my father, King Eglon, kept me sheltered 'cause he used to live his life on social media. So I knew no one would know me as a princess. I needed to hide so that I could grieve."

The words tumbled out like a storm breakin'. Ruth hadn't realized how tight she'd been holdin' it in until it all spilled. Her chest loosened for the first time in cycles.

Mosh's eyes shimmered as she leaned over, pullin' Ruth into her arms. Her hug wasn't frail. It was strong and steady, like an anchor. Ruth melted into it, silent tears spillin' down her face. She didn't even know she was cryin' until she felt the wetness against her cheek.

"How you feel now?" Mosh asked gently as she pulled back.

Ruth wiped her face, still breathin' uneven but lighter. "Better," she whispered. For the first time in a long while, her lungs felt open, her heart less heavy. "That was a lot to tell someone you don't even know."

They both laughed, the sound almost absurd after such rawness. But it felt good, like laughin' through tears at a funeral.

"I needed that," Ruth admitted. "It feels good to let it out."

"I know." Mosh nodded slow. "Talkin' helps you heal. I had to do it plenty before I moved here and even after I arrived. Every stitch, every dress, every bead, it was me workin' through my own pain."

Ruth tilted her head. "Your pain?"

Mosh smiled, bittersweet. "Fashion holds memory, child. Every piece I make carries a story. Some stories end in sorrow, but when someone wears it, dances in it, marries in it, it transforms. That's why I keep sewin', to turn grief into somethin' beautiful."

Ruth's eyes welled again, but this time the tears didn't sting. They felt like balm. She thought of Mahlon, of his laughter, of how he used to say the Barley Harvest was for the forgotten. Maybe this was Yah's way of remindin' her that she wasn't forgotten either. For the first time since his death, Ruth felt like she could step forward wit'out leavin' him behind.

Ruth twisted her face at Mosh, curious. "Why did you choose Neo-Eden?"

Mosh laughed quick, like she'd been waitin' for the question. She always enjoyed tellin' this story. "Well, after I received the money from your family, I went home to relax. Randomly, a message popped up in front of me. It said, *Neo-Eden?*, clear as day. I didn't even press nothin'. I just said yes, and the next thing I knew, I was here. And there was a mansion prepared for me."

Ruth blinked. "A mansion prepared for you?"

"Yes," Mosh nodded, her eyes glintin'. "As if someone had gone ahead and set it all up. The place had everythin' I needed, fabric rooms, design tables, even a garden filled wit' flowers I loved from Moabolis. The move was seamless, almost like Yah Himself carried me here. And my business back home? Thrivin' more than ever. I can do vendor booths for fun now instead of survival. And the best part?" She grinned, leanin' forward. "No one recognizes me."

She laughed hard at that, slappin' her knee.

Ruth squinted at her, disbelief wrinklin' her brow. "No one recognizes you?"

At first, she couldn't believe it. How could a woman whose designs crowned weddin's across Moabolis hide in plain sight? But then she thought back. She hadn't even recognized Mosh herself. The more she turned it over in her mind, the more it made sense. Fame didn't always follow you across worlds.

"Yes," Mosh said, catchin' her breath. "But enough 'bout me." She leaned across the table, slidin' a bag into Ruth's hands. "You need to experience Barley Harvest."

Ruth's eyes widened bigger than the cloud-storage space. "You're kickin' me out?"

Mosh nodded firmly, though her smile stayed warm. "Yes. As much as I enjoy our talk, and I could sit here all day gossipin' 'bout fashion and Moabolis wit' you, you need to experience Barley Harvest. I got a feelin' it'll keep on healin' you."

Ruth chuckled softly, though her throat tightened. "You know… Mahlon, my husband, he wanted to take me to Barley Harvest. He always said it was for the ones the world forgot, but Yah remembered. And now I'm startin' to see that." Her voice caught, but she smiled through it, glancin' at Mosh wit' gratitude.

Mosh stood, motionin' her to follow. Together, they stepped toward the booth's entrance. Outside, the noise of the festival swelled, music, vendors shoutin', the thrum of hover-drones. Just before the curtain opened, Mosh paused and turned, her eyes steady on Ruth.

"Ruth, you got this. I promise you'll not only enjoy yourself, you'll find joy again, like I did."

She pulled Ruth into another hug, firm and certain, like a blessin' wrapped in fabric. Ruth hugged her back, feelin' tears rise again. But these tears weren't the same as before. These carried hope.

"Now," Mosh said, steppin' back wit' a grin, "let's see this outfit."

Ruth smiled, shakey but excited. She shook her Hallelujah, and her honey-and-black balsam outfit downloaded into it like a beam of light. She shook it again, and suddenly she was adorned in the two-piece ensemble. The fabric clung perfectly to her frame, bold blossoms of gold thread stretchin' across the black like sunlight over night. She spun, the skirt catchin' the air, her laughter spillin' out in a squeal. For the first time since Mahlon's death, she felt… beautiful. Alive.

She reached over, huggin' Mosh once more. "Thank you—for everythin'."

"You're welcome," Mosh said, squeezin' her hand.

"This ain't goodbye," Ruth whispered. "Just see you soon."

"Yes, Ruth. See you soon."

Then, as if confirmnin' the moment, an arrow of light burst into the booth. Both women froze, eyes wide, before lookin' at each other.

"I think it's for you," Mosh said, smilin' knowingly.

"I think it is." Ruth's chest swelled.

The arrow zipped out into the crowd, cuttin' a clear path through the chaos of the festival. Ruth didn't hesitate this time. She followed, her honey-and-black outfit gleamin' as she stepped into the sea of people, her heart lighter than it had been in macrobytes.

CHAPTER 25

Ruth followed the arrow, mazin' her way through the crowded Barley Harvest that engulfed the entire city. The arrow led her to a corner where it went inside a buildin' before disappearin' back into her Hallelujah. She looked at the sign outside, noticin' it was a hair salon. She peeked in real quick, observin' the beauticians, and everyone seemed booked. There must be a reason why I'm here, outside of my hair, she thought as she took a few steps in.

The receptionist was endin' her Hallegraphic message when Ruth approached. "Hi, how may I help you?" Ruth heard her smile through the question.

"Yes, I need someone to do somethin' to this." Ruth swung her waist-length locs in front of her, brushin' 'em wit' her hand.

The receptionist glanced over her shoulder, checkin' to see if any chairs were open. She noticed one all the way in the back. "Yes, I do have availability. The special thing about our salon is that there are no bookin's. It's first come, first serve."

The receptionist began leadin' her to the empty station.

"Right this way!"

Ruth passed the many cyborgs and beautibots that were beatin' faces and slayin' wigs. She glanced over, watchin' the many customers swipe through Hallegrams before choosin' the hairstyle they wanted. She smiled as she arrived at her chair.

"Have a seat." The receptionist motioned for her to sit before walkin' away. "Have a great day!"

A small flyin' gizmo zipped out from the back, circlin' around the shop before descendin' to meet Ruth eye-to-eye.

"Greetings!" the beautibot spoke. "I am Glamzmo. I am here to glam you."

The beautibot ran a scan of Ruth's entire face before showcasin' Hallegraphic projections of hairstyles in a carousel.

"Do any of these suit you?"

Ruth immediately shook her head. She liked the selection but didn't love what was presented. Glamzmo circled around Ruth's head three times, then flashed a Hallegram of a new hairstyle.

"This is the Medusa," Glamzmo displayed, showin' a 360 Hallegraphic projection of a style inspired by Medusa.

"You mean the lady that can turn people into stone?" Ruth questioned.

"Absolutely," Glamzmo affirmed.

"Why that hairstyle?"

"Because, upon doin' a face recognition, I discovered that you've never been to this salon, so I assumed it was your first time at Barley Harvest. Am I correct?"

Ruth nodded her head in agreement. It was her first time here, although she had always wanted to come wit' Mahlon, Orpah, Chillion, and her in-laws, but life had other plans.

"So," Glamzmo began, "I decided to choose a hairstyle that will make you not stand out so much, which is a hard thing to do at Barley Harvest."

A look of genuine admiration crossed Ruth's face. She had never really needed to make a statement, bein' royalty. She was used to bein' the center of attention, and now she just wanted to blend in wit' the crowd. No one here knew of her royal status, and she would like to keep it that way. *This is my first time not bein' royal,* she smiled at the idea.

"Okay, Glamzmo!" Ruth said enthusiastically. "Make this happen."

The chair automatically spun as Glamzmo began workin' on Ruth's new do. Ruth couldn't see anything, but she felt her faith growin' stronger as she believed in somethin' she had not yet seen or experienced. She looked around the salon, noticin' the great detail, digital frames showcasin' the many people who had visited the salon. She saw cyborgs, hair-droids, and other gizmos doin' hair and servicin' clients. She was amazed at how well the hairdos were turnin' out.

She began to think of home, Moabolis, and remembered what the hairstyles were like there.

"So, what were the hairstyles like in your place?" the robotic voice of Glamzmo spouted out.

Ruth furrowed an eyebrow as confusion followed behind.

"When I did a scan of your face, I broadened my search and you came up in Moabolis."

Not even tryin' to protest, Ruth just nodded.

"Yes, I'm from Moabolis. Where I'm from, people tend to conform and we all look alike. It's customary for everyone to wear a tracksuit wit' matchin' sneakers. For guys, it's typically a buzz cut, and for women, almost always a ponytail. We always look like we're gonna play sports, although barely anyone can move."

Laughter filled the room as Ruth realized that her country really was just a bunch of people who barely moved but were always ready to move at any given time.

"Stop movin'!" Glamzmo's frustration showed as his digital eye turned red. Ruth quickly stopped laughin' so Glamzmo could return to its work.

"Sorry," she smiled.

She sat there just thinkin' through the events that led up to this moment. Some made her feel awful, while others put a positive glow in her life. She decided that she would focus on the positive, like bein' at Barley Harvest. *I wish Mahlon was here,* she thought. She truly wanted to experience this wit' him, as he and everyone in his family always talked 'bout it.

Before she could think another thought about him, she was bein' twirled around like the merry-go-round she rode in the park to see her new look.

"Ta-dah!" she heard the robotic voice say as he revealed her new style.

Ruth couldn't believe her eyes. She blinked multiple times, hopin' she was awake. She even leaned closer to the mirror to get a better look. She saw her locs movin' around wit' snake heads attached to the ends. The heads seemed alive as their hiss rang through her hair like the bell that tolled when she married Mahlon.

"Oh my!" Ruth exclaimed. "I love it." She gently touched her hair, makin' it recoil. "How did you do it?"

"Well," Glamzmo said, "I took a few of your locs and braided them up to ensure they had the look of a snake. Then, I attached toy snake heads to the ends. I did all this after attachin' a chip to your head."

Ruth swung her body around in terror.

"No, nothin' like that," Glamzmo reassured. "The chip can be removed at the end of the day or week and thrown away, or you can keep it for your hair."

Her shoulders relaxed as she finally breathed after that explanation.

"The chip is attached to your Praise and to you. So whatever mood you're in, your locs will reflect it."

Her locs began to bounce up and down. Ruth was happy at how everything looked.

"I notice that you are happy."

A Hallegram spat her a message: "Pay wit' Tip?" She pressed it. Ping! she heard from Glamzmo behind her.

She stood, observin' her newfound look. She felt different in this new outfit. She was used to the simple tracksuit and sneakers from Moabolis, but now she wasn't there no more. I guess this is the new me, she thought as she twirled.

She made her way to the door wit' a new pep in her step. She waved goodbye as she walked through the door, lookin' at her surroundin's.

No arrow appeared, but Ruth didn't mind that. She felt at ease walkin' through the crowd, noticin' the different attire that fully represented the Barley Harvest.

Two girls stepped from the meshgate shadows, clad in yellow-black tactical pants laced wit' chain mesh and scuffed combat boots. One wore a crop top wit' glowin' glyphs and magenta-streaked hair; the other, a chest rig patterned wit' biomech roses, fishnet synth-weave, and a wire-wrapped collar that scrambled signals.

She walked a little further and discovered a couple walkin' hand-in-hand, gazin' and struttin' like they owned the place. She wore a mesh-armored bodysuit laced wit' tactical rings and chained straps, her boots laced to the knee like battle spires. A feathered collar framed her bold proclamation: "Know That I AM Yah," printed across a relic-shirt of ancient resistance. Her eyes glowed behind yellow visors, and a red beret marked her as high command.

Beside her, he moved like shadow and flame, shirtless under a long, tattered vest, tribal beads swingin' wit' each step. Round crimson lenses veiled his eyes, and a tophat crowned his dreadlocked silhouette. Gloves and combat boots completed the look, half preacher, half warrior, all legend.

Ruth watched them as if they were a celebrity couple who needed someone to ask for their autograph. Their presence screamed, *Take a photo to savor the moment.* She was captivated by how much they commanded their surroundings without sayin' anything.

She smiled as she kept walkin', seein' an assortment of different fashions and hair expressions that would cause the average Moabite to short-circuit. She was used to everyone dressin' alike and actin' one way. It wasn't that her parents forced people to dress like them; it was just an unspoken rule, dress like the Royal Family. Even her in-laws had started dressin' like typical Moabites.

I see why Mahlon wanted me to experience this, she thought as she observed the many different people this festival summoned. She went close to the vendors, tryin' to see what was bein' sold. She saw baskets glowin', and, intrigued, she stepped forward to see what they were 'bout.

"Baskets! We got baskets!" The lady adorned a simple dress that seemed to change colors every few steps. "These baskets are called Woven! They're signal amplifiers woven from memory-conductive fibers, able to store sound, light, or ancestral data passed down through encoded touch. Get one now and start your legacy today!"

Ruth smiled as people swarmed the booth, eager to purchase the baskets. She mozied her way down to the next vendor. She saw a few people showcasin' some beaded necklaces and chokers unlike anything she had ever seen.

"Hallelujah," she spoke into her Praise to activate it. "What are these necklaces and chokers?"

The Praise let out a flashin' red light before answerin'.

"Beaded necklaces and chokers glint wit' embedded microchips and kinetic sensors, designed to track emotional frequencies or emit low-level energy shields. Some beads pulse softly, reactin' to the wearer's biofeedback or nearby movement."

Ruth couldn't believe her ears. Even her snakes were startled. She knew that Neo-Edens were ahead of the technology game, but she never knew they were literally centuries ahead. *My country is only in the testin' phase of these gadgets,* she thought. Her head raised as she remembered Mahlon's words: 'Hallelujah is the highest Praise. Hallelujah increases all the waves.' It all made sense. What was on her arm was the sole reason the Neo-Edens were lightyears ahead of the tech game.

She shook her head in awe and kept strollin' through the crowd. She turned her head in many directions, realizin' there was a subtle hint of music playin' in the background. She recognized it from her weddin'. This is Lo-Fi, she thought. She remembered listenin' to it at her weddin' and Mahlon tellin' her this was the music of his people and that it only came out durin' Barley Harvest.

She found herself flowin' wit' that music ever so slightly. She caught the beat and began steppin' to it as she moved through the crowd. She noticed her hair was groovin' right along, and she smiled. She realized that every Neo-Edenite was, in some way, movin' to the Lo-Fi music, and when the music changed, so did their walk and movement.

She realized she had so much to learn about this place and these people. She felt as if each time she passed a vendor, swatted a gizmo, or brushed past a bystander, it was not only bringin' her closer to learnin' 'bout this new world she left her home for, but also keepin' Mahlon's memory alive. She loved him, and she loved hearin' 'bout his time growin' up in Neo-Eden and attendin' the Barley Harvest. She finally understood why. This event and these people were amazin'.

She mozied herself really far down until she ended up smellin' somethin' divine. She spun around, lookin', searchin' for that smell. She took several paces forward and stumbled upon the place where it was comin' from, The Threshin' Floor.

CHAPTER 26

The Threshin' Floor was established as a diner, at least durin' the day. However, at this time, the Threshin' Floor maintained a lounge environment all day. It was custom durin' the Barley Harvest that the most popular place in town be welcomin' to everyone, terrestrial and extraterrestrial, no matter the occasion. The music danced wit' the smells as people danced around, while others took bites of freshly made food on beat. Some people were sittin' around eatin' and laughin'. Service-droids served food and took orders by typin' on their arms, sendin' it to the kitchen.

Ruth was surprised to see people dancin' in the corner, livin' their best lives at this time of day. However, she remembered that the Barley Harvest was an all-day and all-night event. These people could be leftovers from the night before.

Ruth stepped into The Threshin' Floor wit' amazement. She was quickly greeted by a service-droid.

"Hi, welcome to The Threshin' Floor! Just one?"

"Uh, yes!" Ruth was startled by the droid's question.

"Follow me!"

The service-droid quickly walked toward the side of the restaurant, and Ruth followed behind as best she could. The droid sat Ruth at a table.

"Thank you!" Ruth said. "Hallelujah," she spoke, and the menu appeared as a Hallegram. She swiped through before decidin' on the cornbread and collard greens. Yum! she thought. Mahlon and his family used to make it all the time, so she didn't waste time wit' another reminder of him.

As she waited patiently for her food, she enjoyed the scenery The Threshin' Floor had to offer. She especially enjoyed seein' the fashion of Neo-Eden. She once assumed Mahlon was goin' to a costume party when she saw old photos of him. She never realized how eccentric and alternative his family grew up dressin'. She never realized she would embrace it, like he embraced her customs when they lived in Moabolis.

If you could see me now, Mahlon, she thought, mesmerized by the smells and fashions of The Threshin' Floor. She was so lost in the clothin' until she heard a scream.

"AGAIN! What is wit' these droids?"

A tall, dark man wit' a manager tag was yellin'. Ruth and other patrons hurried toward the situation to see what happened. She made her way through the crowd, observin' a malfunctionin' service-droid twitchin' and freezin'. The manager yelled so loud that everyone stopped to watch him.

"These pieces of garbage! The boss is not goin' to be happy 'bout this! All this money wasted. All these glitches!"

Ruth felt bad for the android, realizin' this must've been an issue for some time. She looked around and noticed everyone was now focusin' on the situation.

"Nothin' to see here, anyone, just go back to your food and dancin'."

The manager tried to refocus the crowd's attention, but they weren't havin' it. They were invested, just like Ruth. She looked down and noticed her Praise begin to glow brightly. She had been instructed years ago that whatever the Praise wants to do, it will do. Don't try to stop it. Ruth, focusin' on the Praise, didn't see the manager walkin' up on her.

"Where have you been? We been callin' for days!"

Ruth was confused, but she felt she must play along in this scene. "My apologies."

She figured the manager must've thought she was here to fix the service-droids. It wasn't like she could say no, since the whole restaurant was now starin' at her. What she tried to hide on her face was only revealed by her hair, designed to mimic her emotions. Everyone was starin' at her hair, the patrons, and now the angry manager, whose face was redder than the sea.

He tried to guide her to the back of the restaurant where their Word of Yah was, but she stayed put.

"Umm, don't you need to check our Word of Yah? It controls all our droids."

"No, I am quite alright."

Ruth lifted her right arm and exposed the Praise.

"The Praise!" the manager marveled.

Ruth smiled as she tapped her Praise. Instantly, a 3-D projection of the restaurant's network appeared. All patrons were stunned at the sight of the massive 3-D display.

So, let's see! Where is the issue?

She slowly turned the projection around to find the problem. After a few minutes, Ruth started to get frustrated. Yah! Where is the problem? she asked.

Her eyes widened as she heard a still, small voice give instructions.

"Stop! Look up! Then glance slightly to your right!"

Ruth listened and saw a small red dot. She reached up and grabbed it.

"Eureka!" she screamed.

She clapped her hands, and it disappeared. Afterwards, she began to rearrange the blue dots for maximum optimization. She knew this problem could happen again if she didn't rearrange the Word of Yah into its proper order. Suddenly, all service-droids began to work properly. The patrons and workers screamed and cheered as the lifelong problem was finally solved.

"Thank you!" Ruth was stopped by the manager as she returned to her seat.

"You're welcome!"

As the crowd settled, the boss, Boaz, walked in. He ran toward the manager in the corner.

"I'm here! I came as soon as I heard. What's up?"

"It was a disaster," said the manager. "They glitched again and shut down durin' production."

"Okay."

Boaz was that dude who cared about his business and, more important, his employees. Regardless if they were human or droid, he gave all creatures respect and did not discriminate.

"Yeah, but it's fine. The people from M.O.E.E. came and fixed it."

"Really? Are they still here?"

"Yes, she's right over there."

"What's her name?"

"I dunno. I ain't ask."

Boaz headed toward Ruth, chucklin' along the way. He could always count on the manager to know what's goin' on, yet never fully know what's goin' on. It made for a good laugh and a good story to tell his friends. That has to be the reason I keep him around, Boaz thought.

Boaz sat down in front of Ruth and smiled as she took a bite of food. Ruth wiped her face and sat up.

"Hello there, my name is Boaz. What's your name?"

"I'm Ruth!" She noticed that even as he sat, this man was tall.

"Well, Ruth, I'm the owner of The Threshin' Floor. I want to extend my dearest thanks to the Ministry for comin' and fixin' my droids."

"You're welcome. But I'm also not from the M.O.E.E."

"You aren't!? Where are you from?"

Ruth knew she shouldn't talk wit' her mouth full, as it wasn't how a princess was raised. She took a sip of water, then waited three seconds like her mother taught her.

"I'm from Moabolis. I was just enjoyin' the Barley Harvest and all it had to offer when I realized that I originally came through to eat. I saw y'all needed help, so I helped."

"Well, thank you anyway. You know, I could use someone like you on my team, just in case." He smiled.

"Well, I'm open to a job!"

"Great, you start tomorrow! Also, your food is on the house. If you need anything, talk to me. If I'm not around, then speak wit' the manager."

Boaz smiled before he stood up and walked back to the manager. Ruth was blushin', though she didn't want to admit why. Her food materialized into a "To-Go" order as she was gettin' up to leave. She walked past Boaz, both of them exchangin' smiles before she walked out the restaurant.

"I see that look in your eye," the manager said.

"I have no idea what you mean." Boaz turned away.

Ruth arrived home, happy and eager to talk about her encounter. She saw Naomi watchin' her favorite soap opera, The Bolt and The Beautiful, wit' her favorite snack on hand, popcorn and Elime's Drink. She knew there were two activities you didn't interrupt Naomi from doin': prayin' and watchin' her stories.

So she sat the food down in front of her, and Naomi instantly snapped out her trance. She was startled at Ruth and her appearance.

"You okay, Mama?"

Naomi couldn't find the words. She had never seen Ruth dressed like this.

"Look at you! I can tell you enjoyed yourself at the Barley Harvest."

Ruth stood up and gave her mother-in-law a spin. At the same time, the snakes laughed wit' Ruth as she admired her new look.

"So, you left me as a Moabite princess wit' your red and white tracksuit and KE-3s and came back the mistress of the Barley Harvest." Naomi laughed. "You have to tell me 'bout how all this," she motioned toward Ruth, "happened!"

Naomi started to eat as she listened to Ruth talk 'bout her day.

"So, it all started wit' this arrow that shot out of my Praise and led me to Mosh—the one that made me and Orpah's weddin' dresses."

"Oh wow, you finally met her? How was that?" Naomi sipped her Elime's Drink.

"It was everything and more. She was the one that gave me the outfit." Ruth did a quick 360. "I had to keep the sneakers. I couldn't imagine doin' all that walkin' in heels."

"And people do it! Shoot, I have done it before." Naomi swallowed a handful of popcorn.

"You did the Barley Harvest in heels?" Ruth couldn't believe what she was hearin'.

"Yes, now go on!"

"Okay." Ruth sat back down. "So afterwards, the arrow brought me to a hair salon. This is where I got the Medusa." The snakes at the end of Ruth's hair smiled.

"Hmm." Naomi pondered. "They are emotion-based?"

Ruth nodded wit' a smile.

"I thought so." Naomi grinned.

"Then," Ruth continued, "I began walkin' around and enjoyin' the Barley Harvest. I saw so many cool people dressed so differently than what I'm used to. I also saw technology so advanced that even me, bein' a royal of Moabolis, didn't have access to it. I'm used to people wearin' the same outfit every day and dealin' wit' the same gadgets. Here, everyone is somethin' different, and the technology that would seem advanced in Moabolis is elementary."

Naomi raised her right arm slowly. "The highest Praise gives the highest waves!" She gestured at her Hallelujah. "This is why we are so ahead of the tech world that, and the Word of Yah that's built in. It's a game-changer."

Ruth looked at her differently. She always heard from Mahlon 'bout the Praise and the Word of Yah, but she never knew how powerful it truly was until today.

"Mama, do you think Yah would allow others to utilize the Praise?"

"He already has." Naomi smiled.

"Really?" Ruth gasped. "So I'm not the only one?"

"Of course not." Naomi swallowed another handful of popcorn. "If you read the earliest blueprints of the Praise and the Word of Yah, it speaks of a mixed multitude. Not everyone in that mix was Neo-Eden. Yet they still were able to receive the Praise and the Word of Yah."

The snakes reacted before she could. She had no idea there were others like her who had this opportunity. She felt honored to be among those Yah had chosen for this gift.

"So, what happened after that?"

"Well, I met Boaz."

"Really? How ya do that?" Now, this wasn't what Naomi expected, but it sure was what she needed.

"I went to The Threshin' Floor, and the droid system malfunctioned and apparently had always malfunctioned. Thankfully, I listened to Mahlon when he talked 'bout work. So I offered my assistance and was able to fix it. Anyway, Boaz came in to check on e'erythin', but by the time he got there, I had e'erythin' under control."

Naomi sipped her Elime's Drink wit' focus. She didn't wanna miss a detail.

"He came over and we chatted. He even offered me a job."

"What did you say?"

"I said yes! It gets me out the house and next to my favorite thing in the world—food."

Ruth and Naomi shared a laugh. The laugh felt good, like it had been needed for a long time.

"Actually, I'm nervous," Ruth said softly.

Naomi got serious. "Why you nervous?"

"Mama, what if I miss you? I never worked a day in my life. I still don't need to work; the company can sustain the both of us until the end of time."

The revelation hit Naomi like the Red Sea hit the Egyptians. Ruth had spent her entire life bein' a princess. From the time she was born, she and her sistah Orpah were groomed to be royalty and diplomats. She wasn't conditioned to be a workin' girl. Now that Mahlon was gone and she chose to stay wit' Naomi, all that changed.

"Yes, it is somethin' different," Naomi assured, "but let me ask you this, are you able to do the job?"

"Yes. It's quite simple, and doin' this type of work reminds me of Mahlon. I want to be close to him any way I can."

"Okay, I understand that." Naomi nodded. "Also, who you workin' wit'?"

"I believe myself, but I did have lunch wit' Boaz. He told me to always check wit' him, and if not him, the manager."

"You stay wit' the women there, is that understood?"

"Why?"
"'Cause someone might get the wrong impression, and I might have to kill that someone."

Ruth and Naomi laughed uncontrollably. They laughed so hard they worked up an appetite for their unfinished food. Yet it had been a very eventful day.

"I'm tired."
"I bet. Doin' what my husband and sons did is tiresome. That's why I don't do it."
"Mama, you know how to do all that?"
"Absolutely! Elime made sure I did, whether I wanted to or not. That was my entire marriage to that man. Wouldn't trade it for anythin'."

Naomi was starin' into space, reminiscin' 'bout Elime. Ruth was starin' at her in awe, reminiscin' 'bout Mahlon. They truly missed them. "So I don't cry myself to sleep, I'm goin' to bed. Night! Love ya!"
"Love ya more, Ruth!"

Naomi was grateful she had Ruth in her life. She didn't think she'd survive if Ruth wasn't here. *What am I gonna do wit' Ruth? She can't take care of an old bat like me. She needs to go find love and be happy.*
"She will," I responded.

Naomi spun around instantly, almost knockin' over her Elime's Drink. She sat down, knowin' where that voice came from. She felt it in her spirit, but she knew she heard it out loud. She took a giant gulp of her Elime's Drink before placin' it back in the floatin' cupholders her sons had made her a year ago.
"Ruuuaaaaaccccchhhhh! I know it's You. Come out so we can talk!"

Luckily, the rooms in the house were soundproofed at a certain time, 'cause that yell surely would've woke Ruth up if they weren't. I chuckled to myself as I appeared in my signature all-black attire, sittin' right on the edge of her couch. Naomi didn't even flinch as I spoke.
"Hello, Naomi!"
"Ruach. Pleasure's all mine."

I knew she didn't want to see me, but I AM Ruach Hokadesh. She didn't have a choice.
"So, what's this 'bout, Naomi?"
"Whaddaya mean?"
"Naomi, my natural body manifests when there's a great need. So what's the need?"
"Ruth needs to find a husband! Someone to love her and help take care

of me."

"Haha! Well, at least you're honest. Do you have any prospects?"

I suddenly moved to the arm of the sofa. It wasn't on purpose. My natural state can't stay still, as I AM the presence of Yah. So, as His presence, I have the tendency to move wit'out wantin' to. Think of it as literally bein' everywhere, all at once. Luckily, Naomi had been wit' me for years and was used to it.

"I mean, I haven't lived here in many macrobytes. I don't know who's single and who ain't."

"Well, let's start small, and then we can grow! Who do you want for her, Naomi?"

Naomi finally decided to look me in the eye. The last time she did that, I was helpin' her process her grief over her husband's death. This time she looked at me as a friend. It made me smile and want to help her more.

"Someone like MAHLON! Someone who's gonna love on her and show her the love of Yah! Someone who understands technology, as we run a billion-dollar tech company."

"That's nice, dear. However, tell me the truth!"

"What'chu mean?"

"You explained the interior, which is awesome like Yah, but how 'bout the physical? It's okay. You can be real wit' me!"

Naomi walked toward the kitchen 'cause she didn't want to admit I was right, but I AM. All that "inner-self" and "be kind to me" was great, yet she knew Ruth would rather have all that in someone attractive than in someone who was facially challenged.

I was already sittin' at the table, waitin'. I loved that the real me could just be everywhere, all at once. It meant no one could escape me or outrun me.

"What? You just upload and download like that?" Naomi said, actin'
brand new like she'd never seen me do this before.

"I AM the motherboard and fatherboard. So travelin' through servers is
who I AM! You know this already. Stop playin' games. Give me the
truth!"

"Okay, okay. I want her to be wit' a dude that's tall, above 6'3, dark-
skin, and slightly muscular, but not too muscular. You get it, right?"

I already knew that, but I needed her to say it. It made it real when
the words are spoken. Once the words are spoken, then the world can
form. I wrote down her criteria on a hallegraphic screen that appeared on
the table.

Dark-skin ✓

Above 6'3 ✓

Loves Yah ✓

Slightly muscular ✓

Got it!

Naomi gave me that "You bettah have it" look she gave her
husband, sons, and now Ruth. There was only one man that fit all the
criteria she wanted for Ruth. I hoped she would be ready for this—but
deep down, I knew she wanted that.

"I believe You. So, who do You got for me?"

I turned the screen to reveal the gentleman to Naomi.

"BOAZZZZZ! Why him?"

"Why not?"

Naomi pondered the question. Boaz was basically a clone of her late
husband. He literally embodied everythin' she wanted in a husband for

Ruth. He would be lucky to have her as an asset. She was so into her fantasy for Ruth that she didn't realize I was givin' her a "hurry up" look until she snapped back.

"You right. I really couldn't find a reason. I was just shocked he's still single. Boaz is a great catch."

"I know. So, who better to marry Ruth than Boaz?"

"Good point. How do I get them together?"

"You'll figure it out!"

In a twinkle of an eye, I was gone. I gave her many things to think about. She had to make these two people fall in love wit' each other. That couldn't be too hard. Naomi knew wit' Yah on her side, anythin' was possible. All she had to do was believe.

"To Yah be the Glory!"

CHAPTER 27

Ruth's brightly colored bedroom was decorated wit' anything and everything that reminded her of Mahlon. She gazed at her reflection in the vanity. Her hair was still styled from the night before since the Barley Harvest hadn't ended.

She swiped through outfit options on her vanity, wantin' somethin' different to wear for work. She settled on a houndstooth top woven with neuro-reactive thread that synced to crowd energy. Photonic mesh pants filtered ambient data, chargin' her wit' each step. A solar-brimmed hat tucked the snakes just slightly out of sight.

She thought 'bout applyin' makeup but realized she didn't need to. She wanted to check out The Threshin' Floor before her first day began.

"Vanny! Show me The Threshin' Floor!" she commanded.

Her VXT 2000, a custom weddin' gift from Mahlon, lit up. It gave her access to the surveillance cameras at The Threshin' Floor wit'out bein' detected. I'm so glad Mahlon taught me how to hack into people's mainframes, she thought. Isn't Yah great!?

Naomi sat quietly in her kitchen, munchin' down a stack of pancakes. Ruth materialized next to her, causin' Naomi to fall to the floor. "Now, girl! Why you scare me like that?"

"Sorry, Mama!"

"Since when do you load so quietly!?"

"Always! Mahlon always said it was dangerous but worth the excitement to do it that way."

"That does sound like him…" Naomi laughed as Ruth helped her back into her chair.

Once seated, Naomi looked Ruth up and down, noticin' she was all dolled up.

"Where you goin'?"

"Work. Remember, I got a job at Boaz's restaurant."

"You did tell me 'bout that! What time you leavin'?"

"Soon as I'm done wit' you!"

"Okay! You can go. Just remember, don't be workin' wit' the men, okay?"

Ruth rolled her eyes but smiled. This was her first job ever. She kissed Naomi goodbye.

"I know! Love you!"

"Love you more!"

Ruth downloaded directly in front of the restaurant, nearly scarin' the patrons. Loadin' was dangerous, and those that did it were always met wit' weird gazes. It was the same weird gaze that Ruth gave when Mahlon first showed her photos of the Barley Harvest. Ruth didn't show an ounce of care as she walked past the onlookers and into The Threshin' Floor.

Like the day before, the music blended seamlessly wit' smells of food at The Threshin' Floor. People and extraterrestrials were sittin' around, eatin', and laughin'. Service-droids were servin' food and takin' orders by typin' in their arms and sendin' 'em to the kitchen. People and aliens were dancin' in the corner, livin' their best lives.

Ruth enjoyed soakin' up the new culture, fashion, and food in Neo-Eden. It didn't take long for her to at least look the part as her fashion mirrored those around her. She discovered, quite quickly, that The Threshin' Floor was the "It" spot for all of Neo-Eden. She wanted to make a great first-ish impression at her new job, and she guessed so did others, 'cause the Manager spotted her and made a direct line to her.

"Hey! Boss man wants to see you."

"He does?"

"Yes! His office."

Ruth tried to maneuver through the busy restaurant wit'out much grace or poise. It was hard to move wit' service-droids comin' from one direction and happy couples dancin' from another. She finally pushed through and found herself starin' at the door to Boaz's office. Excitement and nerves bubbled up, but she pressed them down.

She opened the door and stepped inside. The set-up was modest: digital pictures of friends and family, a hoverin' desk, and a hallegram CPU monitor. Behind it, Boaz was typin' somethin' important when he noticed Ruth standin' in front of him.

"Ruth! Whaddup Doe?"

"Nothin' much! Thank you for askin'. And you?"

"I'm good, good!" Boaz ran over to give her a hug. Startled, she wanted to step back, but decided to hug him in return. That's when Boaz let go as he realized he might have crossed the line. "Sorry, I was just so happy that you came back!"

"I can see that!" She blushed. "So, what do you have planned for me?"

"Well, I was gonna have you stay here and run the system," Boaz said, gesturin' to the holographic monitor hoverin' above his desk.

Ruth tilted her head. "Run the system? What exactly does that mean?" Ruth knew what that meant, but she wanted Boaz to talk more. He had a way wit' commandin' the aura in the room wit'out tryin'.

Boaz smiled, appreciatin' her eagerness. "It's pretty simple, really. You'll monitor orders comin' in from the tables and service-droids, make sure the kitchen gets everythin' in real time, and resolve any glitches before they affect service. If a droid gets stuck or crashes, you'll reassign its tasks through the interface. Think of it as keepin' the whole place runnin' smoothly from behind the scenes."

Ruth nodded, her confidence growin'. "So, I'm like the brain of the operation?"

Boaz laughed. "Exactly! And don't worry, I'll be here to back you up if anything gets overwhelmin'. Just remember, the most important thing is keepin' the customers happy and the droids movin'."

"That sounds… fun," Ruth said, a mixture of nerves and excitement bubblin' up inside her. "I think I can handle that."

"I know you can." Boaz smiled warmly, leanin' back in his chair. "You've got this, Ruth."

"Stay here? I won't be out there wit' you?"

"No, you will be here by yourself where no one can disturb you."

"Circuits!"

Boaz stared at her like she was crazy.

"It's somethin' my husband and I used to say."

Boaz wanted to say more, but he was afraid of where it might go. So, he left it alone and nodded his head in agreement.

"Well, I'm gonna go run the restaurant. If you have any questions, please Halle at me!"

"Okay!"

Ruth watched as Boaz walked out the office, leavin' her by herself. She stared at the chair for a while before she had a seat. "Hallelujah," she spoke loudly, allowin' the system of The Threshin' Floor to surround her in a 3-D projection. Ruth observed her surroundin's, makin' sure that all the systems were operatin' smoothly. She performed a quick diagnostic check, which she learned how to do wit' her Praise, and was happy wit' the results. She was so glad she paid attention to Mahlon when he was showin' her all the joys and wonders that can come wit' knowin' how to operate the Praise. You can get through anything wit' Praise, she thought.

The systems improved 200% from my minor tweaks yesterday, she thought.

Ruth really had nothin' to do as everythin' was runnin' efficiently from yesterday, so she fell asleep.

What she thought might have been a catnap turned into a 45-minute slumber. What made it worse was Boaz bein' the one to wake her up. He walked in and chuckled slightly as Ruth was in a good sleep. He leaned over her to get her attention. "Helloooo! Ruuuuth! Wakey, wakey!"

Ruth's eyes fluttered open to see Boaz leanin' over her. Startled, she toppled right out of her chair. "Ouch!" she winced, rubbin' the side of her head.

Boaz bent down instantly, extendin' his hand toward her. "Are you okay?"

"Yeah."

"I came to check in on you, but you were knocked out."

Ruth's face turned whiter than a soul dipped in His blood. She could not believe that she fell asleep on her first day of work. Sayin' that she was embarrassed would have been a colossal understatement. "Sorry 'bout that! I dunno what happened. One moment I was awake and the next moment, I was asleep. It won't happen again."

"It's fine. It happens to the best of us!" Boaz and Ruth's laughter was broken by their gaze into each other's eyes. They turned away quickly to hide the blush. "I was comin' to see if you wanted lunch." Ruth's face and eyes went wide in sheer panic. Boaz showed a million-dollar smile, calmin' her panic to an ease.

"It is lunchtime already?!"

"Yeah! We close down for lunch so everyone can take it at the same time."

"Really? Circuits."

Boaz's eyebrow furrowed at Ruth. "You know it's a sayin' my husband and his brother used to say all the time."

"I know. They get it from their papa."

They laughed so hard that they started to tear up. They had to catch their breath and wipe the tears from their eyes.

"Whoa! Come on!" Boaz gestured to Ruth to follow him outside the office. She was still wipin' tears as she followed him out of the office. The once hustlin' and bustlin' diner had transformed into a six-star, dinin' restaurant. Their diner was now a fancy restaurant. Ruth's eyes displayed her disbelief at the new restaurant.

"God, do I love technology!" she whispered under her breath.

"What was that?"

"Oh, nothin'!"

Ruth made her way to the center table where Boaz's nameplate was listed. She sat down and noticed all the traditional Neo-Eden food placed in front of her. Boaz turned to her, smilin' at her innocence.

"Before we eat, I would like to ask Ruth to do two things: turn the droids off and say grace."

"Sure! Hallelujah." The Threshin' Floor's CPU system appeared from her Praise. She touched a white dot, and simultaneously all the droids left the diner and went into the kitchen. She grabbed hands wit' Boaz and the few other humans in the restaurant and prayed. "Dear Yah! Thank You for food, friends, and forgiveness. I love the fact that You gave me a job that allows me to utilize my talents and gifts. I am grateful for everyone here, includin' Boaz. Bless him and all his businesses. Amen."

"AMEN!" Everyone echoed. They all began to eat, laugh, and talk. Ruth sipped lemonade when Boaz interrupted.

"So, Ruth! You from Moabolis?"

"Yep! Born and raised!"

"So, you came back wit' Naomi, right?"

Ruth's frozen expression met Boaz's smile. He had a way of calmin' her down and keepin' her on her toes at the same time. She ain't even know why he did, and they had just met.

"How'd ya know that?"

"I know everything that happens in my city! Plus, I asked around. After you left yesterday, I realized that you weren't M.O.E.E.!"

"How? And what's M.O.E.E.? Y'all kept sayin' that yesterday when I finally had the courage to tell you that I wasn't wit' them."

"First, M.O.E.E. is never that efficient! Also, M.O.E.E. stands for Ministry of Eyes and Ears. It is the main department that monitors and fixes our droids and all tech in this country."

The other staff members in the restaurant laughed 'cause they knew just how true it was. Ruth looked around, confused. Everyone was laughin'.

"Is M.O.E.E. really that bad?"

"They aren't bad per se, but it would have taken them a lot longer to fix the problem!"

"Really?"

"Yeah!"

Everyone was listenin' to Ruth and Boaz's conversation. There wasn't much else to do other than surf the web. Let's face it, other people's lives were way more interestin'.

"I am thrilled that she has a daughter-in-law like you."

"Yeah, she is dope!"

"So, tell me, tell us, 'bout your family."

Ruth's eyes widened as a nervous expression crossed her face. She didn't know what to do. She didn't want people to look at her differently. After all, it's not every day a princess leaves her life of luxury to work at a diner.

"Well, I have a sistah named Orpah. We are super close. Lately some stuff has happened, and she hasn't been able to reach out consistently, but she does respond. I love her."

"Dope. How 'bout mom and dad?" Boaz swallowed a bite of food.

Ruth's Medusa hairstyle betrayed her inner conflict, their furrowed brows and dartin' eyes hintin' at the weight of her dilemma. Did she tell them who her parents were or not? Of course not. He didn't need to know everything. She had just met everyone today. She would eventually tell them, but not yet.

"Umm. My parents are awesome. They work from home and have a successful business. Me and my sistah never went wit'out."

"Dope! I would love to meet them."

"You will!" Ruth went back to eatin', and everyone followed suit. The food tasted so divine that people stopped talkin' for a split second, except Ruth. She wanted to know who made this food.

"This food is bussin'. Who cooked it?" Everyone pointed at Boaz. Ruth was shocked once again. Boaz smiled.

"You!?"

"Well, I used to, but now I have droids that I programmed all my recipes into. They do it for me!"

"I am impressed. I'm probably gonna find them recipes and use 'em."

"You can. I got nothin' to hide."

Ruth and Boaz smiled at each other. Of course, everyone in the restaurant noticed. It was obvious they had a thang for each other. However, Boaz was respectful and Ruth needed a job, so fraternizin' was not on the list, yet.

Everyone finished up, and Ruth turned the droids back on so they could clean up. Boaz walked toward the back and Ruth followed his lead. Ruth and Boaz entered and shared a smile. They could not stop smilin' at each other. It didn't make leavin' easier.

"I will leave you to do your work!"

"Yessir!"

He left the office quickly. Ruth waited a second before runnin' to the chair. She almost stubbed her toe tryin' to get there. She leaned back and processed what just happened and how her life has been. She knew she had to call her girls.

"Ay yo! Dash! Juju! Lemme halle at'chu real quick!"

Suddenly, her Praise began to glow. It began projectin' two 3-D hallegraphic images of Black women: Dash de Souza, a petite brown-eyed cinnamon-skin-tone Black woman wit' an afro almost bigger than she is; and Juju Bethulian, a thick gold-eyed dark-skin-tone Black woman wit' long dreadlocs.

"WAZZZZUUPPPPP!"

"WAZZZZUUPPPPP!"

They all laughed. Ruth knew that the only girls to keep her up and goin', besides her mother, sistah, and Naomi, were these two right here. They regained their composure after their moment.

"How's my girls?" Ruth asked.

"I'm good!"

"I am better than ever!" Juju smiled strongly. She knew exactly what Ruth was goin' through. They both lost husbands and cried on each other's shoulders. This time was especially sensitive as Juju lost her husband durin' the Barley Harvest some nanobytes back. They had so much in common. They never thought that they'd be widows.

"You okay?" Ruth asked Juju.

"Yes. Are you?" Juju responded. Ruth nodded her head. It was somethin' she did not like to discuss or talk 'bout. It was still a fresh wound.

Dash, ever the mood-lifter, jumped in. "Thanks for askin', but I'm good!"

"Of course, you're good," Juju teased, turnin' to Ruth. "She ain't got no man to stress her out!"

Dash gasped in mock offense, placin' her hand over her heart. "I beg your pardon? I live a stress-free life because I'm smart, thank you very much."

"You mean lazy," Ruth said wit' a sly grin.

"Excuse you!" Dash shot back, narrowin' her eyes. "Just because I ain't cryin' over no man doesn't mean I'm lazy. I'm just peaceful. Zen. You two should try it sometime."

Juju burst out laughin'. "Zen? Girl, you ain't zen, you're just single and nosy!"

"Okay, nosy?" Dash raised an eyebrow. "I am investigative. There's a difference!"

"You mean 'all up in our business,'" Ruth added, laughin'.

"That's called support," Dash quipped, flippin' her hair dramatically. "You're welcome."

Juju and Ruth laughed; leave it to Dash to lighten up the mood. She was, and had always been, single. Her bein' a point of comic relief helped ease the others through this period of loss. "So, what's new wit' you, Ruth?"

"Well, first I have a job."

Dash and Juju dropped their jaws in shock.

"J-job?" Juju stammered. "But you are a princess?"

"I know, but I gave that up when I came back wit' Naomi."

"I ain't know that you went back wit' her," Dash rebutted.

"I texted y'all!"

"She did text us," Juju admitted. "Dash, you just take forever to read and respond."

Juju and Ruth laughed at the truthful statement about Dash's lack of respondin' to texts. Dash rolled her eyes and stared back wit' a blank expression.

"You heffas done?"

"Nope!" Juju and Ruth continued to laugh wit' tears, and Dash continued to stare at them blankly.

"Anyway! Tell us 'bout this 'job' you have!"

"OK. So, I went to a restaurant to eat. The server-droids were havin' issues, so I fixed it on the spot. The owner offered me a job, and I accepted it."

"Groovy! So, what's the goal?"

Ruth was shocked and confused by the question. She ain't really have a goal and wasn't really lookin' for a job. She just wanted some food and happened to be in the right place at the right time.

"What do you mean?" Ruth questioned.

"I mean, do you got a plan on doin' this forever? Do you want marriage? Kids?" Dash interrogated.

Ruth ain't know how to answer the question, but she tried her best. After all, marriage and kids was somethin' that she always wanted ever since she was a kid herself. When she was married to Mahlon, she thought that she would have her 'happily ever after' wit' him. But when he died, so did that childhood dream. She never gave it too much thought to have it wit' someone else until now.

"I will get married. Naomi wants that for me, and I do too. I will have kids. These things take time. You know how I feel, Juju! Back me up!"

"I do, but I can honestly say that I do not want marriage or kids. I'm fine."

"Me too, as of now!" Ruth was ready to change the subject quickly, and she did.

"Dash, when you gettin' married?"

Dash froze wit' fear. She was not expectin' that from Ruth. She was completely caught off guard, and Dash never liked to be caught off guard.

"That's a great question!" Juju added.

"When the right man comes and demands it!"

Ruth and Juju started laughin' at Dash. Dash wasn't a warrior, but she was willin' to obey Yah's command to get what she wanted. They regained their composure. Dash stared at them, slightly annoyed.

"Soooo! When are you done?" Dash asked.

"In five minutes. I am ready to take a nap."

"So am I," Juju added.

"Me too! We'll call you later," Dash chimed.

"K. Bye!"

"Bye!"

The 3-D hallegraphic projections disappeared. Ruth was relieved. She ain't realize how exhaustin' mental work can be. She began packin' her stuff up to go home when Boaz walked in.

"Hey, you 'bout ready to go?"

"Yeah! I'm tired. I need a nap!"

"Yeah, I know! Workin' here can be tiresome, but fun!"

Ruth and Boaz walked out of his office into the busy street of people and hovercars.

"So, did you enjoy your first day?"

"Yeah, it was—"

"Great?! I will see you tomorrow?" He cut her off and ain't realize it, but she ain't mind it at all.

"You sure will!"

Ruth and Boaz blushed as their smiles grew for one another. Suddenly, a black SUV stopped in front of them and the door opened up. Ruth was scared. The kind of scared that made her chest tight, her breathin' shallowed, and her legs felt as if they'd forgotten how to run.

"I called you a car to take you to your crib."

Ruth calmed her nerves down now that he explained what was goin' on.

"Wow! Um… Thank you so much. 'Preciate it."

"You're welcome!"

Ruth stepped into the car, the door closin' behind her wit' a satisfyin' thud. The interior smelled faintly of leather and freshly cleaned upholstery, a stark contrast to the dusty roads outside. She adjusted her seatbelt, her hands fidgetin' as her mind raced wit' thoughts, fragments of conversations, questions she wanted to ask Naomi, and a swirl of emotions she couldn't quite pin down.

What had Boaz meant earlier? His words lingered in her mind like the warm glow of the harvest sun. She wasn't sure why, but she knew they had somethin' to do wit' her and Naomi's future. Her gut told her it was important, but the pieces weren't fallin' into place just yet.

As the SUV's engine roared to life, Ruth glanced out the window. Boaz stood by the roadside, his hands tucked into the pockets of his well-worn jacket. He wasn't doin' anythin' extraordinary, just watchin' her, yet there was somethin' in his gaze, steady, thoughtful, almost protective. When their eyes met, he waved, a small gesture that sent her stomach into a strange, flutterin' dance.

The vehicle flew off, the scenery blurrin' past. Ruth turned away from the window, her thoughts shiftin' to Naomi. She couldn't wait to get home and tell her everythin'. Naomi always had a way of unravelin' the mysteries Ruth couldn't solve on her own.

"What would she say about this?" Ruth muttered to herself. Her voice was barely audible over the hum of the tires on the road.

Naomi had a way of seein' straight to the heart of things, even when Ruth couldn't. And she had a way of talkin' 'bout Boaz that made Ruth's cheeks burn. He's a good man, Naomi would say, her voice thick wit' admiration and somethin' else Ruth couldn't name. Maybe Naomi saw somethin' Ruth didn't, or maybe somethin' she wasn't ready to see.

The car jolted as it hit a bird, snappin' Ruth back to the present. She glanced at the driver, who stayed locked on the windin' road, oblivious to her inner storm. Ruth sighed, foldin' her hands in her lap and tryin' to untangle her feelin's.

What was it about Boaz that left her so unsettled? Kind, yes. Generous, absolutely. But there was somethin' deeper, somethin' unspoken, that she couldn't quite grasp. Did Naomi see it? Did Boaz?

By the time the truck pulled up to her large home, she still didn't have answers. But as she downloaded in front of the door, a flicker stirred inside her—hope, maybe. Whatever was comin', she knew she wouldn't face it alone. Naomi would be there, and maybe, just maybe, so would Boaz.

CHAPTER 28

Naomi was sittin' on the couch watchin' her stories, The Bolt and the Beautiful, when Ruth came in, tired from work. She slumped onto the couch, lookin' half-asleep. Wit' the snap of Naomi's fingers, the TV went on mute.

"How was work?" she said loudly, makin' sure Ruth ain't fall asleep.

"Lil' borin', but okay!"

"Why borin'?"

"He stuck me in his office all day by myself to monitor the systems!"

"That is borin'. I remember when Elime made me do that!"

Ruth sat upright, unable to believe her ears. Her eyes grew to the size of saucers at this revelation. "He did?"

"Of course!" Naomi laughed. "I told you he taught me everythin' he knew!"

Ruth and Naomi shared a smile, both thinkin' 'bout their deceased husbands. They always focused on the good memories but not for too long. Stayin' there too long only brought back the kind of pain no one wanted to feel.

Ruth rose from the couch, stretchin' her arms. "I'm tired. That place is mentally exhaustin'. I'm goin' to take a nap."

"Okay!"

Naomi watched Ruth leave completely before sittin' back and turnin' the volume up on her stories. But I couldn't let her get too comfortable just yet.

"Now is the time, Naomi!"

Naomi sat up on the sofa, irritated that she had to mute her stories again. I tried my hardest not to laugh, knowin' she didn't like her stories bein' interrupted.

"Ruach," she spat. "What'chu want? I was just 'bout to find out how Jonah ended up in the belly of the big fisha, and I been waitin' for this for months."

I appeared on the arm of the couch, greeted by Naomi's annoyance. She truly didn't like interruptions, but she loved me almost as much as I loved her.

"Naomi, remember what we talked 'bout?"

"I know. Ruth! Boaz! Perfect match! Got it!"

"Yes! But it has to be soon!"

"How soon?" Naomi completely turned off the television so she could look me in the eye. I appeared beside her on the couch. Ruth turned her head toward me, tryin' to focus.

"You have seven days!"

Naomi looked shocked and appalled at my response, but I do have a job myself. Keepin' cosmic balance is not as easy as it looks.

"A week! You gotta be kiddin' me…" Her voice slid into a whisper since Ruth was asleep.

Clap. Clap. She clapped her hands twice, signalin' the room to soundproof itself so she could talk to me. Then she gave me a mini stare-down. She knew I was gonna win, but it was always nice to see her try.

"Naomi, go make love happen between them!"

"How?"

"You're creative. Make somethin' up!"

It was true. Naomi was extremely creative. I knew she could make anyone fall in love; she just had to do somethin'. She didn't have much time, so she had to get on it.

"What happens if I don't get them together in a week?"

Now, I was tryin' to be nice wit' Naomi, but she was testin' me. So I had to be blunt wit' her.

"The same fate that happened to your husband and sons."

Naomi stood up wit' fire in her eyes. She was angry, and I knew it.

"It's the truth! They ain't want to listen to the commands of Yah, so they suffered His judgment!"

Naomi tilted her head slightly. "When did Elime ever disobey? That doesn't sound like him at all.

"You're right," I smiled. "It doesn't, which is why when he did, Yah's judgment was harsh."

"Harsh as in?"

I motioned around the room as if they were an audience. "You see he's not here."

She wanted to attack me, but 'cause she knew the relationship I had wit' Elime, she sat back down.

"Naomi, Elime had a secret. A secret he wanted to bury, but instead, it buried him and those around him. Don't be like him, be like Yah."

She slumped forward, face buried in her hands, and let out a muffled scream. All she ever did was follow Elime as he followed the will of Yah. It just dawned on her to take her focus off of Elime and place it on Yah since, he's the one that Elime said we must be like. "Okay, I'll tell her. Today."

I was happy when I got my way. My smile showed that. Naomi, though, wasn't so happy. Her face said it all.

"Great! See you soon!"

"Yeah, see you soon." Naomi rolled her eyes.

I poofed, and Naomi sat back on her couch, ponderin'.

"I swear this life ain't easy, but I do love the life that I live. I just gotta tell Ruth to get wit' Boaz. That shouldn't be hard, right? Hallelujah."

A Hallegram appeared. She started brainstormin' ideas on how she could get Ruth and Boaz together.

"What 'bout dinner and a movie?" she pondered before scratchin' it off. "Too cliché."

She wrote down other suggestions like beach date, cyber surfin', and a walk in the park. Once again, she scratched them off. She needed to think of somethin' that would catch Boaz's attention as well as Ruth's—but what?

Her face flared up as she aggressively scribbled new ideas, crossin' each one out just as fast.

"Why can't I get this?" she screamed out loud.

She quickly put her hand over her mouth, hopin' she didn't wake Ruth. Then she dropped it, realizin' the room was still soundproof. She chuckled, rememberin' why she had done that in the first place.

Naomi looked down, amazed to see her once Hallegraphic projection now playin' the memory of many nanobytes ago.

She was watchin' her stories and yelled when the scene showed Abram 'bout to slay Izzy, but the A.N.G.E.L. intervened, savin' everything.

Elime uploaded into the livin' room wit' steam comin' out of both ears. Naomi had just woken up her twin boys, and Elime had only just put them down for bed. She knew she messed up, so she did what she always did when she made Elime mad—smiled and hugged him.

She felt his icy anger melt at her warm touch. She watched him, listenin' as he told her that since she kept wakin' the boys up, he decided to soundproof the room wit' a voice command. She laughed, realizin' he wasn't lyin'. She really had been wakin' them up a whole week straight.

The memory slowly went back to the page, snappin' her back into reality. She looked down, feelin' defeated. She closed her eyes and began to pray, rememberin' that Yah's grace is made perfect in our weakness.

"Dear Yah, I need you to help me come up wit' an idea that will get Boaz and Ruth together, amen."

Naomi opened her eyes, noticin' that words were appearin' in her Hallegram at rapid speed. "Thank you, Ruach." She smiled as she waited for it to stop before even attemptin' to read it.

I always get joy when I not only get to help My people, but when I AM invited to do so.

She read it and reread it wit' satisfaction. "This will work. Thanks be to Yah." She tapped the Hallegram, causin' it to disappear back into her Praise. She took a sip of her drink, placin' it back in the air to hover.

She turned back to her stories, ready to find out how Jonah ended up in the belly of the big fish. Ruth strolled down the steps, awake from her nap, seein' Naomi sittin' in the same place she left her.

"Hey, Mama!"

"He-hey, Ruth! How'd ya sleep?"

"Good. Thanks for askin'!"

Naomi turned off the TV and faced Ruth. Ruth ain't realize what was goin' on, still half-asleep. Naomi knew this news needed her to be a bit more awake.

"So, we need to talk."

"'Bout what, Mama?"

Naomi looked away from Ruth. She couldn't keep eye contact wit' her, but she knew she had to if this was gonna go smoothly.

"'Bout… how you are doin' at work!" Naomi forced a smile. She thought she could go through wit' it, but somethin' wouldn't let her.

"Well," Ruth began, "work was like I said awesome, but borin'."

Naomi nodded her head. "Can I make a suggestion?"

"Sure, mama!" Ruth smiled. She was familiar wit' the idea of work and always open to suggestions on how to make it more enjoyable.

"You could ask Boaz if he could move you out into the diner to work. I mean, you proved that you were able to concentrate and complete work in front of the patrons, right?"

Ruth nodded.

"So why not just have a table in the corner or work remotely? That way, you can still experience the Barley Harvest and do your job."

Ruth nodded again. "I can ask and see what he says. I can always pray that Yah will move on him, as it is written, 'He has the king's heart in His hand.'"

"Great." Naomi's clap complimented her smile. "I am sure he will agree to one of those suggestions. Boaz is understandin'."

Ruth smiled. She was so happy that she talked to Naomi. "I know that I just woke up from my nap, but I am still tired, so I'm gonna call it a day. Night!"

Ruth embraced Naomi before Loadin' to her room.

Naomi slumped her face into her hands, wipin' off that last encounter. She gulped her Elime's Drink before I reappeared next to her.

"Naomi?" I began. "What did we just discuss?"

"Now, Ruach, I got a plan, okay." She was lyin' through her teeth. She must've forgot that I AM all-knowin'. I don't know why folks lie to Me like I AM not the embodiment of truth.

"A plan?" I questioned.

"Yes, a plan. One that will lead these two love wires together."

"Okay, so does this plan end in seven days?"

"Yes, it does. I promise you that." Naomi knew she was bein' dishonest wit' Me, but she wouldn't admit to it. So I AM just gonna nod My head.

"Thank you, Ruach. I promise You that I got this. You can trust me."

"Okay, I will trust you."

I vanished. I didn't want this girl to keep lyin' to Me like I AM one of these humans that have error—an error I never wanted, might I add. I decided to fall back and only come when needed, and I AM always needed.

CHAPTER 29

Naomi sat up in her bed, rubbin' her eyes. She tried to sleep off the events that happened yesterday wit' me and Ruth, but she couldn't shake it. She slipped on her silk bathrobe that warmed her body and made her way to the kitchen. Her eyes flickered open wide when she saw a huge 6 plastered on the kitchen counter. The moment she blinked, it disappeared.

She swiveled her head left and right before lookin' back down at the counter. She knew exactly what that 6 meant. She only had 6 days left to do what I asked, and if she didn't, she would face Yah's judgment. She knew, from bein' married to Elime, that no one wanted to be on the receivin' end of Yah's judgment. She tapped the kitchen counter, and a Hallegram projected different choices for breakfast. She settled on a glass of water just as Ruth came down ready for work.

"Hey, Mama! How'd you sleep?"

"I slept well, and you?"

"I slept the best I have in a long time."

"Work can do that to you." They shared a laugh.

"Well, I'm gonna use some of the suggestions you gave last night. I pray he says okay."

"I'm sure he will. Well, you better get goin'. You don't want to be late."

Naomi received a quick kiss on the cheek before Ruth loaded out of there.

Naomi began sittin' down when a portable seat zoomed underneath her. She was feelin' what her husband felt all those nanobytes ago. Keepin' a secret was rough, but she knew she wouldn't let what her husband went through become her story. She learned much from him, but the one lesson she never wanted to be a student in was secrets. She realized that her husband hid information from her, and now it was affectin' her and Ruth. She had to break the cycle if it was the last thing she did.

While Naomi was dealin' wit' the secrets she had to keep, Ruth was loaded to what had become her new favorite place, The Threshin' Floor.

She downloaded right in front of The Threshin' Floor like she always did. She giggled a bit before steppin' into the hustle and bustle. Walkin' in, she went straight back toward the office, mazin' her way through the crowd as best as she could. She pushed open the door, noticin' Boaz sittin' behind the desk, waitin' for her.

"Hey, Boaz!"

"Hey, Ruth!" He stood up, leanin' in for a hug. Ruth enjoyed huggin' Boaz and always cherished the moment. He smelled like hard work and cinnamon, and he stood like a Goliath compared to her.

"So, I've been thinkin'," he said, releasin' her and lookin' down at her gaze. "Yesterday, I had you in this office all day, and I know how borin' that can be."

Ruth agreed wit' a nod.

"I remembered how you fixed a mezzobyte of problems in just minutes when you were out in the diner. So, I decided to give you the option—either work here in the diner, or go out into the Barley Harvest and fix any problem that comes up, remotely."

Ruth's smile widened. This was confirmation. She couldn't believe Boaz was givin' her the option she truly wanted. She knew she would make the most of it.

"Well, Boaz, I decided to work remotely so I can enjoy the Barley Harvest—under one condition."

"What's that?" Boaz asked.

"I want you to come wit' me to enjoy the Barley Harvest." Ruth smiled, eyes gleamin'.

Wit'out even thinkin', Boaz spoke. "Absolutely." He returned her smile.

"Hallelujah," Ruth said into her Praise, instantly downloadin' them both into the center of the Barley Harvest.

They turned in every direction, takin' it all in. The Barley Harvest had a way of commandin' attention from everyone who stepped into it.

Ruth felt her hand get grabbed as she was pulled into Boaz's chest. Before she could protest, her body melted into his arms, and an array of emotions flooded her. She snapped back to reality as Boaz shifted away.

"Sorry," Boaz began. "I know how fast the Barley Harvest can be, and we can end up gettin' separated if we're not careful."

Ruth only caught bits and pieces, noddin' her head. It wasn't until that moment she realized she felt safe wit' Boaz. That shocked her, since she had only known him for a few days.

Boaz took her hand again, leadin' her through the Barley Harvest the same way the arrow guided her some nanobytes ago. They weaved through the crowd until they reached a pastry shop. Steppin' inside, Ruth felt the ambience right away—it was calm and invitin'. The color scheme and artwork reflected that peace.

"Where are we?" Ruth asked as Boaz motioned for her to sit.

"This is the best pastry shop in all of Neo-Eden. They sell the best vegan carrot cake this side of the Jordan."

"Hallelujah," Boaz spoke, and instantly two slices of vegan carrot cake materialized in front of them, along with forks and a tall glass of oat milk. He wasted no time takin' a bite, savorin' every second. Ruth mirrored him and was pleasantly surprised.

"You're vegan?" Ruth asked.

"Yes, so is everyone from Neo-Eden." Boaz took a sip of oat milk. "It's part of the culture and who we are."

"Wow." Ruth leaned back in her chair. "I remember Mahlon tellin' me everyone in his nation was vegan. I thought he was overexaggeratin', but I guess I was wrong."

Boaz nodded between bites. "What did you eat where you're from?"

"Well, we ate everything." Ruth paused, lettin' the next bite give her time to think. She didn't want him to know yet that she was a princess— or that she could inhale a whole carved turkey in one breath. She knew she'd tell him eventually, but not now. "My family was open to a variety of foods. There were animal products as well as non-animal products. But I changed my diet 'cause of my in-laws."

"How was that?" Boaz leaned in, intrigued.

"It was hard for me and my sistah, but eventually we got it."

"You have a sistah?"

"Yes, I do. Two sistahs married two brothers." Ruth's voice softened as memories of their double weddin' came rushin' back.

"Wow, that must have been excitin'!" Boaz said, impressed.

"It was. But enough 'bout me." Ruth finished her bite of cake and leaned forward. "Tell me more 'bout you."

"Okay, well… I'm Boaz. I'm from Neo-Eden. I'm intelligent, carin', and an amazin' businessman. My most popular venture, The Threshin' Floor, is one of my joys. We get everyone—some from this dimension and some that aren't. We've even attracted life from other planets as the popularity grows."

Ruth watched closely. Wit' every word that left Boaz's lips, his face lit up brighter.

"Wow, that's impressive." Ruth nodded. "I remember my first time there. It almost rivaled the experience I'm havin' now at the Barley Harvest. The amazin' people, the awesome food, and the cherry on top was the Word of Yah. Although I rearranged a few spots, whoever installed or designed it specifically for your store knows what they're doin'."

A smirk crept across Boaz's face. He chuckled. "I'm surprised you asked that. It was Naomi who designed it."

"Really?" Ruth's eyes widened. "I mean, she did say Elime taught her 'bout tech, but I would've never guessed to that level."

Laughter burst from Boaz like lava from a volcano. "Hahahahaha!" He laughed for a good thirty seconds before finally catchin' his breath.

"Elime teachin' Naomi 'bout tech." He broke into another chuckle. "That's a good one."

Ruth scrunched her face like discarded paper, annoyed.

"Oh, you really don't know." Boaz sobered instantly, his voice serious.

"Know what?" Ruth asked, confused.

"Naomi is a genius." Boaz smiled. "And before you even ask, let me show you somethin'."

He sat up straighter, then spoke, "Hallelujah."

A Hallegram flickered to life, staticky at first before clearin' up. Ruth grabbed it and placed it on the wall next to them for a better view.

The screen split, revealin' two younger figures—Elime and Naomi. Each side showed them workin' furiously in a lab, designin', creatin', and buildin' technology that could revolutionize the world. Slowly, the two halves merged until it was clear they were in the same lab, workin' side by side.

"Looks like I beat you again." Naomi leaned her head into Elime's chest. They had been workin' on an equation to optimize the AI in their house.

"I guess you did." Elime hugged her back. "You are one of the smartest people I know, and what you come up wit' can only be attributed to the power of Yah."

"To Yah be the glory." She faced him for a moment before restin' her head back on his chest. Elime's eyes wandered, noticin' scattered blueprints on the table he hadn't seen before. He reached over her, causin' her head to follow his hand.

"What is this?" He studied the blueprint with admiration. "You been holdin' out on me." His smile widened as his eyes scanned the details.

"Oh, these?" Naomi pulled the paper gently from his hand, placin' her finished work on top. "That's a gift for Boaz. A thank you for introducin' me to you."

Her finger traced up his chest, almost makin' him forget what he wanted to say. Almost.

"Nice try." He caught her hand and kissed it. "That won't work today. I want details."

She rolled her eyes with a playful smirk. "Fine. I designed Boaz a diner-by-day, lounge-by-night restaurant. The entire system will run on the Word of Yah, through the power of Ruach, and can be controlled by our Praise." Naomi's voice grew brighter with every word.

Elime picked up the design again, seein' it with new eyes. He couldn't believe someone invented somethin' so genius.

"I didn't think I could love you more than I already do, but you never cease to amaze me." Wrappin' his arms around her waist, he pulled her in for a passionate kiss. "I thank Yah every day I listened to Boaz when he told me to marry you."

"I am thankful as well." She held him tighter. "I was skeptical, but from the moment I met you, you made me feel safe."

Elime tilted his head. "Why were you skeptical?"

Naomi smiled softly. "Elime, you are extremely competitive when it comes to bein' an inventor. That's what I admire the most—and what I fell in love wit'. But the very thing I loved also made me hesitant. I didn't want to spend my whole marriage competin' wit' my husband."

"You really think I would've competed wit' you?"

"Elime, it's not like you would've tried on purpose. It would've been subconscious—always tryin' to outdo me. I didn't want that, so I prayed on it. And Yah came through."

"He sure did." Elime squeezed her tighter.

"He did, which is why I made a decision." She pulled back, lockin' her big brown eyes on his soul. "After I finish this blueprint for Boaz's restaurant, I'm shiftin' my focus to other areas of my life."

"What does that mean?" he asked.

"I'm gonna use my intelligence to help my family." She smiled.

"Family? It's just you and me." Elime chuckled, but Naomi's eyes told a different story. He froze. "Wait!" His head tilted as realization hit him like the flood in Noah's day. "Naomi! You pregnant?!" His shout echoed with joy.

Naomi just smiled as he scooped her up and spun her around. He couldn't believe it—he was gonna be a father, and Naomi was gonna be a mother.

"Well, there's another surprise."

He set her down on the table, scatterin' blueprints and papers. "What surprise?"

"We're havin' twins."

Elime's eyes rolled back as he passed out cold. Naomi sat on the table, chucklin', before whisperin', "Hallelujah."

The AI glitched for a split breath, then corrected itself: "Water, provided."

She splashed it in his face, wakin' him slowly. Settlin' onto his chest, she laid her soft afro against his heart as it raced beneath her ear. He wrapped his arms around her, still in disbelief. I'm gonna be a dad to twins, he thought.

"We're gonna be parents to twins," he whispered.

"Yes, we are." Naomi closed her eyes, wantin' to savor the moment for life.

The screen went black before the Hallegram zipped back into the Praise on Boaz's arm. Ruth sat quiet, unable to find the words. Happiness and Naomi were like distant cousins, not really wantin' to meet. Ruth knew Naomi loved Elime, but seein' to the depth of how far her love stretched felt truly divine. She gave up everything for her family and now her family wasn't here.

"After she finished my blueprints for The Threshin' Floor," Boaz broke the silence, "she left the tech game and poured her intellect into the place she loved the most her family."

"How did she do that?" Ruth asked, puzzled.

"Well, Naomi enjoyed bein' a woman, a wife, and a mother. So, she invented gadgets and gizmos that helped her be all that she could be." Boaz sipped his water. "She merged her tech brain wit' her woman's brain and the results were revolutionary."

"So…" Ruth hesitated. "What exactly did she invent?"

"Hahaha! For starters—" Boaz motioned to Ruth's hair. "She created Glamzmo."

Ruth's hair came alive, mirrorin' her face. She gasped, hands flyin' to her curls as they moved around her palms.

"Wow! She never told me that!" Ruth shouted, then quickly caught herself, simmerin' her voice down.

"She invented that so she could always have her hair did. Havin' twins makes even the simplest tasks difficult."

Ruth nodded slowly. "So, she gave up life in tech for her family?"

"No." Boaz smiled. "She used tech to advance her family." He cut another bite of cake. "And when she, or Elime, saw somethin' that needed to be shared wit' the world, she shared it. Remember, she was the one who told the world 'bout the vanity Elime made her. And look what that brought her." He gestured toward Ruth.

Ruth smiled, realizin' she was an answer to Naomi's prayer. But her smile faded. "Wait… hold on." She shook her head. "How did you even get that memory?"

Boaz chuckled. "She hid it in her blueprint. When she gave it to me, I noticed a small QR code in the corner. I scanned it, and that memory appeared." He stared out the window, lettin' his emotions settle into his words. "Those memories always reminded me to love and to love hard. I hope one day I can find someone to share my love wit'." His voice angled toward Ruth.

"I hope I can do it again." Ruth's gaze met his, before driftin' back to the window. The people at the Barley Harvest outside looked like background characters in her world.

"Ruth, what was it like to be in love?" Boaz's question snapped her focus back.

"Wow." Ruth searched for words she couldn't find. "I… uh… never been asked that before. Give me a second." She breathed deep, then spoke. "Bein' in love was the greatest surprise gift I ever got. My marriage was arranged at first. My sistah and I were promised to Mahlon and Chillion."

"Why was it arranged?" Boaz asked.

Ruth didn't want him to know she was a princess, so she brushed it off. "Rich people doin' rich people' things."

Boaz caught his laugh in his throat, forcing it down. He knew that statement all too well.

"Now," Ruth continued, "at first we protested, me and my sistah both. We wanted to find love on our own. But our parents sat us down, explained it was the best decision of our lives, and told us to trust them. So, we trusted and, we had the best husbands we could ever ask for this side of Jordan." A tear tried to break loose, but Ruth wiped it away. "Then they passed away. My sistah, with Naomi's help, went back to our parents."

Boaz slid his chair closer, draping a warm arm over her shoulder. "I'm so sorry you experienced that. I did send my condolences when it happened."

"Really?" Ruth looked up.

"Yes. I paid for all their home-goin' ceremonies."

"You did?"

"Yes. I loved Elime, Mahlon, and Chillion. Their deaths crushed me. I grew up wit' Elime and Naomi. I watched Mahlon and Chillion grow up—I even babysat sometimes. They're my family. I loved them."

Ruth hugged Boaz like an old friend she hadn't seen in years. Outside of Naomi, she had no one she could share her grief wit' who truly understood. She could always call her sistah, but her sistah carried her grief like a weapon, anger first, tenderness later. Ruth didn't want to stand in that fire again.

Boaz held her tighter, his embrace steady, like he was silently tellin' her I got you. For the first time since Mahlon's death, Ruth felt the weight in her chest loosen just a little. She didn't want to let go.

But slowly, they eased apart.

As their arms slid down, Ruth's face lingered close to his. Their eyes met. For just a breath, the world around them blurred into silence. The Barley Harvest crowd outside, the clink of dishes, the hum of Praise devices. It all faded like there was only him, only her.

Their lips brushed, a spark so quick it could've been an accident. But the heat that followed was undeniable. Ruth's heart raced, panic and curiosity dancin' in the same rhythm. She froze, realizin' what just happened.

Boaz stiffened too, his hand twitchin' like he wanted to reach for her again but stopped himself. Both of them pulled back at the same time, like children caught sneakin' sweets before dinner.

An awkward pause swallowed the air between them. Ruth tucked a strand of hair behind her ear, pretendin' to focus on her half-finished slice of carrot cake. Boaz cleared his throat, slidin' back into his seat like he hadn't just almost kissed the woman sittin' across from him.

Their eyes avoided each other until a patron walked by, breakin' the tension.

"Well," Ruth said at last, her voice softer, careful. She made herself look at him again. "I'm thankful you brought me here. I'll be back."

Boaz's smile returned, but this time it carried somethin' else, somethin' unspoken, heavy in the air. A knowing.

Before either could say another word, a ping came from Boaz's Praise, confirmin' his payment was accepted. The sound snapped the moment in two, bringin' them both back down from that edge.

He stood up, helpin' Ruth to her feet. He held her hand as he led her through the door, back to the hustle and bustle of the Barley Harvest. The busy scenery contrasted the pastry shop's quiet ambience. Ruth didn't have much time to process as Boaz led her through the crowd of people. She didn't mind havin' him lead. It felt like home to watch him do this, almost as if she had been doin' this for a long time. They finally made it to a quieter part of the Barley Harvest, regaining their composure.

"You okay?" Boaz asked. "I know it can be sometimes overwhelmin' for new people."

"Yes." Ruth finally felt her breath steady. "It can be, but I love it. I'm glad I get to experience this wit' someone like you."

Her words pulled a smile across Boaz's face, and she mirrored it without even thinkin'. He reached for her hand, leadin' her back toward The Threshin' Floor. Normally, Ruth would've suggested loadin', but walkin' beside Boaz made her want to savor every second.

This time she didn't let herself be dragged. She chose to walk with him, closin' the gap between them, slidin' her fingers between his and restin' her head lightly against his arm. Boaz looked down at her, sheer happiness stretchin' across his face. It felt natural like she belonged there.

As they strolled, Boaz pointed out the shops, vendors, and restaurants she'd only ever find in Neo-Eden. Each story gave Ruth another piece of the city, and another piece of him. She laughed at the tales, especially the ones where Mahlon, Chillion, and Elime made their appearances. Those memories made the walk more than a tour. It felt like she was bein' woven into their world.

Ruth was enjoyin' herself so much wit' Boaz that she barely noticed when they finally arrived at The Threshin' Floor. They stood together for a moment, admirin' the diner's familiar glow. Ruth took a step forward, but Boaz held her back.

"What's wrong?" she asked.

"It's almost time!" His voice was charged, excitement spillin' into the air around them.

"Time for what?" Ruth looked around, then back at him.

"You'll see."

They stood side by side, gazin' at The Threshin' Floor. Ruth glanced at Boaz's face, and the look in his eyes told her somethin' was about to happen. She turned her head just as the diner began to shift before her eyes.

The plain daytime diner shimmered, its frame morphin'. Red bricks materialized, stretchin' upward, while black-tinted windows formed along the walls. The neon sign that once flashed bright colors now deepened into a bold crimson glow. Two tiny nanochips dropped in front of the entrance, one on each side. Ruth's eyes widened as the chips stacked on themselves, buildin' faster and faster until two massive bouncer-droids stood guard. Both wore sleek all-black, from shades to shoes, looming like silent sentinels.

"Wow…" Ruth whispered. It was the only word she could find. She had never seen anything like it. "So, your restaurant does that every day?"

"Yes." Boaz grinned, pride glowin' in his face. "And I'm still amazed by it to this day."

"I bet," Ruth said, still searchin' for words. "I've never seen anythin' on this scale."

"I know." Boaz took a step toward the building, motionin' her forward. "C'mon."

Ruth stayed planted. "I can't. I have to go home and check on Naomi."

Boaz pouted, his lips curvin' like a kid denied candy. "But I wanted you to see the lounge side of my restaurant." He pulled her a little closer, and she stumbled right into his chest. "Please."

She looked up, caught in the spell of his deep brown eyes. For a second, she almost said yes. "Tomorrow. I promise. But tonight, I have to check on Naomi."

"Okay." His voice dropped, small and reluctant, like a child acceptin' a no from his mama.

"I promise I will. Tomorrow." Ruth tapped her Praise, uploadin' herself home.

Boaz stood in front of the glowing lounge entrance, a little defeated— but deep down, he knew tomorrow would come.

Ruth downloaded right into the livin' room where Naomi was watchin' her stories like it was the best thing in the world. She plopped down next to her, knockin' Naomi out of her daze and back to reality.

"Hi, Mama!"

"Hello, Ruth." Naomi paused the story. "How was your day? Did you give the suggestions like we discussed?"

"My day was amazin', and I didn't even have to give the suggestions!" Ruth turned her body toward Naomi, her smile stretchin'.

"Really? Why?"

"Well, when I got to work, Boaz saw that bein' in the office by myself, alone and bored, wasn't the place for me. So, he let me work remotely and even took me for some cake."

"Cake? Really?" Naomi tilted her head. "How was that?"

"It was amazin'." Ruth sank deeper into the sofa, relivin' the moment in her head. "We talked, learned more 'bout each other. He even taught me so much 'bout you."

"'Bout me?" Naomi raised a brow. She was puzzled why Boaz and Ruth would spend their time talkin' about her. "What y'all say?"

"Well," Ruth sat up, excitement brimming, "he told me you were a tech genius in your own right, and that you gave him the blueprints that built The Threshin' Floor."

Naomi chuckled softly. She wasn't shocked Boaz spoke of her that way. He always told her, back when they were young, that she was his inspiration in the tech game. "Yeah, it's true. I am, and always will be, a tech genius."

Ruth tried to hide her surprise, but her snake hair-do gave her away.

"Mama, why did you tell me it was so hard for women to do tech?"

"I said it can be difficult 'cause this is a man's game," Naomi explained, sippin' Elime's Drink. "But I never said it was impossible. The reason I soared in the tech world was simple, I was better than everyone. There wasn't a person alive who could invent, design, or build better than me. That level of intellect was a gift, wit' or wit'out repentance. The only one who could even come close was Elime. And even though I was better, he always pushed me to step my game up."

"Yes, Boaz showed me your memory." Ruth smiled faintly.

"That makes me happy 'cause I can never watch that memory again."

"Why, Mama?"

"'Cause…" Naomi's voice dropped. "Everyone in that memory is gone."

Ruth and her Medusa hair both gasped. They hadn't realized it until Naomi said it out loud. Ruth suddenly understood why Naomi avoided tech now. It carried too many ghosts.

"Yes," Naomi sighed. "And now every time I open my eyes, I'm reminded of them. That's partly why I don't talk to Boaz much. He was the one who told Elime to marry me when Elime had the chance." She smiled to hold back her tears. As much as she wanted to cry, her memories with Elime kept her goin'. "Truth is, seein' Boaz makes me sad, 'cause he reminds me of Elime and my boys. I know I have to get past it, but I'm not ready yet. One day, very soon, I will be."

Ruth wrapped Naomi in her arms, and Naomi clung tightly back.

"You know," Naomi said softly, "when I left the tech game to focus on my family, people thought I was crazy. They said I was wastin' my brain. What they didn't understand was that I used my brain for the people I loved. And because of that, I invented things that still benefit the world."

"I know." Ruth smirked. "Boaz told me you created Glamzmo."

"Haaaa!" Naomi burst into laughter. "I sure did. I made Glamzmo 'cause I had twin boys and my husband and, we couldn't keep our hair done while carin' for them." She laughed harder, then added, "I'm glad the things I invented back then are still bein' used like the hoverin' crib, the automatic baby bottle that mixes and warms itself without help… all of it."

"Wait!" Ruth's eyes widened. "I remember that! I found my old bottle one day and asked my mama what it was. I can't believe you created that."

"Yeah, I did." Naomi nodded proudly. "I'm glad we were always around each other even before we knew each other." She smiled at Ruth. "So, since I have your attention, what else did you and Boaz do?"

Ruth looked away, caught off guard. "Well… we went to the pastry shop. Then we walked back to The Threshin' Floor, and he showed me different spots at the Barley Harvest each wit' a story."

"That sounds fun."

"It was." Ruth's face lit up. "I also saw the diner transform into the lounge. It was magnificent. You outdid yourself."

"Yeah, I did," Naomi smirked. "The Threshin' Floor was my fifth greatest accomplishment. One, my relationship wit' Yah. Two, Elime. Three and four, Chillion and Mahlon. And five, The Threshin' Floor."

Ruth nodded slowly, her eyelids heavy. Naomi noticed.

"Ruth, go on to bed. I know what it's like to work and be tired. I'll join you shortly."

Ruth nodded, whisperin' "Hallelujah" into her Praise, uploadin' to her room. Naomi laughed softly, grateful Ruth had stayed by her side.

"You seem to be enjoyin' yourself," I appeared next to her, smilin'.

"Hello, Ruach." Naomi's tone carried little enthusiasm. She knew why I was here and she wasn't fond of me right now.

"Naomi, why you gotta be like that? You should be happy to see me."

"I am," she said, finally meetin' my eyes. "I promise."

"Uh-huh. Anyway, you know after today, you only got five days left. I'd hate for Ruth to bury you."

Naomi stood, carryin' her dishes to the sink, not because she cared to clean 'em, but because she wanted space from me. "I'm workin' on it."

"Really? What have you done?"

"Well, thanks to my suggestions, Ruth and Boaz spent time together today. That's what we all want, ain't it?"

She was right. We all wanted them together.

"Okay. But when do you plan on tellin' her the severity of the situation?"

"When I have the chance. I still have five more days. I'll tell her."

I didn't argue. Naomi thought she had it all figured out and with me in her corner, she had a chance. "Okay, Naomi. But after today, you'll only have five. Tell her sooner rather than later."

I vanished. Naomi dropped her dishes into the sink, lettin' it wash them automatically, before slumpin' into her soft bed. Her whole body, not just her eyes, grew heavier by the second.

If this is how Elime and my sons felt… then I have to tell her, she thought as her mind drifted into sleep.

CHAPTER 30

·

Naomi's eyes flickered as she slowly started to wake from her dream. Before her mind could fully catch up, she saw a giant number 4 pulsin' in front of her. She flung her head up nervously, lookin' around the room, realizin' that the giant number 4 was nowhere to be found. She tossed her head back on the pillow, tryin' to control her breathin'. Once she settled down, she made her way to the kitchen, which was already preparin' her orange juice.

She sat at the bar, downin' a full glass in one gulp. The glass instantly refilled, and she downed it again. The cycle almost repeated for a third time until Naomi heard footsteps.

"Good afternoon, mama!" Ruth's voice sang through the kitchen. She was still in a good mood from what happened last night wit' Boaz.

"Wait… what?" Naomi blinked, confused at Ruth's words.

"Good afternoon?" Ruth hesitated. "You do know it's the afternoon?"

Naomi twisted her hover-seat, starin' at the clock in disbelief. She couldn't believe she had slept the whole mornin' away. "I'm sorry, Ruth. I can't believe I slept my mornin' away. This ain't like me."

"Yeah, it isn't," Ruth agreed. "Ever since I met you and your family, you've always been an early riser." She tapped the counter, and a glass of water appeared. "I went to check on you, but you were sound asleep. I didn't want to disturb you, so I let you rest." Ruth downed her water in one gulp.

Naomi smeared her hands across her face, tryin' to process what Ruth said. She hadn't slept that long since before she met Elime. Back then, she enjoyed bein' up in the mornin', especially when she had a family to wake up wit' and care for. Now, she was sleepin' half the day away. She knew this was all tied to her disobedience in not tellin' Ruth. Ruach was serious, and she just didn't realize how serious He was 'bout doin' the will of Yah.

"Thank you for lettin' me sleep in. I appreciate it." Naomi focused her gaze on Ruth. "Wait, why are you here? Don't you have work?"

"Haha," Ruth laughed. "Yes, I still got work. Boaz asked me to come in durin' the evenin', and I agreed. I'm 'bout to head out soon. I just didn't wanna miss you before I left."

Naomi's heart melted. She loved that Ruth always cared for her and put her first. She knew she needed to return the favor before there was no more Naomi left. "Thank you, my child. Now go on, you don't wanna be late."

Ruth leaned in for a hug before she uploaded out of there. "Bye. Love ya!"

"Love ya too!"

Naomi rested her head against the counter, wishin' all this could just be over. "What am I gonna do?" she whispered to herself.

"I have some suggestions," I said audibly to her spirit.

"Ruach, not now, please!"

"Haha, okay!" I chuckled. She knew I was gonna be right, and she didn't feel like bein' wrong. Even though she was feelin' the weight of not doin' Yah's will, I still had hope she'd get it done. While Naomi wrestled wit' her own battles, Ruth was already preparin' for what had to come.

Ruth downloaded right in front of the Threshin' Floor like always. She walked straight in, wavin' to patrons and worker droids, then made her way to Boaz's office, where he was waitin' by the door.

"Ruth, how are you?" He hugged her, engulfing her in his arms. She mindlessly hugged him back, enjoyin' every second.

"I'm doin' fine." She lifted her head as Boaz towered over her. "How 'bout you?"

"Good." He grabbed her hand, leadin' her back to the lounge. "I wanted you to experience the Threshin' Floor at night. But before that, you need to experience the Barley Harvest first. C'mon."

He whispered Hallelujah into his Praise, and they were suddenly downloaded right in the middle of the Barley Harvest. Ruth jumped into Boaz's chest on instinct, knowin' how much hustle and bustle the Harvest usually came wit'. But this time was different. She pulled away, lookin' around at how mellow the crowd seemed. Large, yes, but more relaxed than the rush of mornin'.

"Ruth," Boaz said, "welcome to the Barley Harvest afterdark."

As if his words were a trigger, the Harvest lit up wit' dimmed lights floatin' in the air, creatin' a glowin' path to follow. Boaz took Ruth's hands and they started walkin' slowly. She looked in every direction, amazed at how the crowd's elegance matched the ambience. Their attire still carried the boldness of daytime, but now mixed wit' black-tie flair, makin' Ruth smile from ear to ear.

Boaz led her to a small vendor. The smell drifted into Ruth's nose and down to her taste buds, dancin' to the beat of the night's music.

"Oh my," Ruth said. "What's that excitin' smell?"

"Those are the roses." Boaz motioned toward the glowin' flowers. Ruth focused as each one lit up brightly.

"Uhh!" She struggled to find words. She remembered Mahlon talkin' 'bout these flowers, but she had never seen them up close. "I remember hearin' 'bout these from Mahlon. What are they again?"

"These are Glozes: glow roses," Boaz explained. "They're uniquely grown in Neo-Eden and only bloom at night."

Ruth's face lit up like the flowers themselves.

"How may I help you?" a gentleman in all black asked, liftin' his head from his screen.

"Yes," Boaz said. "I'll take two: black and purple."

"Yes sir, comin' right up!" The man swiped across his screen, and two Glozes materialized into Ruth and Boaz's hands. Ping! Boaz tapped his Praise, sendin' payment.

Ruth clutched his arm as they walked away, inhalin' the sweet glow. "Thank you!" She squeezed his arm. "I always wanted one." The Gloze's scent felt familiar yet unlike anythin' she'd ever smelled.

"Ruth, you know what you're supposed to do wit' your Gloze?" Boaz smiled.

"No," she admitted.

Crunch! Boaz bit into his rose, savorin' it. Ruth's eyes widened, then she tried a bite. Her face lit up as she realized it tasted like butter pecan ice cream. Wit'out thinkin', she inhaled the rest in one breath.

Boaz gave her a disturbed look.

"Umm, is somethin' wrong?" she asked.

"Uh, no. No," he stammered. "I just never seen someone eat like that, like you didn't even have to bite."

Ruth held her composure, the same way Boaz held her hand carefully. She had forgotten until moments like this that she ate different from most people. Mahlon had been the first to point it out, askin' why she inhaled her food instead of chewin'. She always blamed her father, since that's how he ate and his body showed it. Sometimes she forgot to turn off the Moabolis princess mode that let her consume differently.

"Yeah, it was so good I couldn't just take one bite." Ruth smiled, avoidin' the details of her life as princess.

"I can tell." Boaz finished his Gloze. They continued strollin', admirn' vendors and spectators.

"This atmosphere feels so different after dark," Ruth said.

"Yeah, it is." Boaz nodded. "That's why I only do Barley Harvest afterdark."

"Really?"

"Absolutely. It reminds me of family."

Ruth's ears perked up at the word.

"When I was younger, we always went durin' the day. It was overwhelmin' for me as a kid, but you learn to handle it."

"What changed?"

"I don't know." Boaz scrunched his face. "One day we were supposed to go, but somethin' happened. My mom told me to wait."

"She's beautiful!" Ruth said, seein' the image on his Praise.

"Yeah, she is." He swiped it away. "That time, she took me afterdark. Ever since, that's the only way I experience it as a spectator. Workin' the Harvest is one thing, but enjoyin' it is different."

"I can imagine."

"Look at it—it's calm, peaceful." He motioned to the scene. "I'm sure your first time here caught you off guard."

Ruth nodded. When she first downloaded to the Barley Harvest, the chaos had her mind racin' everywhere.

"You see the difference? Your body's calmer too. You're holdin' my hand different. Not as tight as in the day."

He was right. She hadn't realized until he mentioned it.

"Now don't get me wrong, Ruth. The day Barley Harvest is holy too. That rush of adrenaline, meetin' folks from this planet, other planets, galaxies, even universes… even other moments in time."

"Other universes? Other moments in time?" Ruth's attention sharpened.

"Yes, Ruth!" His voice brimmed with excitement. "That's one of the Harvest's biggest secrets. We get people from other universes and timelines."

Boaz glanced around, lowerin' his voice. "When time travel went public, word spread fast. The Harvest started attractin' not just extraterrestrials, but travelers from different places in time."

Ruth nodded, maskin' her familiarity. As Moabolis princess, she was used to such things, but Boaz couldn't know that yet. "Wow. So… have you actually met anyone from a different timeline?"

"Yes, I have. Wanna see?"

Ruth nodded eagerly. Boaz hurried them to a park bench, tapped his Hallelujah, and a screen flickered into view, snowin' before revealin' a video.

A younger Boaz stood in the corner of his restaurant, lookin' around proudly. He'd only had the Threshin' Floor a few years, but it was already one of Neo-Eden's most thrivin' spots. Thank you, Yah, he thought as the service droids bustled around servin' patrons. Thank you, Naomi, he added, knowin' how much both had done to get him this far.

"Everything okay, Boss?" the manager asked, walkin' up.

"Yeah, just takin' it all in."

"Good. This restaurant is a hit. You really outdid yourself."

Boaz smiled. "This wasn't me. I have to give it to Naomi and Yah. They did it all."

"Of course!" The manager nodded and went back to directin' the service droids.

Boaz let his gaze drift back over the restaurant, joy wellin' up inside him. He couldn't have asked for a better moment. Then his eyes caught on the door. A man and a woman had just walked in. Somethin' about them struck him. It wasn't their clothes, which matched the Barley Harvest crowd but their presence. They didn't feel like they belonged to this place.

He watched as a service droid led them to a window table. Curiosity gnawed at him until he finally made a beeline to greet them.

"Hello, how are you?" he said, arrivin' just as the droid stepped back. The droid paused, then quietly moved away.

"We are both fine," the lady answered with a smile. "How are you?"

"I am great. What can I get for you?"

The pair shook their wrists, pullin' up their menus. They scrolled with deliberate care.

"We'll take BBQ jackfruit sandwiches with fries," the woman said. "And two large waters, no ice."

"Absolutely." Boaz tapped his Hallelujah, summonin' their order. "Enjoy your meal. If you need anythin', let me know."

"I do, actually," the woman said with another smile.

"Yes?" Boaz leaned in, eager to know more.

"Have a seat."

Boaz tried to hide his excitement, but he felt like he was about to erupt like a new piece of tech launchin'. "Yes?"

"First, introductions." The woman extended her hand. "My name is Didi. This is my husband, XV."

Boaz shook both their hands. "Hi, I'm Boaz." His smile stretched wide. For some reason, he needed to know more about these two.

"So," Didi asked, "what made you want to take our order personally? Be honest."

Boaz chuckled. "I saw you across the room, and somethin' about y'all stood out. Like you're… different. I wanted to know how."

"Hmmm." Didi tilted her head. "What would you like to know? We're open books."

"Where are you both from?"

"We're from a place called Axum," XV replied.

"Axum?" Boaz frowned, scrollin' through his mind for any trace of the name. Nothin'. "Where's that?"

"It's very far away," XV said.

"How far?"

The two exchanged a look before Didi leaned forward. "Different universe," she said with a smile.

Boaz's eyes shot wide, soarin' like a shootin' star. "A different—" he caught his voice mid-shout, "—universe?"

"Yes," Didi nodded. "One that's more mystical… or mechanical."

Boaz studied them carefully. "That phrase… wait. Are you A.N.G.E.Ls?"

Didi shot XV a quick look.

"Somethin' like that," XV said, "but not the way you think of A.N.G.E.Ls."

Didi leaned in. "What he means is, your A.N.G.E.Ls are based on science. Ours are rooted in the supernatural."

"Really?" Boaz's wonder only grew. "I'd love to learn more about this."

"We'd love to share," Didi said, standing with her husband, "but we have to go." She clapped her hands, and their food packed itself neatly into to-go containers.

Boaz's eyes burned, near tears. "Wait, don't go. I want to know more."

Didi took his hand, noddin' for XV to take the other. "We know you do. And you will learn. You can always come visit."

"How? How do I visit you?"

"That, you'll have to figure it out yourself," Didi said gently. "Nana Buluku told us we couldn't show you."

"Nana who?"

"The One you call Yah." Didi smiled.

Boaz looked down, strugglin' to wrap his mind around what just happened. "Wa—" He looked up and they were gone.

He spun in a frantic circle, then tapped his Hallelujah, pullin' up the security feeds. Screen after screen, nothin'. No trace of them. He sighed, wipin' his face, and walked back to the manager, defeat written all over him.

"Boss, what's wrong?"

"I met these amazin' people… and I don't know if I'll ever see them again." Tears pooled like he'd just lost old friends.

"Boss, you will see them again." The manager squeezed his shoulder. "Remember, it is written: 'Faith is actin' on the Word of Yah with confident assurance that what I hope for has already happened, even if I haven't seen it yet.'"

Relief swept over Boaz like a calm wave. Yah's words always put him at ease. "Yeah. I just gotta have faith."

"Absolutely, sir." The manager smiled.

Snow flickered on the screen before vanishin'.

"So, what do you think?" Boaz asked, facin' Ruth. Her expression stayed blank.

"Yeah, uh… wow. Cool." Ruth finally raised her head from his arm. "Did you ever meet them again?"

"No." Boaz sighed. "I tried. I'm still tryin', but no luck." Defeat was written all over his face. He desperately wanted to see Didi and XV again.

"Hey." Ruth gently pushed his head toward her. "You will meet them again. I promise. Like your manager said in that memory, have faith."

"You're right." Boaz nodded, though sadness lingered. "It's just… it's been years since that day. I tried everything to find them. And before you ask, yes, I did invite Yah in before I did anything. But nothin' worked. Sometimes I feel like Yah doesn't want me to meet them."

Boaz's hand tensed in hers. Ruth massaged it softly until he relaxed, his head droppin' in defeat.

"Boaz," Ruth said firmly, "I don't believe for a second that Yah doesn't want you to find those two A.N.G.E.Ls. He wouldn't have sent them to you otherwise. He knows you. He knows you've got a heart that befriends everyone. That's how I met you. So have faith. It'll happen again."

Boaz leaned into her, embracin' her for a hug. Ruth had been hopin' for it, and excitement bloomed as she hugged him back.

"You ready to head back?" Boaz asked, feelin' lighter, still holdin' tight to her hands.

"Absolutely." Ruth jumped to her feet, pressin' her head back on his arm as he led her out. They didn't say much. They let the ambience of the Barley Harvest afterdark do the talkin'. Ruth knew after tonight she could never go back to the day Harvest. Somethin' about the night about Boaz, made it unforgettable.

When they arrived at the Threshin' Floor, Ruth noticed a long line stretched outside.

"What's that?" she asked.

"Oh," Boaz smiled. "There's always a line for afterdark. Everyone usually makes it in. If not, they come back when it's a diner."

He walked past the line, the bouncer lettin' them in without hesitation. Boaz guided Ruth like it was her first time, and she looked around wide-eyed, realizin' she'd been so wrapped up in bein' with him earlier that she hadn't noticed how transformed the Threshin' Floor became at night.

The lounge shimmered like a hidden jewel under the stars. Its walls curved and pulsed with ancestral symbols carved in bioluminescent circuits. The air hummed mellow and thick with spiced hibiscus and sandalwood incense. In the center, a lo-fi artist named Luna Moon sang honey-smooth into the night, her voice meltin' into the down-tempo rhythm of her kora-synthesizer. Above her, digital constellations glowed in motion, while the crowd swayed slow, glowin' cups of obsidian drinks in their hands.

In the back, the VIP section glowed gold and indigo, veiled in velvet mesh that shimmered like stardust. Crescent-moon couches cradled guests draped in silk robes, whisperin' secrets, cuttin' deals, and dreamin' out loud beneath holograms of ancestors watchin' over the rhythm.

Ruth spun a full circle, overwhelmed by how chic and elegant the place was. She couldn't believe Naomi had built somethin' like this. Memories of Naomi flooded her until Boaz reached for her hand and brought her back to the present. She leaned into him as he led her onto the floor.

Couples swayed slow, bodies intertwinin' like they were tryin' to become one. Ruth and Boaz joined in, laughter trailin' behind them like a second song. He turned her, his frame brushin' hers as they fell into rhythm. He was a Goliath beside her, but his touch was gentle, his lead certain. When his arms wrapped around her, the world melted away. She felt safe. She felt infinite.

When Luna Moon's set ended, Boaz led Ruth into a private suite. He tapped his Hallelujah, and a soft bubble wrapped around them, mutin' the outside world. Ruth watched him gulp his water, quiet but intent, which he took as an invitation to talk.

"Tell me what you think." He leaned closer, wantin' her honest opinion.

"Well…" Ruth smiled. "This place is amazin'. I've never been anywhere like it." She caught herself before ramblin'. "I still can't believe Naomi built this!"

"Believe it," Boaz said, slidin' a little closer. "She built everythin' in this place off smart work, prayer, fastin', and almsgivin'. I'm honored to carry it. She usually tells people no."

"Really?"

"Yeah. Even before she retired. If someone asked her to build or help, she'd tell 'em no. Not 'cause she was mean, but because she believed people relied on shortcuts. She's anti-shortcuts. She wanted folks to learn on their own. If she did help, she always brought Elime."

He slid closer again. This time, Ruth noticed and leaned in too. When he leaned back, arms stretched across the seat, she rested her head on his chest. She heard his heartbeat sync with hers. Neither of them pulled away; it felt natural, like they'd been made for this moment.

"Hey," Ruth tapped him gently, lookin' up. "As much as I'm enjoyin' myself, I need to leave. I should check on Naomi."

Boaz wanted to protest, but her devotion was one of the things he loved most. "Okay, I understand." He hugged her tight, then tapped the table. In an instant, Ruth uploaded back home.

Boaz sat there, tryin' to soak in the moment, but it didn't last. His homies piled into the suite, crashin' his sectional, pepperin' him with questions about the new girl he'd been spendin' time with.

"Haha," Boaz laughed, sayin' nothin', just smilin' as the music carried him back into the night.

CHAPTER 31

Naomi was sittin' on the couch, tryin' to watch her stories. Normally, she would have a bowl of popcorn and Elime's Drink. Today though, she was sittin' wit' her virtual blanket that rose and lowered in temperature dependin' on her body heat. She looked at it wit' joy every time she used it. It was one of her family's inventions that she kept to herself.

Elime once told her to share it wit' the world, but that was when she was already done inventin' for the world. She smiled softly, knowin' this gentle reminder of her family now kept their memory alive.

Naomi didn't even notice that Ruth had downloaded in, full of joy.

"Hello! Mama?"

Shakin' her head, Naomi snapped back into reality and turned the TV down.

"Sorry 'bout that. I was into my show."

"Haha!" Ruth chuckled. "I can tell."

She slouched down next to her, causin' the virtual blanket to extend over her legs.

"I have so much to tell you."

Naomi shifted her body to listen.

"Well, as stated, Boaz wanted me to come to work at night to see The Threshin' Floor after dark."

Naomi nodded.

"It was amazin'. First, he took me to the Barley Harvest, and I must say I prefer it at night. It felt so different, so warm. Then he bought me a Gloze."

"Ahh, a Gloze." Naomi chuckled. "I remember my prototype for them."

"Wait." Ruth blinked twice, her mouth slightly open. "Mama, you invented the Glozes?"

"Yes, I did, when I was a teen." Naomi shifted to get more comfortable. "It was one of my first lucrative inventions. That invention moved me from six figures to eight figures. I still collect checks from it. I own all my and Elime's patents."

If Naomi was anythin', she was always a businesswoman. She prided herself on ownin' every invention she created.

"Wow, you really did live many lives before I met you." Ruth tilted her head, still takin' in the revelation.

"I tell people that I've lived three lives, before Elime, durin' Elime, and after Elime."

They both laughed.

"That's true." Ruth thought on it, realizin' she described her own life the same way. "Anywho, I had an amazin' time wit' Boaz. He even showed me a memory he had wit' people from another dimension. He said he only met them once and has been tryin' ever since to meet them again."

"I know," Naomi said. "I remember when that day happened, and Boaz told Elime and me 'bout it. I believed him instantly 'cause I've met my fair share of multidimensional and multi-universal people."

"Mama, really?" Ruth asked, surprised. "You met them as well?"

"Not them per se, but others. I can't go too far in detail 'cause I was told not to say so by my best friend, Ruach."

Ruth nodded in agreement. She had met Me before and could tell that although I was comfortin', I was also stern.

"But you must mean a whole lot to him," Naomi continued, "for him to show you that. He doesn't just show anyone that."

Ruth giggled, thinkin' back on the few days she had spent wit' Boaz.

"Umm, yeah, we mean a whole lot to each other."

"Keep goin'."

"I mean, when I go to work, all we do is spend time wit' each other. We hold hands, we talk, and we have even danced some of the night away. I have never felt this way wit' anyone since Mahlon. I truly enjoy him."

Naomi just stared at her, but felt a nudge from Me. She knew what she had to do, and I endowed her wit' the strength to step forward and break this curse.

"Okay, so… he's someone that you can see yourself wit' for the rest of your life?"

"Wait, what?" Ruth asked, thrown completely off balance.

"You heard me!" Naomi said with a confidence she hadn't felt since her family's death. "You told me that you basically have feelin's for Boaz, and that when you do spend time together, it sounds like two people datin' and slowly fallin' in love wit' each other."

Ruth didn't even realize it until that moment. She replayed her memories wit' Boaz over and over and saw the truth—

She had already fallen in love wit' him.

"You are right," Ruth said quietly. "I have fallen in love wit' Boaz."

Naomi smiled. This was goin' smoothly, and she was overjoyed that Ruth was takin' it well. She was so happy Ruth wasn't goin' to end up like the men in her family.

Death doesn't look cute on me, Naomi thought.

"And I mean, I do love you," Naomi said softly. "I just want you to love again. Also, you can't stay wit' me forever. You gotta live your life. Mahlon would want that."

Ruth's emotions flared up like her acne did when she was fifteen. She loved Mahlon. Anytime anyone brought him up, her love ignited like it was the first time she met him.

"You right!"

Naomi quickly faced Ruth, surprise written all over her face. She didn't think Ruth was goin' to agree wit' her.

"You right," Ruth continued. "I don't wanna argue wit' you. I have found love again! I don't wanna be a perpetual widow."

She paused.

Ruth realized what she had just said and knew those words could easily be misinterpreted. The last thing she wanted was to hurt Naomi. She braced herself for Naomi's wrath.

"You right. I am a perpetual widow. I don't wanna find another. I am older, and I wanna stay married to my husband. I love Elime."

Ruth was relieved when her mother-in-law didn't yell. Naomi didn't play 'bout her emotions when it came to Elime. She was in love and never wanted to love anyone else.

"I know you're in love wit' my son," Naomi said. "I also know you will make a great wife."

Ruth couldn't believe her ears. She knew Naomi wanted her to get married, but she didn't expect her blessin' so soon.

"I guess you're right. So… what do we do next?"

"Don't worry." Naomi smiled. "Leave that to me."

CHAPTER 32

Boaz entered from the back, makin' sure the lounge was ready for operation. It was one thing when it was the diner, but a whole 'nother when it was the lounge, he thought, movin' through the crowd. He was so used to the technology haywirin' that relaxin' felt impossible at first. But ever since Ruth fixed the systems, the lounge had been runnin' better than ever. Usually, it would glitch, revert to the diner, then stutter back, but tonight it held steady. Thank You, Yah, for Ruth, he thought as he made his way to his friends.

Boaz and his crew were posted at a private sectional, sharin' drinks and laughs. Every night he made his usual rounds to keep things afloat, but now, with Ruth's touch on the systems, he realized he didn't need to. For the first time, he could just be himself. And man, was he himself.

Boaz may not have been the loudest or the life of the party, but that never stopped him from bein' the center of attention. He was the most respected and beloved man in all of Neo-Eden, and he wore that respect with humility. Leanin' back in his chair, he soaked in the vibe.

He loved watchin' people truly enjoy life, and he had made it his ministry to help them do just that. But even ministry took its toll. He felt the weight of it in his bones and knew it was bedtime.

"Imma head out," he announced, settin' his glass down on the sleek tray of a service-droid zippin' past the table. Risin' from his stool, he headed for the exit but misjudged the path and stumbled over a hoverin' chair.

"Ay yo, Bo! You good?" one of his boys called out. "Need a ride?"

Boaz waved him off wit' a grin. "Nah, bruh, I'm good. Just got ahead of myself. Swear I'm straight." He chuckled, steppin' outside as he pulled up his Halle app to hail a cab.

The cool night air brushed his skin while the neon glow of the club's sign flickered on the wet pavement. Moments later, a sleek automated vehicle pulled up, its doors hissin' open. Boaz uploaded inside and leaned back. The car hummed softly as it glided toward his house in the hills.

The ride was smooth until they hit the top of his driveway. That's when he noticed someone standin' in the shadows near his mansion's entrance. His instincts kicked in fast. Without a word, he shifted his wrist, slidin' his Praise into a ready position, the weapon concealed beneath his sleeve.

"You see that?" Boaz asked the cab's AI driver.

"Negative, sir," the synthetic voice replied.

The car eased to a stop at the gates. Boaz stepped out slow, eyes sharp, every muscle taut. But the figure was gone. The only thing left was silence, broken only by the low hum of his home's security drones driftin' overhead.

The mansion loomed like a relic from a forgotten future, where Soulaani craftsmanship met zero-point energy. Its curved walls shimmered wit' adaptive alloys that shifted hue wit' the passin' sun, while solar tesserae harvested light in fractal precision. Ancestral motifs etched by plasma cutters pulsed wit' bioluminescent data, tellin' stories only machines and memory could decode.

Drones flitted through anti-gravity corridors like chrome insects, their paths guided by a central AI rooted in tribal lore. His butler-droid, Williams, opened the front door just as Boaz approached.

"Ah, Master Boaz, how was your evenin'?" the droid asked in its crisp, polite tone.

Boaz managed a smile, but his mind was elsewhere. "It was good, Williams. I spent time wit' Ruth, and then my boys and I had a great time." He hesitated, glancin' back toward the driveway. "Hey, did anyone come by while I was out?"

Williams tilted its mechanical head, its emotion scanner lightin' up faintly. "No, Master. Why do you ask?"

Boaz frowned but shook his head. "No reason. Just thought I saw someone. It's probably nothin'."

Williams gave a reassurin' smile, as much as its metal frame could muster. "The property is secure, sir. If there is anythin' to report, I will notify you immediately."

Noddin', Boaz headed inside. But the uneasy feelin' lingered. Even as he climbed the grand staircase to his bedroom, he couldn't shake the sensation that he was bein' watched.

"Hello?" he called out, his voice echoin' faintly in the expansive hallway. Silence answered him.

Shruggin' it off, he entered his room and prepared for bed. The day had been long, and his body welcomed the cool embrace of his sheets. Sleep came quickly, pullin' him into a dreamscape where he saw her— Ruth. Her face was clear, her smile radiant. Though they had just met, he felt a deep connection to her, as if their souls had always been intertwined.

Boaz awoke in the middle of the night, drenched in a cold sweat. The dream had been so vivid, so real. Reachin' for the glass of water on his nightstand, he took a long gulp to calm himself. Tossin' the covers off, he turned his pillow to the cooler side and laid back down.

"AAAAHHHHHHH!" Boaz's scream pierced the silence as he jolted upright.

Standin' at the foot of his bed was Ruth, holdin' a tray of brownies.

Williams arrived at the door moments later, poundin' on it like an officer on a raid. "Master! Master! Are you alright? I heard a scream!"

Boaz's eyes darted between the beautifully melanated woman standin' in his room and the closed door where Williams waited. "Everything's fine!" he called out, tryin' to regain his composure. "Just a bad dream!"

Turnin' back to Ruth, he blurted, "Ruth? What'chu doin' here?"

She smiled, settin' the tray on a nearby table. "I came to see you."

"Why?" he asked, still tryin' to make sense of her sudden appearance. "How did you get past my security system?"

Ruth met his gaze wit' a smile. "Naomi."

Boaz threw his hands up. He knew there was only one person who could hack his system wit'out even tryin'.

Ruth started laughin'. "Let's not act like you didn't want me in your house."

Boaz couldn't protest, 'cause truth be told, he had planned on invitin' Ruth over so they could get to know each other. "Well, okay. You're right, but what could you possibly need me for? It couldn't wait until tomorrow?"

Ruth sat down on the edge of the bed, her expression turnin' serious. "Doin' business as a woman is doable, but most of the time, they'd rather deal wit' a man. I was thinkin'… we could work together. You'd make a great partner. Plus, let's be real. You look like you need a wife to help you keep this place in order, and I could use a husband to handle things I don't want to do like reprogrammin' my Praise. We like each other, right? So why not give it a go?"

Boaz stared at her, his mind racin'. He'd never had a woman propose to him, and he definitely hadn't expected it tonight. He grabbed his water glass and drained it, tryin' to buy time to think. He was searchin' for the words, but decided to freestyle and hope for the best.

"Naomi can't run the company? She's done it before."

"Now you and I both know Naomi don't wanna do that. I don't even know why you asked." They both laughed. They knew how serious Nami was 'bout stayin' in the background of the tech game.

Settin' the glass down, he met her gaze. "Ruth, I know the Almighty Yah has already blessed you now and forever. And yes, I do want to be wit' you forever. I do want to marry you. I just gotta follow customs. If a closer relative is willin' to marry you, it's his right first. If he's not interested, I'll marry you. I promise. I know it sounds strange, but this is how we do things in Neo-Eden."

Ruth's disappointment was visible, but she nodded. She really wanted Boaz to say "yes." She followed Naomi's plan wit'out rewritin' or missin' a beat. She forgot that Neo-Edens do things differently than how she did it in Moabolis. It was times like this she wished she was home so she could get her way. She stood up, brushin' invisible crumbs from her dress.

"Where you goin'?" he asked.

"Home. I can't stay at my boss's house all night, wit' brownies and no milk."

Boaz chuckled. "Why not?" He snapped his fingers, summonin' two large glasses of oat milk.

Ruth turned back, her eyes lockin' wit' his. A slow smile spread across her face as she picked up a brownie. Boaz grabbed one too. Their eyes never wavered as they took a bite together. Wit' each chew, Boaz hoped and prayed that he could marry Ruth. The brownies alone were enough for half his estate in holy matrimony. He took a sip of oat milk the same time she did. They never said a word, they just kept eatin' brownies and drinkin' oat milk all night long.

The next mornin', Ruth woke up singin' praises to the Mighty Yah as she gathered her belongin's. She couldn't believe she had just sat up practically all night, eatin' brownies and drinkin' oat milk wit' Boaz. She hadn't done somethin' that fun since she and Mahlon were first married, tryin' to find what they had in common. They both realized they loved brownies wit' oat milk. Ruth chuckled at the memory as she felt hands on her shoulders and jumped back.

"Whoa, whoa! It's just me! Where you goin' so fast?" Boaz said.

"Home! I have to get home and see Naomi. She needs me."

Boaz lifted his Praise, whispered in it, and smiled. Ruth felt hers tinglin' up her arm. She checked her Praise to discover Boaz had blessed her account. She loved the fact that he was generous wit' money, just like her father and how Mahlon used to treat her.

"Wha—what am I supposed to do wit' this?" Ruth was pleased. She was royalty in Moabolis, but since movin', makin' money through work was a struggle she wouldn't wish on her worst enemy.

"Take it home wit' you. If anyone asks, you worked all night bakin' brownies." They both chuckled. "Also, you shouldn't be goin' home empty-handed. Do you need a ride? I'm headin' into town right now." Boaz shot Ruth a smile that made her melt.

"I'm cool! Appreciate it!" She didn't wanna get too swept up in him, so she ran out the door wit' a huge smile on her face. She almost knocked Williams down as she was runnin' out of the house.

Williams wiped his suit down. "Master, who was that?"

"My wife!"

Boaz smiled before headin' back to his room to get ready. He was thinkin' 'bout his night wit' Ruth and how it went. He wished he could have gone wit' her, but he had to follow the customs and traditions laid out by his forefathers.

Ruth decided not to upload to her home but left through the front gate. She was thankful that Boaz didn't have neighbors, 'cause leavin' a man's house early in the mornin' was not the vibe. It wasn't like a princess to do what she was doin', even though she knew nothin' happened. The real reason she wanted to walk home was to call her friends wit' an update. She had plenty of juicy details 'bout Boaz they needed to hear.

"Ay yo, Dash, Juju! Lemme Halle'atchu for a second!" Suddenly, two 3-D Hallegrams of her friends projected from her device.

"Dash! Juju!" Ruth exclaimed. "Y'all ain't gonna believe what happened. I spent the night wit' Boaz. Sorta."

"No way!" they yelled in unison.

"Yes way! It was amazin'. He's a real gentleman. I am smitten." Ruth strutted down the sidewalk while tryin' to focus on both the conversation and where she was goin'. She was realizin' it was harder than she thought.

"Gentleman? But he got you walkin' like—?" Dash took a bite of her snack, waitin' for a response.

"I CHOSE to walk home. I wanted to tell my girls what happened."

"Darlin', what exactly did happen?" Juju was a bit too concerned. She was the mom of the group, and Ruth loved that.

"My troubles leavin' my life faster than these girls' edges!" Ruth shot back.

Dash choked on her chips from laughin', and Ruth felt her spit through the Hallegram.

"Hrrk! Hrrk! Hrrk!" Dash tried to control herself.

"Dang, girl, cover your mouth!" Ruth wiped her face off.

"Seriously, have some respect for yourself!" Juju rebuked.

"My bad, can I not choke and laugh in peace?" Dash chuckled.

"NO!!!!" they screamed together.

Dash took a drink of water, payin' her friends no mind. Ruth realized that the Praise upgrade for physical touch wasn't what it was cracked up to be. She might have to disable it as soon as she got home.

"Well, tomorrow he's gonna help me wit' the problems. Thanks be to Yah!"

"Tomorrow? Why not today?" Juju asked.

Ruth knew she was gonna get the third degree from her friends, but she knew it was comin' from a lovin' place. "Because, he gotta go make the moves. Oh, I gotta talk to Naomi. This chat was much needed, as always. I'm gonna Halle at y'all later."

"Alright, girl. I'll Halle!" Dash hung up.

"Ciao." Juju followed.

Ruth couldn't help but laugh. Her friends were literally the best, and they always kept her grounded. She regained focus only to realize that their conversation carried her all the way to her home wit' Naomi. She started to knock on the door, then realized this was her home and she lived there.

"Honey, I'm home!" Ruth sang into the room.

"Ruth, where you been?" Naomi questioned her like she didn't send Ruth on that mission wit' precise details to do exactly what she said.

"You knew where I was." Ruth and Naomi both laughed. Ruth began to tell Naomi all the excitin' and amazin' details that happened wit' her and Boaz.

Naomi lifted her Praise to her lips. Suddenly, a bowl of popcorn appeared on her lap, and a large Elime's Drink hovered next to her.

"This story gettin' good, I need a snack!" Naomi shoved a handful of popcorn in her mouth.

Ruth started laughin', rememberin' why she loved Naomi.

"You remind me so much of Mahlon," Ruth said. "He always did that when I told him a story."

"Where do you think he got it from? The Saturnians? The Nephilim?"

The women laughed while Ruth continued the story, not leavin' any details out. She really wanted Naomi to get her popcorn's worth. Over an hour later, she realized they were far into the afternoon.

Ruth smiled. "Well, it was great talkin' to you. I gotta call my sistah and fill her in."

"Tell her I said hello. I do miss her tremendously. Please, tell her to stop ignorin' my Halles!"

"I will!" Ruth made her way upstairs toward her bedroom. She hurried over to her vanity, excited to share the news.

"Ay yo, Orpah! Lemme Halleat'chu for a second!"

The mirror faded into black for ten seconds. Then an image shimmered of a young woman dressed in purple pajamas, sittin' up in bed. Her room was in total chaos, with many people cleanin', rearrangin' furniture, and bringin' her food. Before anythin' could be said, Orpah clapped her hands three times, and the room cleared out.

Ruth chuckled. That was typical Orpah behavior. Finally, the two were alone and quiet.

"ORRPPAAHHH!" Ruth yelled as she always did when she saw her sistah.

"RUUUTTHHH!" Orpah yelled back. "How you doin'? How has it been? It feels like it been forever."

"Orpah, it's been a month."

"Yes, but that is a looonngggg time for us. You are my sistah. We used to be together every single day and now…"

"I know, but you could have stayed. She told BOTH of us to go, Orpah. You could've ignored her too!" Ruth really did miss her sistah. Sometimes it felt like a mini-death, goin' from seein' so many people every day to suddenly not seein' them at all.

"True, but I feel that it was directed towards me. It was no secret that your husband, Mahlon, was her favorite."

Ruth's silence spoke volumes. She, as well as the entire family, knew that Mahlon and she were the favorites. She tried not to make it so obvious, but Naomi and Elime didn't make it easy. Even in their strength they fell short and did ask for forgiveness.

"Ruuuth? You gonna respond? Or nah?"

"You're right." That's all Ruth could say. She never thought she would admit that part of her life to her sistah. But since both their husbands were gone, there was no reason to hide the truth.

Orpah blinked in surprise. "I wasn't expectin' that."

"Well, it's true. But the past is the past, so let's move forward and be sistahs again."

Orpah smiled. "We will always be sistahs!"

Orpah loved her sistah Ruth, and Ruth loved Orpah. They would always have each other. They sat there and chuckled at each other. They truly had a bond like no other. Their parents raised them to be their sistah's keeper.

"Orpah," Ruth said. "I found someone. He is older, but he is amazin'. His name is Boaz. He is nice, kind, and rich. He is willin' to marry me if no other man will."

"Okay, I see you. Well, the same has happened for me as well. A king, tho. His name is Abi, and he is the King of the Philliez!"

Ruth was pleased that her sistah found someone. She never wanted Orpah to be alone and did plan on movin' her down here, had she not found anyone. She knew Naomi wouldn't mind, as she loved Orpah as well.

"So, we both found men. This is dope! I am super happy for you."

"Same to you. We have to talk more, but I gotta go and tend to Abi!"

"Same. I have to go to sleep so I can meet up wit' Boaz in the mornin'. Love you! Oh, wait!"

Orpah froze, concerned 'bout what Ruth could possibly say.

"Naomi wants you to call her."

Orpah relaxed wit' a smile. "I will. Love you!"

And wit' that, the screen went black before fadin' into the reflective glass it once was.

Ruth ran to her bed to lay down. She pulled up a picture of Mahlon on her Praise. "I love you. Everything I do is in honor of you. Tomorrow, we will conquer!"

Ruth decided to stay in the house and not go anywhere. After her night wit' Boaz and her mornin' wit' her sistah, Orpah, she knew she needed to stay in this bed and rest. Whatever happened, it was in Yah's hands, and Ruth would accept the outcome.

Accept what Yah allows, Ruth thought, as her eyes slowly felt heavier and heavier wit' each second.

The next mornin' a call from Boaz knocked Ruth right off her bed. She quickly turned off the video on her Praise as she slowly got up from the floor.

"He-hello?" The sleep in her voice hadn't quite caught up wit' her.

"I'm headin' to the city to meet up wit' some family to help you. You able to come?"

Boaz's voice woke Ruth faster than Lazarus. "Yes, I'll Load."

"See ya soon."

Ruth was thankful that Mahlon had taught her how to properly Load through the servers of any city. She didn't realize how many people still were scared 'bout what could happen. As long as you believe, everything will be fine, she thought. She hung up the Halle, runnin' to the bathroom. She looked at herself in the mirror, tryin' to calm down. She couldn't believe she was one step closer to bein' married and hopefully to Boaz. She knew this had everything to do wit' Yah, and any and everything wit' Yah is "Yes and Amen," but that "Yes and Amen" was somethin' to fight for.

She finished gettin' cleaned up when she realized she didn't have anything to wear. She went to her vanity and started searchin' for somethin'. She knew the Barley Harvest was still goin' on and her snake hair was still holdin' up, but she wanted somethin' that was Barley Harvest yet simple for a possible weddin' proposal. She scrolled, and scrolled, and scrolled until she saw it. She clicked "OK," and it materialized on her.

It moved like a glitch, cloaked in emerald camo-silk that shifted wit' light and code. Gold leg coils tracked her vitals, mirrored lenses scanned timelines, and her platform boots anchored her to defy gravity.

She stood in front of her vanity, ready to take on the world.

"Ay yo, Neo-Eden, what'cha doin'?"

Suddenly, the mirror faded black, showin' Neo-Eden. She felt the molecules in her body start movin' toward the screen. Wit' one blink of her eye, she was in Neo-Eden. Boaz was standin' off in the distance.

I really wish this transportation would eventually put me next to the person, she thought as she was glidin' toward him.

Boaz was posted up in Neo-Eden. His whip, the RBG 1920, was the illest. He sent a Holla to all of Naomi's closest male relatives. All ten of them answered, each pullin' up next to Boaz. Once Boaz saw everybody was there, he yanked off his Praise and threw it to the ground.

"Hallelujah," he spoke.

The device hit the floor and instantly expanded, growin' five times its size. Then it began to spin, its panels unfoldin' like petals of a metallic flower. Each petal was etched wit' glowin' ancestral code, symbols stretchin' across time itself. The ring rose, hoverin' above the ground, its hum deep and resonant like the voice of creation.

Gasps echoed through the crowd as streams of light shot upward, forming a halo that surrounded everyone present. The Praise wasn't just a device anymore; it was a covenant made visible, a contract between the seen and unseen.

Boaz stepped into the center, and wit'out a sound, his body began to levitate. The ancestral symbols reflected off him, markin' him like Yah's chosen redeemer. He rose higher and higher 'til he hovered above the entire crowd like prophecy fulfilled.

"Naomi is gettin' older and seeks a male investor in her business. So, I decided to bring this to the people so they can be a witness. If you don't invest, then I will."

"I will buy the land. I need more land to give to my kids," one of the male relatives responded immediately.

Boaz lowered himself to the ground to face the man. "Oh, okay! I like to see it. So you agree to also marry Ruth?" Boaz tried to slide that last comment in, hopin' he wouldn't catch it.

"The devil is a liar," the man shot back. "I will lose my land if I do that. You know what all of this entails. I am not you, Boaz. I don't have the money and resources to recover if somethin' goes south. You need to buy it."

He stuck his hand out, and Boaz began to dab him up. At that time, Neo-Edens performed certain handshakes to demonstrate different levels of agreements.

"Now, y'all all see that I am investin' in the business that belongs to Naomi and her family. Wit' that, I am also marryin' Ruth. Amen!"

"Amen!" the crowd shouted in agreement.

An elder approached Boaz. "Boaz, what you are doin' is great and mighty." He placed a hand on Boaz's shoulder. "You will be blessed because of the decision you made today."

The crowd roared in support, which made Boaz smile from ear to ear. As everyone cheered, Ruth walked into the crowd. The people stepped aside, allowin' her to reach the center where Boaz was still floatin'. She reached him, and before she realized it, he was on one knee wit' a weddin' ring.

"Ruth," said Boaz. "Will ya—"

"YEEESSS!!!" Ruth shouted, cuttin' him off.

The whole crowd cheered as Boaz and Ruth passionately kissed.

CHAPTER 33

Ruth gazed at herself in the same vanity that Mahlon gifted her when they first married.

SWOOSH! SWOOSH!

Ruth felt Glamzmo place the brushes on her face like an artist to a blank canvas. It had just finished doin' her hair in an elegant updo wit' nanochips fashioned into the shape of lilies, the flower of Neo-Eden. They complimented her face as well as her earrings, which were in the shape of balsam flowers. These were the same flowers placed strategically in her bouquet along wit' lilies that sat off to the left over the vanity. The exquisite smell added a unique fragrance that reminded Ruth not only of her home, Moabolis, but of her marriage to her deceased husband, Mahlon.

She snuck a peek at her weddin' attire while Glamzmo was changin' brushes. Originally, she couldn't decide on what weddin' dress to wear, and even reached out to Mosh for some samples, but nothin' felt right. It wasn't until she discussed her concerns wit' her soon-to-be husband, Boaz, that he suggested they invite Yah into the equation. She was so glad he did, because they decided they would honor Ruth's heritage as a Moabolian and both wear tracksuits wit' the latest KE 5's shoes that haven't been released.

She chuckled a bit, never imaginin' that Yah would say to get married in traditional Moabolian attire. His ways are not our ways and His thoughts are not our thoughts, she thought, as she realized where she was.

"All done!" Glamzmo's methodical voice said.

"Thank you, Glamzmo!" She tilted into the mirror, smilin' at the work Glamzmo did.

"You are welcome." Glamzmo flew off and out of the room, leavin' Ruth alone wit' her thoughts

However, before she could wonder 'bout today, a familiar face strutted in.

"Hello, Ruth!" Naomi placed her hand on her shoulder.

"Hello, Mama!" She jumped up for a hug. Naomi returned the hug, enjoyin' huggin' Ruth.

"How are you?"

"I'm fine, li'l nervous, but fine. How are you?"

"I'm fine as well. Just put on my attire for the weddin'." Naomi did a 360 spin, displayin' her lavender tracksuit wit' all-black KE 5's. "You like?"

Ruth smiled. "Absolutely. You look great." Ruth mimicked Naomi. "How 'bout me?"

"You look fabulous." Naomi looked at Ruth like a proud mother, which she was. "I know you're nervous as I would be, too, if I had to get married in this day and age."

Ruth nodded.

"So I decided to make sure you had somethin' that would calm your nerves."

Naomi whispered, "Hallelujah," when King Eglon, Queen Lani, and Orpah wit' her fiancé, Abi—downloaded into the room beside Ruth.

"Ahhhhhhhhhhhhh!"

A piercin' scream went through the entire room. Ruth charged toward her family and tackled them to the ground wit' a giant hug. She even knocked her dad out of his hover chair. They all laughed as they stood up and embraced each other more formally.

Pop! Naomi tapped her Praise when Ruth noticed her family's ears had bubbles on 'em that disappeared.

"I knew you were gonna scream, so I came prepared."

"Hahaha!" Everyone laughed at how well Naomi not only knew Ruth, but how prepared she was.

"Anyway," Ruth smiled, "how are you? I'm so glad that you all came."

"Ruth, we all talked yesterday 'bout how we're comin' to your weddin'." Orpah gazed oddly in her sistah's direction. "We were at the dinner party slash bridal rehearsal last night."

"I know, but after that period of not speakin' to you all, I always allow myself to feel surprised when I first see you." Ruth responded.

"You look beautiful," Queen Lani interrupted her daughters' banter. "I can't believe, even at this age, I still have to mediate between you both."

"Thank you, Mom." Ruth hugged both her parents. "And Dad, thank you for the KE 5's. I didn't think you were ever gonna release 'em."

"Hahaha!" King Eglon's laugh roared around the church. "I would do anything for you. And technically, they aren't released but, for my daughter, my princess, I would do anything."

Ruth hugged her dad tightly as a thank-you for always bein' there.

"So, how did Boaz feel when you told him you were a princess?"

"Well," Ruth started, "I never did. I just waited until he met you all those many nanobytes ago, and then I told him after the fact."

"You didn't tell him prior?" King Eglon took a bite of his chocolate-chip cookie that dispensed from his hover chair. "Cookie?"

"No, Dad. We are all good." Ruth smiled. "I kept that to myself for the duration of our relationship. You and Mom's presence was the first time he realized I was a princess. I'm glad you kept us out of the public eye. It made him fallin' in love wit' me feel so real."

"I am so glad that both of my daughters found love again." Queen Lani smiled at Ruth and Orpah. Ruth knew their parents were worried 'bout their daughters when both their husbands died. She could see their emotions were on the up since discoverin' both had found love again.

"Yes," Queen Lani added. "I can't wait for that love to blossom in Ruth like it did in Orpah."

Curiosity washed over Ruth's face as she turned to her sistah, who lifted her jacket, exposin' a baby bump.

"Orpah!" Ruth screamed.

Orpah nodded wit' a giant grin. Ruth grabbed her sistah for a hug and received one back.

"I am so happy for you. I'm gonna be an aunt!"

"Yes, you will be an aunt," Orpah smiled, then focused her gaze on Naomi. "And you will be a grandma."

Naomi immediately ran wit' open arms to Orpah as they embraced.

"I will always love you, Naomi," she whispered in her ear.

"I will always love you, Orpah," Naomi responded. "So, do you guys have a name?"

"Goliath." Orpah smiled.

"Why that?" Ruth questioned.

"It's from his culture, our culture, and I wanted to honor that."

"I completely understand. I want to name my child from Boaz's culture, our culture, as well."

Ruth and Orpah smiled at each other. Sharin' a sistah moment never got old wit' them.

"Well, Ruth," Naomi spoke, "we shall be off. We'll be lined up, waitin' for you at the entrance. We love you."

Naomi whispered, "Hallelujah," uploadin' them to their destination.

Ruth released a sigh before returnin' to her seat. She was mentally tryin' to prepare herself for what was 'bout to happen. She was gettin' married to Boaz.

Before she could really let it settle in, she heard someone download behind her.

"Hey, Ruth," Juju spoke.

Ruth jumped out her chair, jumpin' into her friend's arms.

"How are y'all?" Ruth smiled.

"Fine," they both grunted as they set her down on her feet. "You?"

"Great." Ruth strutted over to a couch that was hoverin' off to the side. She motioned for her friends to come join her. Juju gracefully sat in her seat while Dash slouched. Ruth chuckled—she loved seein' that even in their mundane tasks, their personalities stood out.

"I am so glad you guys are here. I needed to see you in person."

"Well, we're glad to be here," Juju said.

"Ditto!" Dash smiled. She looked around, then stared directly at her friend. "Ruth, why weren't we in your weddin'?"

The smile Ruth held fell faster than ⅓ of the A.N.G.E.L.s. "Dash, you know why."

Dash threw her hand up, not tryin' to hide her frustration. "We're friends, best friends, like sistahs. Don't sistahs usually end up in the weddin'?"

Juju could see Ruth's frustration. "Dash, you know the rules. We aren't allowed to do anythin' that could draw attention. Attendin' the weddin' is one thing, but bein' in the weddin', where we'll draw attention and questions, is a whole nother thing."

Ruth sighed, directin' her smile toward them. "Thank you. But anyway, y'all look amazin' in your tracksuits."

Juju and Dash did a once-over of their lavender tracksuits wit' KE 5's.

"Yeah, why did you choose lavender?" Dash questioned.

"Well, I met someone who changed my life when I was seven. She had lavender hair and, I wanted to honor her," Ruth answered. "I remembered when Boaz told me his story 'bout meetin' other bein's from other dimensions, and it prompted me to give her a call—and eventually tell him I met some of my own."

"Is she comin'?" Dash retorted. "How did he handle that?"

"She is," Ruth smiled. "She's actually sittin' on my side wit' her husband, who I also met—and two very special guests. And he handled it quite well. He was suspicious of how well I took the information the first time."

"Special guests? And that's a relief."

"Yes, Dash," Ruth tilted her head. "Special guests for Boaz."

Ruth ignored Dash's comment 'bout her extraterrestrial friend. Both Juju and Dash stared at Ruth peculiarly. They never knew Ruth to keep secrets from them. They told each other everything that ever happened in their lives.

"Okay, so Boaz met two bein's from a different dimension years ago, and he tried to find 'em but couldn't." Ruth fixed her jacket. "So, I called in a favor and got them and my guest here."

Dash and Juju's eyes jolted.

"Ruth, you did what?" Dash yelled.

"Ruth, typically I would've told Dash she's overreactin', but in this instance, I agree," Juju said. "What were you thinkin'?"

"Okay, okay! Relax, everyone!" Ruth held her hands up, tryin' to defend herself. "All I did was ask, and surprisingly they said yes. I didn't even have to do any paperwork. They called it a weddin' gift."

Dash and Juju looked at each other before starin' at Ruth.

"Yeah, so nothin' to worry 'bout."

Once again, Dash and Juju looked at each other before returnin' their gaze to Ruth.

"You guys trust me. I've never called in a favor before and it's my weddin', so…"

"Well, it is your weddin', and only the best and brightest for our sistah-friend," Juju smiled at Ruth. Juju knew how to keep things calm and stay level-headed.

"Yeah, yeah! We love you," Dash said. She knew how to be a fighter and headstrong even when she wasn't tryin'.

Juju glanced at Dash before turnin' her attention to Ruth. "Well, we'll be off. We have to get back to our seats. Isn't that right, Dash?"

Dash just nodded wit' an eye roll. Juju shook her right wrist, causin' both of them to upload.

Ruth released a giant sigh as she made her way to her vanity, lookin' at her makeup and hair. She glanced at the time in the corner, realizin' that in less than five minutes she was gonna be Boaz's wife. She felt an array of emotions that left her with only one thing to do in that moment: pray, as Mahlon had taught her to do when she felt overwhelmed.

"Dear Yah, let this day go well. Allow everything that is supposed to happen, happen. Let Your will be done on Terra as it is done in the Cloud. Amen!"

In that moment, Ruth felt peace that passed all understandin'. Her whole body breathed and relaxed for the first time in a long time. She looked in the mirror and smiled. She not only saw the girl from Neo-Eden; she also saw the princess from Moabolis, the widow of Mahlon

Efrathat, but now a combination of all three of those would make Boaz a very lucky and happy husband.

She tapped her Praise, downloadin' her way into the entrance of the sanctuary. There she saw every single one who made her who she was, and she was glad they could be here to welcome the new person she was becomin'. She heard the music and realized that she arrived on time.

In the distance, she saw Boaz in his all-black tracksuit wit' KE 5's. He looks so good, she thought, before he disappeared down the aisle of the sanctuary. Ruth watched as, two by two, each group went down the aisle that made up some portion of their weddin' party.

Finally, it was her turn. Her father was seated comfortably on his hover scooter, and she was ready to go down the aisle when she looked down, noticin' that her father had a chair added for her to sit in so he could "carry" her down the aisle. Tears welled up in her eyes as she took a seat next to her dad.

The slow melody of Luna Moon strung through the sanctuary as every person including Boaz was cryin' while Ruth's father carried her down the aisle.

"Who gives this woman to be married to this man?" the minister droid asked.

"I do," King Eglon responded.

Boaz helped Ruth out of her seat. They both wiped each other's eyes, but the tears kept rollin' down. They finally gave up. Ruth handed her bouquet to her sister and itertwined her fingers wit' Boaz. The minister droid continued on wit' the service, and there wasn't a dry eye in the crowd.

Once the weddin' was over, everyone stood and watched as the sanctuary transformed into a reception hall filled wit' an AI band and a dance floor, while each table received a private chef-droid that could make any dish their heart desired. Even wit' all their experience wit' technology, everyone was still amazed at what it could do and how it could make 'em happier if used properly.

"Would everyone remain standin'," the AI DJ commanded, "and help me welcome Mr. & Mrs. Boaz Efrathat!"

The music played as Ruth and Boaz entered in, dancin', while everyone clapped around 'em. They danced for a few minutes before the music became real somber, and they started their first official dance as husband and wife. The crowd watched in awe as their waltz blended so seamlessly wit' House music. Once again, there wasn't a dry eye in the crowd as friends and family gazed at their dance.

They finally walked to the head table as a signal for their guests to begin eatin'. Once food was devoured, everyone made their way to the dance floor.

Ruth grabbed Boaz from the dance floor and led him to a table for two special guests.

"Hey, so I have a surprise for you."

"Really?" Boaz was intrigued. He did enjoy surprises especially when they came from Ruth.

"Yes." Ruth stopped at the table where the special guests sat.

"Ahhhhhhh!" Boaz's screams were muffled by the loud dance music. He felt as if his eyes were deceivin' him, so he rubbed 'em just for clarification. He blinked several times before rushin' into the arms of his old acquaintances, Didi and XV, wearin' gold tracksuits wit' KE 5's. They all smiled as if they were long-lost siblin's finally reunited.

"Hallelujah," Ruth spoke, as a soundproof bubble engulfed 'em. "I knew I would see y'all again. How are you both?"

"We are both fine," Didi said. "We knew the same thing." They all hugged again, savorin' the moment as best they could. "Congratulations on gettin' married."

"Thank you!" Boaz grabbed Ruth's arm, pullin' her closer. "You did this? How? Thank you! I love you!" He hugged Ruth tightly like it was their second encounter meetin'. "I love you even more than I knew I could. How did you do this?"

"I had my work cut out for me, but it was worth it."

"I bet." Boaz sat down at the nearest seat, motionin' for the rest of 'em to join. "What have you been up to? It has been many, many macrobytes since I have seen you."

Didi and XV looked at each other oddly, then stared right back at Boaz.

"Umm, Boaz," XV said, "for you it has been years, but for us, it's only been two days. I'm not surprised that time works differently in our different dimensions."

"Two dayyyysss!" Those words slipped out of Boaz's mouth before he even processed 'em. "Wow. I guess time does work differently. However, I'm happy you came on my, I mean our special day."

"We are, too!"

Just then, a couple came into the bubble. The lady and gentleman were wearin' matchin' lavender tracksuits.

"Kidaaaaa!!" Ruth nearly knocked Didi down tryin' to get to Kida for a hug. She held her for a bit before huggin' her husband, XVI. "I am so happy you both could come."

"Absolutely. We wouldn't miss this for anythin'."

Ruth brought her friends over to meet everyone. She stopped mid-stride and stared at XV wit' a fresh pair of eyes. She then turned to XVI, who was smilin' from ear to ear as if he knew exactly where her mind was goin'.

"XV. XVI! Y'all are related!"

"Duh!!!!!!" XVI laughed. "It took you long enough. We were all growin' concerned when you didn't put two and two together."

"Hey, how was I supposed to know you both were related?" Ruth asked.

"Maybe because we look identical, and my name is XVI and his name is XV. You know that it was just a hunch." He laughed, and the rest of 'em joined in.

Boaz grew curious with each passin' word of their conversation. "So let me get this straight: I met two A.N.G.E.L.s when I was younger, and my wife, Ruth, met two A.N.G.E.L.s when she was younger, or at least I assumed she met 'em and they were related?"

"Yes, dear! I met Kida on the playground in Moabolis when we were both seven. Her lavender hair drew me to her, and we would play when she came every so often."

"Also yes," Didi giggled. "Well, actually, my husband and I are the parents to XVI. He's married to Kida. We are, as y'all say in this dimension, A.N.G.E.L.s, but Kida isn't. She is what you all would call part of M.O.E.E., so she's blind in this dimension."

Kida readjusted her sunglasses as a quiet "yes" to what Didi said.

"Kida, I didn't know you were blind!" Ruth exclaimed.

"Well, when I first arrived here, I wasn't. However, from the end of the first time to now, my vision kept goin' and goin' until finally I couldn't see in this dimension, so I stopped comin' back. But because I love you, I came and I'm completely blind, but not really."

"Oh yeah," Boaz began, "you're now a part of M.O.E.E., which is a multifaceted organization."

Ruth's confused gaze fell on Boaz as he started to explain.

"So, when my wife first heard of M.O.E.E., she heard 'bout 'em as tech people that monitor and fix the droids throughout the country. That's true. However, they're also the prophets of the city and are led by the Upgrade to build the latest piece of tech. They do this by seein' in the spirit realm, or cyber realm as we call it. This ensures that we not only stay the leaders of the tech industry but use the technology to worship Yah."

"Really?" Kida stared in his direction.

"So I guess wherever you're from, you must be part of those who monitor and fix issues in your country."

Everyone except Ruth and Boaz looked at Kida wit' a smirk.

"I can feel y'all lookin' at me. Stop it."

"Wait, what's goin' on?" Ruth asked, bein' nosy and wantin' to know.

"I'm not gonna tell you just yet. This is your day and his day, and we are here to celebrate it. Isn't that right?"

Everyone nodded their heads.

Kida made her way to the dance floor wit' a few slight stumbles while everyone followed suit. They all danced the night away for as long as they could.

"Ay, yo!" the DJ said. "We want to take this time to make a toast to the newlyweds, Mr. and Mrs. Boaz Efrathat, before they leave in a couple minutes to go on their honeymoon and start their new lives."

Everyone raised glasses that materialized from their Praise.

"Cheers!"

Everyone took a huge drink before smashin' the glasses on the ground.

An AI band appeared, marchin' them all outside, where they played as Boaz and Ruth were uploaded into a limousine. Everyone cheered and waved as it took them into the night, on to start their new journey.

CHAPTER 34

Ruth and Boaz's beautiful baby boy, Obed, had just been born. Life was truly great for Ruth a year after bein' married to Boaz. Her mother-in-law, Naomi, lived comfortably on her estate and even had a house-droid that handled the cleanin' and cookin'.

Ruth sat outside on the veranda, watchin' nature and technology thrive as one. The sky shimmered wit' hover-screens and Praise signals, but the gentle hum of cicadas mixed wit' the cooing of Obed inside grounded her in peace. She smiled, hearin' the soft "coos" of her son as Boaz played wit' him in the next room.

Her Praise vibrated in her palm. She glanced down. It was the group call she shared with Dash and Juju. Not thinkin' much of it, she answered. But before the connection even stabilized, a scream so sharp tore through the feed that it jolted her Praise from her hand. The device hit the floor and flared, projecting a 5-D feed right in front of her.

"AAAAHHHHHHH!" Dash screamed. Her face was bloody, her hair tangled, her eyes wide. "JUJU! RUTH! HELP MEEE!"

Ruth's body tried to freeze, but she rebuked it. Fear was not what Yah gave her.

"They're comin' for me!" Dash sprinted into a room, slammin' the door behind her. "I can't fight them off much longer!"

"Fight who?" Ruth spun toward Juju's projection, confusion twistin' her face. "Dash, who after yo—?"

The sentence shattered when the door exploded inward. Hulkin' men three times Dash's size and robots towerin' even higher poured in like a flood.

Ruth and Juju gasped, but Dash didn't hesitate.

"Hallelujah!" she roared. Her Praise blazed on both sides like golden blades, floodin' the room in light.

She moved like she'd been forged for war. A roundhouse kick sent one brute crashin' into the wall. She sucker-punched another, dropped to her hands, flipped, and blasted a robot's chest wide open. Sparks showered the air as she slid under another strike and came up swingin'.

Ruth and Juju stood frozen, starin'. They had never seen this side of Dash.

"Juju," Ruth whispered, steppin' closer. "Help me pull her out."

"Huh?" Juju blinked, still stunned.

"I know you're confused." Ruth grabbed her hand, squeezin' hard. "But we can do this. Together."

The latest Praise tech allowed physical interaction through Hallegram. Juju steadied herself, then jumped through the holo-field to stand at Ruth's side. Together, they reached—arms plungin' into shimmerin' light—grabbin' at Dash's figure as she fought and bled.

They pulled wit' all their might, strainin', inchin' her through. Dash was halfway out, still knockin' heads while bein' dragged toward safety.

Then she vanished.

The connection cut. The light collapsed. The room was silent.

Panic froze Ruth's face. Her knees trembled as she stumbled into the next room. Boaz was on the floor, laughin' as Obed gnawed on somethin'.

"What! Happened! To! The! Connection!?" Ruth's scream cracked through the house.

Startled, Boaz jumped up. "I…I dunno. Lemme check." He darted behind the couch and stopped.

Obed sat happily, chompin' down on the glowin' fiber line that powered the Praise system.

Boaz pulled it free, the cord chewed clean through. He held it up with a weak grin. "Found the problem."

"Chewed?!" Ruth's face flushed red hot. "You let him chew the connection?! Do you realize—" Her voice broke.

Boaz had never seen her this furious. He dropped the grin, crossed the room, and pulled her shakin' body into his arms. "Ruth… please. Tell me what happened."

"She's gone." Tears poured down her cheeks. "Dash, she's gone. She Holla'd us bloody and screamin', fightin' off giants and machines. Juju jumped to my side so we could pull her out. We almost had her and then—" She buried her face in his chest. "The line dropped."

Boaz held her tighter, guilt crushin' him. "If I'd been watchin' Obed better, if I—"

"No." Ruth jerked his chin up to meet her eyes. "Don't you dare blame yourself. This ain't your fault. It's whoever took her fault. I can't stand by and do nothin'. Dash needs me. Needs us."

Boaz searched her face. He'd seen her fierce before, but never like this. Her grief and fire mingled, turnin' her into someone unstoppable.

"You helped me when I needed help," she whispered. "Now let's go help Dash."

Boaz hesitated. "Help her? You don't even know where she is."

"Yes and no." Ruth lifted her upper lip, revealin' the mark etched inside—יהוה—glowin' faintly against her skin.

Boaz's eyes widened. "What is that?"

"A sign," Ruth said firmly. "Dash, Juju, me and others too. We all carry it. It binds us. Finds us. If one falls into danger, the rest can reach 'em."

Boaz stepped back, strugglin' to process. "So you're part of some… secret society?"

"Exactly." Ruth managed a tired laugh. "Don't try to make sense of it. Your head'll hurt."

He rubbed his forehead, overwhelmed. "So what now?"

"Now we bring her back."

"But Obed,"

"He'll be safe with Naomi. My people will watch over him too."

Boaz still looked uncertain, but Ruth was already movin'. She scooped up Obed, pressed a kiss to his cheek, and strapped him into the back of the RBG 1920. The car molded a custom seat around him, hummin' softly to acknowledge the child.

Slidin' into the driver's seat, Ruth lifted her Praise. The car absorbed it, its sleek black surface morphin' into a gold-and-purple beast of a machine Boaz had never seen before.

He climbed into the passenger seat, still shaken. "I didn't even know it could do that…"

Ruth gripped the wheel, her eyes set. "Ay yo, Juju! I'm on my way."

"I'm waitin'!" Juju's voice came back steady, though laced wit' worry.

Ruth tapped the rear screen. Obed smiled up at her, gigglin'. Relief steadied her pulse. She turned to Boaz, kissed him hard, and for the first time since Dash vanished, he let go of fear.

Then Ruth's voice rang out through the Praise: "Naomi! Can you watch Obed?"

"Of course," Naomi answered, her tone warm and sure. "Anything for my grandbaby."

Ruth exhaled, her lips curlin' into a grin. She tightened her grip on the wheel.

The RBG lifted from the ground, hummin' wit' sacred power. Gold and purple light split the night sky as the vehicle hovered forward, engines roarin' like a chant sung by the gregorians.

Beside her, Boaz fastened his belt, his confusion turnin' to resolve. Ruth felt it; the shift, the moment her husband stopped resistin' and started fightin' wit' her.

The hunt for Dash had begun.

About the Author

Willie Fordham is a science fiction and fantasy author whose stories blend futuristic technology, myth, and deeply human themes. With a background in education and a passion for exploring the intersections of culture, faith, and imagination, he creates universes where advanced civilizations wrestle with timeless questions of identity, legacy, and what it means to be truly free. When he isn't building expansive worlds filled with hover-cars, intergalactic travel, and mythic creatures, Willie is dedicated to inspiring the next generation of dreamers and thinkers. His work bridges speculative storytelling with a sense of wonder, always aiming to leave readers entertained, challenged, and hopeful. He currently lives in Virginia, where he balances writing, teaching, and community projects with an endless stream of new creative ideas. Visit Williefordham.com for more information